GRAVEL ROAD
Book I in the *Echoes* Series

By: Courtney Baker

To Rhyan and Evynn, my constant proof of God's love. I'm so proud of the little girls you are and the women you will become. And to Matt, my "Callin". I'm so grateful that my Gravel Road on earth led me to you.

PROLOGUE

Get out or you're going to die.

The voice, the feeling, the whisper. She felt it reverberate through her soul and knew that it was so. It wasn't screaming, it wasn't frantic. It was Truth.

She looked at the knife in his hand. Saw the rage in his eyes.

And she ran.

CHAPTER 1

Fear followed her out of town and onto the cracked, weathered highway. Her gas tank was low and the sun was quickly hiding from the night. Light. She craved the light.

The gas station called her in and she felt her heart accelerate with the panic of having to pump her own gas. She felt flushed and light-headed, angry with herself that something so simple would prove to be so difficult. He'd always gassed up her car. She wouldn't have done it right. She never did anything right.

He had never paid with cash before and she faltered, unsure what to do. Her credit cards were hidden away in her purse. The cards would be the easiest way for him to find her and she was at least smart enough to not make that mistake.

She fumbled for her cash and took three deep breaths, willing her heart to slow. Looking around, she calmed knowing that she would see his silver BMW pretty easily from where she was parked. The man at the counter looked at her with interest when she walked in. Her long hair was the color of suede, and her eyes had held the attention of men since she was a young teenager. The man smiled at her when she handed him her money, and then a look of pity swept over his face. She quickly looked away. She didn't want attention. She didn't need attention. She needed to be forgotten.

Her heart continued to race as she pumped the gas. She didn't feel it slow until she was settled back in her car and once again out on the road. She didn't have any idea where she was going. But, if she didn't know her destination, he didn't either. She checked the road signs and headed south. If she had to live out of her car, at least she wouldn't freeze.

As night closed in around her, she made the decision to park at an abandoned car wash and slept in fits until morning. She didn't have much of a plan, except to get a couple days away from him.

She left before dawn the next morning. Along her journey, the highway seemed endless and barren. As the miles passed, her tense muscles slowly began to relax. She realized how different her knuckles looked when her hands weren't clutching the steering wheel, her lifeline. She looked around at the dust and the weeds bordering the side of the road. It was maddeningly symbolic. When would she start to see life?

She saw his face everywhere. Billboards, drivers in the next lanes. Three times she thought she saw him driving the car to the side of her. Her adrenaline would spike as she waited for him to ram her off the road. It hadn't been him. Just a stranger. But, hadn't he always been.

Strangers. Her entire world blended into a mesh of people that should have loved her, but never could. Her mom tried. She had to believe she tried with all she had. But, depression and sickness stole any affection she might have wanted to give.

But, her dad. No. There wasn't room for justification. The evidence of his inability was in every look, every sigh, every motion, every emotion. She wasn't wanted and he proved it by disappearing into the night. Night after night.

Kyle had driven two full days and stopped her car in a little town off the nearest exit to food. She had been living on candy bars and water and was beginning to feel weak and shaky. She needed protein. She only had a little over thirty dollars left of her cash, but she didn't see that she had a choice. She bought a hamburger at the drive-through of a fast food restaurant and ate it so fast she made herself nauseous.

Looking into her rearview mirror, she felt the impact of his fist when she touched the bruise around her eye. It was a week old and turning the cruel colors of healing.
He didn't usually lose his temper so soon after a bad round. If he hit her, he'd wait weeks before doing it again. The days after his punishment were filled with apologies, excuses. Kyle remembered those times as the good days. Her reprieve. But the last time, he'd only waited a few days before he came after her again. Any illusions of calm were fractured.

She ran a finger over her swollen lip. She was able to eat, that was an improvement. She pushed her reflection away and vowed to never forget. How it looked, how it felt. Her jaw was still tender, but nothing was broken. She laughed bitterly when she thought of how she was always so grateful when she'd run her tongue over her teeth and feel they were still there. Who was she? So hated. So despised.

Unlovable.

The sun welcomed her as she got out of her Civic and made her way down the main street. If there ever was a place she'd like to escape into, this town would be the one.

She didn't know why she went inside. She gazed up at the worn sign above her. "Hayfield Feed and Tack" Somehow it looked like a beacon, beckoning her in. Calling her name.

Texas Hayfield found himself staring into nothingness once again. Edith Marie. Oh, how he missed her.

They had met on a double date when they were both seventeen, fifty-three years before. Edith was his girlfriend's best friend at that time. When he and his girl got into an argument at the beginning of the movie, she headed off with his best friend. Texas and Edith found themselves alone, talking themselves right into love. They were married just a few months later.

Their life had been one of dreams fulfilled, hopes realized. She had been his lovely lady and he missed her every second since she'd been gone. She'd had a stroke, tending to her garden. It was such a mean way to die. She'd been alone in the heat of the day for hours before he'd gone home to find her. By the time the ambulance got all the way out to his place, he knew she wasn't going to make it.

For a week, he sat by her side, reading and praying. People would come and go, but he wouldn't leave her room. She woke up long enough to turn her eyes to him and squeeze his hand. When she finally went home to her Jesus, Texas knew that brief moment he'd had with her had been God's gift to him. Her last communication to tell him how much she'd loved him all those years. Every memory, every embrace, every touch. She told him she'd remember always, with one look.

Thirty-six days since he'd buried her. How he wanted to go with her.

The bell jingled over the door and Mr. Hayfield looked up from his recollections. A young girl stood just inside, looking around the store. She saw him and quickly looked down, like she was afraid for him to see her eyes. She was so fragile, like a glass blown bell. And she was beautiful. Just like the little girl he and Edy never had.

They had never been blessed with children. But with the town folk's kids all running around and growing up and having more kids, they never lacked for a child to hold or love. Now, without his Edith, the absence of children was leaving a hole bigger than he'd expected.

The girl didn't move, and Texas took measured steps toward her "Well, hello there. I don't believe I've seen you around here before."

Kyle looked up at him when he spoke and gave a slight smile. Texas nearly grimaced when he noticed her black eye. Black bleeding into brown, bleeding into purple. Her cracked lip made it painful to watch her smile. This little girl standing before him needed him as much as he needed her. He could tell immediately. The Lord was providing him something to help heal his broken heart. Maybe Texas could heal her heart as well.

"My name's Texas Hayfield, but everyone here in town calls me Pops."

"Hi. I'm Kyle Evans." She absently put her hand over her brow. "I just got into town. You don't happen to be hiring here, do you?"

Tears rested in Pops eyes and it took a few moments to speak, "Yes, Kyle. I sure am."

✝

It was clear very quickly to Pops that Kyle had no place to stay, no where to go. She had no one. Pops knew his old barn was a little dusty, but it would be perfect once it had a good scrubbing. He'd had it enclosed as a little mother-in-law suite years before when Edith's daddy had passed on and her mama needed a place near her only daughter. Funny how God worked things out like that. Pops couldn't have known that those nails he'd hammered into those boards decades before would one day be used to shelter this delicate child before him.

He'd been nervous to suggest she come follow him home to take a look at the barn. This world just wasn't the same one he'd grown up in. But, he wanted her to get settled, if she wanted stay at his property. He could tell she surprised herself by accepting his offer.

Pops closed the shop a little early to make sure they'd arrive home when there was still plenty of daylight, and waited in his truck until he saw her little black car pull up to follow. He glanced in his rearview mirror several times to see her behind him focused on his truck, both hands tightly gripping her steering wheel.

It was twelve minutes from the store to his home if he didn't get stopped by a school bus or the one stop light in town. He slowed down to take the corner into his long drive and said a prayer. His life with Edith had always been about changing the world for the better. This was the first time he would have the opportunity to change the world without her by his side.

He put his truck in park and stopped the engine. His truck was an ugly old thing. Light blue with dents and dings, and patches that needed painting. But, it had been his when it was brand new, and he could still see what it looked like the day he paid for it and drove it home to surprise Edith. He didn't know much about body work, but he'd put hours into the engine and it ran smooth as butter. He closed the door and had to open it again to slam it shut. Kyle had scooted out of her coupe and was walking toward him.

"Your house is so beautiful." She was staring at the little white house with black shutters. It was a pretty typical house for the country, but it looked like a home.

"Thank you. My Edith and I bought this little beauty just a few weeks after we were married. It was our first and only house." Pops looked up at their home and then down at the ring on his hand.

"Did Edith pass away?" Kyle knew the answer in his silence.

After a few moments, he spoke. "She had a stroke in her garden. It's been a little over a month now. I'm still in mourning, ya see. It's been a real hard time." A tear escaped and he wiped it so quickly that Kyle almost didn't see.

"I'm so, so sorry. " She didn't know what else to say.

"Oh, Darlin'. Don't mind this old man. I'm a mess, you can see it by lookin' at me. I know we all have our problems and heart aches. It's part of life. You come into town without work or a place to live and I don't hear you complaining none."

Kyle smiled up at him. "After meeting you, I feel like my luck's finally changing."

Pops looked back at her and returned the smile. "Oh, little girl. Luck's got nothing to do with it."

It didn't take much to get Kyle moved in to her new home. She had left Indiana with just the clothes she was wearing and her wallet. She couldn't wait to take a shower, scour the last of his germs from her body. Buy a clean outfit so she could wash the one she was in. The simple things were all she desired.

Pops opened the windows and looked around to assess the barn's condition. There was a small bathroom at the back of the house near the one bedroom. The great room was attached to the kitchen and a little sitting room was positioned immediately before the hall leading to the only door. The walls were white and scuffed, the furniture old. It was small, but suitable.

"I hope this will work for you. I'm sorry it's in such bad shape."

Kyle's eyes were wide as she looked around her new place. "It's absolutely perfect." Pops didn't have to look at her to know she was crying. So, he wasn't alone with his tears. They were quite a pair.

"I have soap, buckets and rags. We can get her cleaned up in no time. And I know there's not a thing worth eating in here except maybe some canned beans. If you'd like, I can get the stuff for you to get a start on your cleaning and I'll go on ahead and make us some dinner. We can eat out on the back porch since it's such a lovely evening, and then I can show you where the town market is tomorrow morning. We'll get you some necessities. My treat."

Kyle couldn't believe how giving this person was standing before her. He was like a guardian angel. If this wasn't luck, she sure wished she knew what it was.

✝

Pops had homemade biscuits with sawmill gravy, sausage and pancakes ready and waiting when Kyle walked over from across the drive forty-five minutes later.

"I love breakfast for dinner." Steam jumped high and disappeared as he set the plates down on the little table on the back porch.

Kyle couldn't remember feeling so hungry, but was grateful she hadn't started to eat before Pops began to pray. She closed her eyes in respect, but felt slightly uneasy. Praying wasn't something she was used to, but if praying and Pops went together, it couldn't be all bad.

They chatted about the weather in Greenville and found that they both enjoyed nature and plants. They talked intermittently between bites, but the dinner was filled with bouts of comfortable silence. Kyle ate two helpings of pancakes and a biscuit covered in gravy before she finally put her fork down. When Kyle had taken her last bite, Pops excused himself and came back minutes later with clean sheets for her bed, a couple towels and an airy cotton dress.

"The dress was my Edy's. It's most definitely not something a young girl would want to wear out and about in town but it will do around the house."

"Thank you, Pops. Thank you so much. I wish I could say more."

Pops shook his head. "That's what we're here on this earth to do, Child. We're here to be a light in this world. If I could shine some of His light on you, then I've done my job for today."

Kyle didn't understand who Pops was talking about, but smiled and thanked him again before running back to the barn to continue cleaning. It was after two o'clock in the morning before Kyle finally fell asleep on her bed, on top of the covers, clean and fully clothed in her borrowed dress.

I'll find you, Kyle. You know I will. You can run as far as you want to. I might even leave you alone for a while and let you start to feel real safe. But, I will come after you. I will find you. And you'll be sorry.

Some day.

Kyle shot awake, her heart beating uncontrollably. She couldn't catch her breath. Sliding off the bed onto the floor, she hid in the corner, trembling. It took her a few minutes to realize where she was and that she had woken from a nightmare.

It was only a nightmare.

✝

Kyle's second day in Greenville dawned with gentle rays of promise. It was nearly ten-thirty by the time she woke and dressed. She made her way across the drive toward the farm house and stopped half way to look at the expanse of the property. She was so caught up in herself the day before to look up and see the beauty surrounding her. She inhaled the scents of azaleas, honeysuckle and blooming dogwood trees.

A warm breeze brushed her cheeks and she stopped where she was and closed her eyes. No flinching. No tears. No running.

No more running.

When she opened her eyes, she saw Pops standing on the top porch step, watching her. She was embarrassed, but smiled to let him know she was fine. Finally. She was fine.

✝

The town's single grocery store and local second-hand shop stocked all she could possibly need. Pops stood up front talking to the Market's manager while Kyle shopped. When she'd made her way through all the aisles, Pops handed the cashier a handful of bills. Kyle felt her face flame red. She didn't want Pops to pay for her, even if she would work for it.

Holding the door open as Pops walked out, Kyle promised him. "I'll pay you back, Pops. Every cent, from my first paycheck."

"This is my gift to you, Sweet Girl. You have no idea how wonderful it is to feel useful. Don't go takin' that away from me, now." Pops put his arm around her shoulders as a smile broke through his lined face.

They walked to the truck that way. From a distance, one couldn't tell if he was protecting her, or she was holding him up.

✝

Kyle didn't want to wait to start working. The sooner she learned the workings of the feed store the better. And the sooner her mind was occupied.

Thursday mornings, the customers were scarce but the occasional purchase gave Kyle confidence with the cash register. When she'd make a mistake, her mind would scream the insults

10

she was so used to hearing out loud.

"You're such an idiot. Stupid. There's no way you can survive on your own."

Pops would reassure her and she'd try again. He was right by her side. The shrill lies would die before they reached her lips, and she began to catch on to the processes.

Nearly three hours into her first shift, a little girl about ten years old came in with her mom and older sister carrying a small bundle resembling a golden retriever puppy.

"Well, hello there, Miss Jana. How are you and your beautiful girls this morning?" Pops greeted Miss Jana like he'd known her all her life, and somehow Kyle guessed that was true. "Looks like you have a new addition to the family."

Jana rubbed the puppy's ears and laughed, "Yes we do. Andy and I finally gave in. We just picked her up last night and we're in need of some puppy food."

"Sure, sure. Miss Jana James, this here's Kyle Evans. She just arrived yesterday, right in time to start helping me out. Kyle, this is Jana and her beautiful girls. Little Townsend is holding the pup and her older sis there is Chandler."

The girls smiled and Chandler said, "Nice to meet you, Miss Kyle." Kyle could tell their mother had worked to instill manners and was being rewarded. Chandler looked to be about fifteen, but had a maturity about her that could make someone question her age.

"It's nice to meet you all, too. What did you name your puppy?"

Townsend was quick to answer, "We named her Princess because she likes pink." The adults laughed and Townsend smiled down at Princess and gave her a kiss on the top of her fuzzy head.

Kyle followed Pops over to the dog food and listened to him tell the James' girls about the different brands of food and which he felt were the best. She wanted to soak in his knowledge so she could repeat it to another customer when they had the same questions.

Once the ladies had decided on a bag of dry food and a chew toy, the met up at the cash register and Kyle rang them up.

Jana quietly regarded Kyle while she was bagging the dog toy. There was no amount of make up that could cover Kyle's black eye. Jana didn't know her story, but she knew exactly who Kyle needed. "We're happy you're here in Greenville, Kyle. If you ever need anything, please let me know. And if you'd like to go to church with us some Sunday, we'd love to have you sit with us."

Church. Kyle hadn't thought of church in years. The few times she'd gone with her mom as a child stirred memories she wasn't prepared for. The smell of the ancient building, keeping a tight hold on her mama's hand until she finally was forced to let go. Fear turning to comfort as the minutes passed listening to stories of Bible heroes.

But that had been so long ago. She remembered feeling loved by the teachers. She remembered briefly feeling something she'd describe as hope. But, it was so short-lived. Almost like it hadn't happened at all. Her dad didn't approve and her mom gave in. She always did. Even as a little girl, Kyle could remember all the battles lost.

"Thank you." It was all Kyle could think to say.

Jana reached across the counter and patted Kyle's hand. Emotions threatened to attack, but just as quickly Jana turned around with her little crew and disappeared out the door.

✝

Saturdays were always busy at Hayfields. There were moments when Kyle didn't feel like she had time to breathe. Millie Brown came in two days a week to help out. And a couple extra guys came in every Friday and Saturday to add muscle, loading hay on trucks. They were all able to help out behind the counter from time to time. Several times, Kyle could feel one of the men staring at her and felt her face heat.

When the day came to an end and Pops switched the sign from open to closed, he turned to Kyle with a smile on his face.

"You did great, Sweet Girl. You did just great."

Kyle felt she could fall asleep right there standing against the counter. "Thank you, Pops. I don't remember ever being this tired."

"I understand, yes I do. We're closed on Sundays, so Saturdays are our biggest days of the week."

Kyle replaced some bags of bird seed and asked, "Why are you closed Sundays? I thought everything was open on Sundays."

"Well, it's the Lord's day. I promised Him when He helped me open this store that I'd save Sunday just for Him."

Kyle straightened and studied Pops. His shoulders stooped and his thin, gray hair was mussed, much like his shirt. She couldn't quite understand what he was saying, but she liked Pops. She liked him very much. Whatever he had, maybe she could have it, too.

Pops drove his pick-up down the drive, slow as a snail. Kyle enjoyed his company, but was excited to make a sandwich and crawl into bed.

When Pops cut the engine, he turned to Kyle. "Thank you so much for all your help today, Sweet Girl. I really didn't know how much I needed you until you were there."

"You're welcome. I need to thank you. Again. You have no idea what you've done for me."

Pops smiled. "Actually, I'd like to help you in the only way that really matters. I'd like to invite you to go to church with me in the morning. I know you might be nervous, or you don't know what to expect. But my church is full of good, honest, loving people."

Kyle looked at her hands folded in her lap and knew she couldn't turn him down. Not after all he'd done for her. He saved her life.

Kyle forced herself to whisper. "What time?"

"Ten-thirty. I'll drive, if that's okay with you. And I'd like to treat you to lunch afterwards. Ma's Kitchen is the best place to get real home cookin'.

Kyle brushed her hair back and met Pops eyes. "Okay. I'll be ready."

✝

The old, white church building was tiny in its original form, but had at least two larger additions on the side and back. The hedges and grounds were meticulously maintained and Kyle could feel the respect that so much care must have taken.

As Kyle and Pops approached the front door, they were greeted with warm smiles and hugs. Most of the congregation was elderly and filled with words. But, their hearts and their love were genuine. Kyle's stomach settled and she was beginning to feel comfortable in the worn pew, with Pops next to her.

Pastor Trevor looked to be in his fifties and one of the youngest in the building. He had a heart and a passion that Kyle was drawn to. When he spoke of the gift Christ gave at the cross, Kyle couldn't look away. When Pastor spoke of scripture, Kyle took longer than anyone to find it, but turned to the scripture in the church Bible along with everyone else.

Pastor Trevor addressed those seated before him. "If you were to die today, do you know for sure that you'd go to heaven?" He looked from face to face and his eyes found Kyle's and he repeated his question. "If you died today, are you sure, to your core that you'd go to heaven?"

He again looked around as he continued. "There are a lot of

people out there claiming that as long as you believe in something, anything, then you'll either go to heaven or just go to sleep forever. Some say that you'll get to heaven by being a good person. Or you'll get to heaven because everyone goes to heaven.

"But, the truth is, there's only one way to get to heaven. We can't earn it. We can't buy it. We can never be good enough for it. The only way to heaven is a gift. It's free. All we have to do is take the gift when it's offered."

Kyle felt like he was talking just to her. "Beloved. The gift is being offered to you right now. Jesus died on the cross to pay for your sins. That's the gift. All you have to do is believe it. Believe that He died for you. Because He loves you that much. Believe that He rose again and is alive. He is God and He is real. Believe that we've all sinned and have fallen short. Believe that He came to forgive us and wash us clean.

"Believe the truth."

Kyle felt something move in her heart. She was a sinner, that much she knew. She had done more wrong in her short life than she could imagine anyone seated near her had done in all their years combined. She'd heard of Jesus before, of course. But, she thought He was a God that condemned, not a God that loved.

Pastor Trevor continued and Kyle looked down at her hands folded in her lap. "Take His gift. Accept His gift. And secure your place in eternity."

Pastor Trevor closed his eyes and everyone else did the same. "Dear Jesus. Touch every heart in this place. If anyone is unsure of their future, please Lord, speak to them now. Open their hearts to hear Your voice. Help them to find Your peace, Your hope. Help them to understand that You came to seek and save the lost, not the perfect."

Tears threatened to fall as Kyle thought of just how lost she was. Just how imperfect. Could she really find peace? Could she really feel hope.

As they left the church and made their way to Ma's Kitchen, her question was answered. Even though she hadn't made a commitment, peace slowly crept over her heart. Hope began to take root.

CHAPTER 2

One month to the day that Kyle parked her car in her new hometown and walked into Pops' store, she was still jumping at the smallest sound. She was angry with herself for being so frightened, like a sapling in a hurricane. But it was always in her thoughts that he would find her. It had only been thirty days, but it felt like it should be long enough. She wanted to quit looking over her shoulder. She didn't want to just be free, she wanted to feel free.

Church with Pops was giving Kyle much to think on. Pops had given her Edith's Bible. As Kyle took hold of it, she knew what it meant for him to let it go. She held it and smoothed her hands over the worn cover, the edges bent and cracked with use. Verses were underlined and highlighted and Kyle spent hours at night pouring over scripture. But after four services with Pastor Trevor, she found herself restless and searching.

She had fallen asleep with the Bible on her chest when a loud noise woke her. She sat straight up in bed and threw the covers off. She had been sleeping with the lights on since she moved in, and kept a knife beneath her pillow. She felt for the knife and grabbed hold, placing her bare feet to the icy floor.

"Oh, God. Oh, God. Help me, Lord." She wanted to scream the words, but they came out in a breath.

There was a light on in every room. It was how she lived. Darkness was her enemy and light, her comfort. She glanced in the bathroom. She had learned immediately to keep the shower curtain open to be able to see if anyone was hiding in the tub. It was empty. The great room was sparsely furnished, but the kitchen had a large island that an intruder could crouch behind.

Kyle's heart rate accelerated as she felt herself inch forward. Repositioning the knife in her hand to attack, she jumped and screamed at the invisible invader. No one was there. She was alone.

A broom was lying on the kitchen floor. How it fell, Kyle couldn't guess, but she began to laugh. After a moment, her laughter turned to bitter, broken tears.

She went down on her knees, then laid down, prostrate on the floor.

With her face pressed to the cold tile, she prayed herself into the Son. "Lord. I believe. I believe You and I believe in You. But, I'm such a mess God. I've sinned so much. I still sin so much. How can You forgive me?"

Before the words were out, she heard a whisper over her heart.

Because I love you, Child. Because I died for YOU.

And just like that, Kyle Evans was written in the Book of Life, by the hand and with the blood of Jesus.

Kyle couldn't go back to sleep for hours, but woke with a new purpose and a desire to tell the world that she was saved. She began with Pops.

She dressed and ran out the door, shoving it closed behind her. She nearly lost her footing on the gravel crossing over to the main house, but she barely noticed. She ran up the front steps and knocked on the front door. When Pops didn't answer, she ran around back to the garden.

Kyle found Pops on his knees in the dirt, planting bulbs and applying fertilizer. He looked up when he heard her and sat back to watch her. He knew by the smile on her face, the glow that hadn't been there before.

"Pops! I did it! I asked Jesus in my heart and I understand now."

Pops slowly got up to his feet and Kyle ran over and gave him a hug. "Thank you. You didn't just give me a job and a place to stay. You introduced me to God. I wouldn't be saved if it wasn't for you." Tears slid down her cheeks as she spoke the words and Pops fought to keep his in check.

"You would have found Him some day, but I'm so glad to have been a part of it."

Kyle backed up and sat in a rocker. "Now what to do I do?"

"Now, we have ourselves a baptism." Pops clapped his hands and dirt flew around him.

"What do I have to do?"

"Well, a baptism, as you probably know by now, is your way of confessing that you've asked Jesus into your heart. It's a way to be obedient to God's word and follow Jesus' example. So, the preacher will ask you if you've accepted Christ as your Savior and believe that He is the Son of God. You'll say that you do, and then you get dunked. It's a symbol of the living water washing away all your sins. It's a beautiful thing, getting baptized, Sweet Girl. A beautiful thing."

Kyle's smile widened. Yes it was a beautiful thing.

CHAPTER 3

Kyle knew she was different. She felt it in everything that she did. She knew it by the way she wanted so desperately to be a better person and live the way God wanted her to live. And she found herself smiling most of the time.

Only one other customer was in the store when the bell sounded and Jana James came in with Townsend and a much larger Princess.

"Hello, Kyle. It's great to see you again." Jana's face lit up to see her and Kyle felt special, a feeling she still needed adjusting to.

"Hi, Jana. Hey there, Townsend. It's great to see you, too. It looks like Princess must be eating you out of house and home. She's getting so big."

"She can eat, alright. I have a feeling we'll be seeing you more and more as she gets older. If she can eat this much now, I can only imagine what the future holds." Jana laughed. She was a beautiful woman, with shoulder-length russet hair and a slight figure. There was nothing flashy about her, but she was someone people noticed by her attitude and smile.

Pops heard her from the back office and came in to say hello. "Jana, Townsend. How are you beautiful ladies today?"

Jana gave him a quick hug. "I was just telling Kyle that our little Princess is a big pig."

"That's good. Means she'll be strong and healthy."

Jana turned to Kyle again. "I wanted to invite you, again, to church. I don't want to bug you, but if I don't ask, you might not ever join us."

"I've actually been going with Pops to his church. I was saved this past week." Kyle beamed.

"Oh! I'm so happy for you. Come here and let me give you a 'welcome to the family' hug." Jana gave Kyle a hug like she would her own child and Kyle found herself, once again, so grateful to be in this town.

"Pops, why don't you and Kyle join us Sunday at our church and I'll make you both a great big dinner afterward."

"That sounds mighty fine. What do you think, Kyle?"

Kyle hadn't realized it was alright to visit other churches, but felt a surge of excitement. "Sure, if it's okay with you, Pops."

"Of course it is. You don't have to go to my church just because I go, Darlin'. You need to figure out the best church home for you. My church has a lot of more mature individuals," Pops chuckled. "Jana's church might be more to your liking. Pastor Jeremy Green is a good man. I knew Jeremy when he was just a little tyke, hiding behind the hay bales until his momma was pullin' her hair out to find him. Now look at him. Three babies of his own."

Pops' reverie shifted to the present. "You need to find a good, strong Christian boy, more your own age. I don't know how easy that will be at my church."

Kyle agreed but was lost on his comment about a good, strong Christian boy. No Christian boy was going to love her.

That night, when her monsters were their strongest, she put her head in her hands and wept.

"God. Who will ever love me? *Why* would anyone ever love me?"

Because you are a new creation in Me…

Because you're Mine.

✝

The James' church building was a deep red brick surrounded by a manicured lawn and large oaks. Flowering bushes bloomed around the perimeter of the structure and seven steps led to the large wooden doors.

A couple stood outside, greeting those walking in. They were about her dad's age and were smiling and laughing with a girl closer in age to Kyle. She thought they might be related by the way they bantered, but her attention bounced from person to person. They all seemed like family.

Introductions seemed to go on forever. Kyle felt like she met everyone in the congregation. She was seated between Chandler and Pops, two of the sweetest people she'd ever met. It was when Pastor Jeremy began to preach that she relaxed and leaned into his words. It didn't take but a few minutes to realize this was her home.

✝

Lunch with the James family was loud with fun and fellowship. Andy, Jana's husband, had a sense of humor that ensured laughter was never far away.

Davis, their twelve year old son, had an easy smile and a contagious giggle. He was going to be handsome young man, with dark curly hair like his mom and blue eyes like his dad's.

All three kids were well-mannered and friendly. Kyle felt an ache that she was missing out on her life's goal.

Like she read her mind, Jana broke into Kyle's thoughts. "So, what are your long term plans, Kyle?"

"That's funny, I was just thinking about that. I went to school up north to be a teacher. I was in the middle of my internship when I left."

The adults were all too gracious to ask exactly why she left her dreams behind when they were almost realized, but Jana knew to carry on the conversation when they were alone.

"You'll be a great teacher." Was all she said and the matter was dropped until the adults retired to the back deck. The children disappeared to different rooms and quiet settled in.

Pops and Andy walked around to the front of the house so Andy could show Pops his motorcycle. Jana took the opportunity pick up the abandoned topic.

"Can you transfer to our community college here?" Jana broached cautiously.

"I don't think so," Kyle was silent for a moment, deciding how much to share. "I left because I was afraid of someone. He actually works at the college I was going to. I'm afraid that if I try to transfer my credits, he'll find out where I am."

Jana let it sink in and then moved forward, "I know someone that works in the Sheriff's office. He could get you a restraining order. Or he could talk to the school for you and let them know not to give out any information.'

For the first time since she'd left Indiana, Kyle felt like she might just end up with her dream after all.

With hope building, Kyle asked "Do you think that would work?"

"I do. His name's Grayson Williams and he's a member of our church. He's actually married to Paige who works at the middle school.

"God's watching over you, Kyle. I know He is."

Kyle smiled through a haze of tears and nodded in agreement.

Monday morning, Jana called Grayson and explained Kyle's situation. When Gray called the school to let them know they needed to keep the transfer quiet, he learned that Professor Paul Garrison was no longer employed. Once the paperwork was filled out and faxed over, Kyle was well on her way to becoming a teacher.

June was hot and dry and Kyle knew she could find Pops in the garden, watering his leafy charges.

"Hi Pops. Can I talk to you for a minute?" Kyle was nervous and it was obvious in her voice.

Pops stopped spraying and turned to look at her. "Sure, Darlin'. What's on your mind?"

Kyle walked over to the back table and sat down facing him. "I don't really know how to say this."

"You want to switch churches." Pops smiled down at her and then chuckled.

Kyle immediately relaxed and asked him, "How did you know?"

"I've lived a lot of years, and I'm pretty perceptive. Life Way Church is perfect for you. Lot's of young folk. Lot's of strong, Christian leadership. I couldn't be happier for you. And, Darlin, I promise you I'm not upset a bit. I want you to grow, and I can see that happening with the Life Way family. It doesn't mean you're not my family. We're all brothers and sisters, it don't matter a bit which church ya go to. Long as it's based on the Good Book. "

Kyle sighed loudly and Pops laughed. "You'll figure it out soon enough. Not much you could do to make me upset with you. You're a fine girl. You need to remember that, now, ya understand?"

"Thank you, Pops. So, it's alright with you if Pastor Jeremy baptizes me?"

"'Course it's alright. Just let me know when so I can be there to see it. It'll be a glorious day. Glorious." Pops turned on the spray again and Kyle nearly skipped back to her little home.

✝

Jana went with Kyle on Friday to talk to Pastor Jeremy. Kyle was uncomfortable walking in, until she felt herself relax with Jeremy's open, welcoming smile. He was in his early thirties and talked often of his wife, two sons and baby girl. He was a person that knew his place in life and encouraged others to find theirs. The fact that he believed she had one was comforting.

"Kyle, I'm so happy you've decided to join our little family. It's obvious that you mean a lot to Jana and Andy."

"Thank you. This is all so new to me."

"Well, I'm sure Jana has given you some advice, but reading your Bible is at the top of the list. Joining a life group or a Bible study will help you so much, too. We'll start those back up in September. And, you can ask Jana, or me or my wife, Michelle, any question at all. It can be confusing, but the Bible never contradicts itself."

"I appreciate that. I've been reading quite a bit. Pops gave me Edith's Bible and it means the world to me for so many reasons. And I can't wait to be baptized."

Jeremy loved to see a new believer, so filled with passion and excitement that so many others had long since lost. He thumbed through his appointments on his phone and his smile broadened. "Well, what do you think about July fourth?"

Independence Day. Freedom. It was perfect.

The day Kyle Evans was to be baptized was cloudless and serene. Not at all what life before life had been. She rode with Pops to the church a half hour early to dress in her white, spotless robe. She pulled it on over her clothes and stared at herself in the full length mirror. She could hear the music playing, starting service. It was almost time.

"Is this really how You see me, Lord?"

Pastor Jeremy knocked, interrupting her prayer.

"I'm all ready." Kyle turned toward the door. Jeremy walked in with a big grin.

"These are my favorite days. How are you feeling?"

"I'm a little nervous, but I can't wait." The robe was slightly too long and Kyle had to lift it up an inch to walk.

"There's no reason to be nervous. How about I pray?" Jeremy didn't wait for a response before he closed his eyes and began. "Dear Lord, I thank you so much for Kyle. I thank you for her decision to accept You into her heart and follow You in your commandments. You cherish and treasure her more than she'll ever realize or understand. Please help her to get a glimpse of how big your love really is. I pray you take away her nerves to just enjoy what this day means. The symbol of sins erased and a new life to live. In Your name, Jesus. Amen."

It was time. Pastor Jeremy stepped into the water of the baptismal and spoke on behalf of Kyle. Then he welcomed Kyle. The water was warm and every step she took led her deeper into the love of Christ. She was immersed in His grace. His mercy. His love. She was submerged, and rose again from the water, drenched in His forgiveness. She wiped her eyes looked out over a sea of faces, beaming up at her. And she listened as those same people cheered and cried.

It was her second very best day ever.

After service, Kyle's hair was damp and she had not one ounce of make up on, but she didn't care. She smiled as she gave hugs, smiled as she received them.

Jana held her tight and whispered in her ear, "I'm so proud of you, Honey." Kyle could almost hear her mom speaking those same words. Maybe God used Jana's voice to let Kyle know that her mom really was proud of her. Either way, Kyle felt a love she could never have imagined. It was real and tangible. It was family.

Gray came up to congratulate her and introduce his wife, Paige. Before he could give introductions, Paige gave Kyle a big embrace. "I'm so glad to finally meet you. I've seen you before, and Gray told me that he helped somehow to get your transcripts here. I hope you don't mind he told me, but he knew I'd want to know. I'm a teacher at the middle school and I can help you get your internship next semester so you can graduate."

Kyle laughed as Paige finally took a breath and Gray shook his head. "She's really like this all the time. That's why most people don't know I can speak."

Paige slapped his arm and led Kyle away. "He's ornery, but he's mine. So, let's get everything started. I also happen to know of a sixth grade teacher that will be on maternity leave at the first of the year. If you got the substitute job for her class, that would be a great way to get your foot in the door."

Kyle was reeling with what Paige was saying and how fast she was saying it. Her dreams were really going to happen. God was working everything out and all she had to do was let Him.

CHAPTER 4

She was anchored in her bed, looking toward the opened door of her bedroom. A dark figure stood in the shadows, filling the frame. Kyle tried to move, tried to scream.

She knew she was in a dream, fighting to end it. Her mind was in one place, while her body willed it to wake.

She fought, begged, to escape the fog. Her head began to clear and she was able to focus. There was no figure, no threat. She was alone.

She sat up and felt for the knife beneath her pillow. She held it in front of her until the sun finally rose and spilled through the windows.

And for all that time, the demons hissed in her ear.

He will find you.

✝

Summer ran slow and steady and Kyle tried to fill her time. She worked as many hours as she could with Pops and frequently found herself over at the James house. She was growing close to the kids, but Chandler was the most interesting to her. To be a teenager and so grounded and secure was something that Kyle couldn't comprehend. It went against everything she had been. When she looked at Chandler, she saw who she wanted her own daughter to become, if she was ever blessed with one.

"So, you've decided already what you want to go to college for?" Kyle was helping Chandler fold laundry.

Chandler's deep blue eyes had a habit of smiling whenever she spoke "Oh, yes. I've known since before I can remember. I'm going to teach, so we'll have a lot in common. When did you know that you wanted to teach?"

Kyle thought about it before answering. "Hmm. I guess before I can remember, too. My mom had been a teacher before she had me. I'm sure that's why it just seemed natural. She taught kindergarten. I would love to teach elementary school, but I think I'll be happy with sixth grade."

"I definitely want to teach the little ones. I've been helping my mom in the nursery at church since I was in there with her. I just love little kids. They're so innocent and funny."

Kyle looked up at Chandler, a towel in her hand. "I can see you being the best teacher ever. I really mean that."

Chandler stopped folding and looked back at Kyle, "That means a lot to me. It all seems so far away."

Kyle put a pile of socks in the basket and agreed "I have one semester left, and it feels so far away. But, don't rush it. Life can go so fast. Enjoy every minute."

School was well on its way and Kyle made arrangements with Paige to go in and look around. Paige was excited to see her when she arrived on campus and gave her a big Paige hug. "I can't believe it's all working out. You'll graduate in December and start working in January. Who could make that happen except God? I love it when He shows Himself like that. How are you feeling? I know the local college is small, but it'll work, right?"

Kyle smiled again at Paige's run-on ways. "I'm so happy. I can't believe how excited I am. I really like my teachers and I only had one class that didn't transfer over, so I'm making that up at night."

Kyle looked at the brick buildings and foliage surrounding her. "This is a beautiful campus."

"Thank you. This building is only about eight years old, so it's still in pretty good shape. Let me introduce you to Kayla. She's the mommy-to-be that you'll be substituting for. It just so happens that she's my team leader, so we'll be in the same block." Paige smiled, knowing that Kyle would be grateful.

"Here, I'll show you my room first." Paige led Kyle down a corridor toward the front of the building and opened a classroom with a key around her neck. Her room was spacious and bright, filled with individual desks and computers. The decorations were intricate and elaborate, Paige's style written in every design.

"This is wonderful. I can tell you like what you do."

Paige looked around and agreed. "I do. I love crafty things, too, so that helps when you're a teacher."

Paige led her through an adjoining door to the next room and they found a very pregnant woman sitting at a large work desk.

"Hey, Kayla. I wanted you to meet Kyle, your future substitute."

Kayla didn't try to stand, but waved and gave Kyle a big smile "Hi Kyle. Paige sure works fast when she wants something. I'm really looking forward to a sub that I don't' have to worry about. I have a great class, though, so you'll be just fine."

Kyle responded before looking around. "I really appreciate the opportunity. I can't wait to get started. Are you having a boy or a girl?"

Kayla rubbed her belly and snickered "I'm having one girl that looks like two boys. She's going to be big like her daddy. He was almost ten pounds. I should have asked him that before I agreed to marry him."

The girls laughed and Kyle felt right at home. Teaching wasn't guaranteed to be easy, but it was guaranteed to be rewarding if she put enough into it. And she knew she would.

✝

The weather started to cool quickly when November approached. Thanksgiving was rushing near and Kyle knew she wouldn't be alone. It meant so much to her that she had others to take her in and make her feel like one of the family. She knew that when she had a family of her own, she would do the same for anyone that was alone. The thought of family sent a tremor over her heart.

She walked into her little house and put her books on the kitchen island before kneeling by the couch.

"Dear Lord. I still don't know how to stop feeling this way. I want to be loved, but I don't see how. I'm damaged."

A word whispered over her heart.

Read My Words.

Kyle reached for Edith's Bible and it opened naturally to Jeremiah 29:11

"For I know the plans I have for you" declares the LORD "Plans to prosper you, not to harm you. Plans for a hope and a future."

Kyle ran her finger over the words, highlighted in yellow. "Plans. You have plans for me.

"And they're good."

Paige and Kyle became fast friends. They went out for coffee occasionally, but mostly they enjoyed running. As soon as Paige discovered Kyle was a runner, she set up a schedule that would fit in for both of them. Three days a week, they would meet to run and talk. Kyle looked forward to her time, and was disappointed when she had to tell Paige that she couldn't come over for Thanksgiving. Jana had already invited her and Pops over to their house for the traditional turkey and all the fixin's.

Thanksgiving morning was dreary and cold, but Kyle didn't care. She pulled on her warmest sweater and her new winter coat. She was going to enjoy this day for the first time in her life.

She didn't remember one holiday she'd enjoyed as a child. Not Thanksgiving, not Easter, not even Christmas. No matter the excitement of baby dolls and carriages, doll houses and fancy dresses, she couldn't escape the din of the ever-present bickering. Later there were no gifts, no arguing. There was nothing at all. Today, and every holiday after this, would hold only happy memories.

Jana and Andy's extended family were there. Aunts and Uncles, a half a dozen cousins, grandparents and an elderly friend. It was a loud and entertaining day. By the time Kyle arrived home, she couldn't wait to fall into bed.

She worked Friday and Saturday and by Sunday, the weather had cleared to a sunny day with higher temperatures. Kyle loved Sundays. Worship and fellowship had become her two favorite things. She would be able to see the James family and Paige. Then she would meet Pops out at Ma's Kitchen for lunch. It was always the perfect day.

Kyle arrived early to church, a normal habit. Jana and Andy were already in their row, saving her a seat. Chandler must have been in the nursery, but Townsend grabbed her in her child-like embrace and held on. Davis waved and went back to drawing on his bulletin.

Jana had asked Kyle what she'd done with the rest of her weekend. Kyle had started to respond when a tall, muscular young man she'd never seen before walked past her down the aisle to a seat near the front. Kyle worked hard at not staring. That boy took her breath along with her focus and Kyle willed herself to look back at Jana to continue their conversation. Jana smiled at her and then laughed when Kyle blushed. A crowd came in and everyone found their seats.

Kyle looked back toward the young man and studied the back of his head. He was close to her age, his hair dark and cut short, his shoulders broad. Her pulse accelerated. There were quite a few young, single people at the church, but not one of them had done what this one just did to her heart.

Paige's parents came in and sat next to him, then Paige and Gray sat on the other side. It didn't take long to figure out that the handsome guy she just blushed over was her best friend's brother. She shook her head and forced her eyes away. Out of the corner of her eye, she could tell that Jana was still smiling.

Service ended with one of Kyle's favorite songs. It was an old song, set to a new tempo and it filled her soul every time she heard it. Her heart was full and happy when she walked out of the building.

She and Jana stopped a little ways away from the door when Kyle saw Paige walking toward her, arm linked with the best looking guy Kyle had ever seen. His green eyes were smiling and he was in the middle of a story when he looked her way and stopped. Paige smiled up at him and made her way in front of Kyle.

"Hey, Ky. I wanted you to meet my little brother, Callin. Callin, this is my sweetest and most beautiful friend in the whole world, Kyle Evans."

Callin remembered to extend his hand, but they both stood looking at each other before Kyle shot her hand up to meet his. "It's great to meet you, Callin."

Callin took her hand. It was soft and so small. He wasn't sure yet if she was sweet, but the 'most beautiful' part was definitely true.

"It's great to meet you, too." Callin had a hard time taking his concentration off Kyle when Paige asked him a question.

They released hands. Kyle couldn't help but be disappointed. His hand was big. Strong. He would make her feel safe if… If what.

"Okay. No one's listening to me. Cal, I asked you what time you needed to leave today."

"Oh. I have to leave after lunch."

"Kyle, can you join us for lunch?" Paige was trying to be a match-maker and it was very obvious to the small group.

"I wish I could. I'm meeting Pops and he doesn't have a cell phone for me to call him."

"Well, next time, then. We'll make plans," Paige tugged at Cal's arm. "Come on, brother. Grayson gets crabby when he's hungry."

Callin and Kyle stared at each other a few moments more before saying good-bye. When they were out of hearing distance, Jana spoke. "Well, those were some pretty brilliant sparks. You couldn't ask to get in on a more wonderful family."

Kyle laughed. "I just met him, I wouldn't go marrying me off yet. Besides, I'm sure he's been a good boy his whole life, with parents like his. What would I have to offer him?"

Jana put her arm around Kyle's shoulders as they walked to their cars. "Sweetie, that's the devil talking. Don't you dare go listening to that liar. You have everything to offer. And you are worthy of being happy with a good boy."

Kyle wanted to believe it. When she watched Callin pull away in his pickup truck, she wanted to believe it more than anything in the whole world.

CHAPTER 5

Pops took Kyle out for her graduation dinner at the fanciest restaurant in town. They ate pizza and celebrated the beginning of a new chapter in her life. Kyle ate three pieces and leaned back in her seat.

"Thank you, Pops. You know we wouldn't be here celebrating anything if I hadn't met you that day I came to town."

Pops finished off his second piece and took a sip of water. "God would have brought you this far, with or without me. I'm just grateful to Him that he chose to include me. You're a special girl, Kyle. You might not believe it, in fact, I can pretty much tell that you don't. But you're as special as they come. When you're feeling down in the dumps and the past is acting up, you remember my words. And you believe them, you hear?"

Kyle smiled. She couldn't have asked for anyone more loving and encouraging. She thought about what the next few months held. In just a few short weeks, she'd have a class of her own. Paige had told her the week before that Kayla had admitted she wasn't coming back after her daughter was born. She wanted to be home with her baby, and it opened up the door for Kyle to move on with her life.

Pops looked at Kyle, deep in her thoughts. How anyone could have ever hurt that child made him mad enough to boil over and want to come out swinging. Her bruises were long since gone, but he wondered how much time it would take the scars on the inside to fade.

"I'm going to miss you around the store, you know. I doubt I'll have as many young gentlemen come in once you've left."

"I'll miss you, too. But, I'll still help out when I can. Definitely on Spring and Summer breaks. It's my home away from home. And we'll still have Sunday lunch at Ma's."

Pops knew it was true. He'd still see her. But the ache in his heart still smarted, all the same.

✝

Christmas was even more festive than Thanksgiving in the James home. Kyle and Pops arrived on Christmas afternoon, but this time Kyle supplied a pecan pie. Chandler gave Kyle a hug and showed her the camera she'd received. She loved photography and this had been on her Christmas list for ten months.

Townsend ran in from the kitchen and nearly tackled Kyle. Townsend was at such a fun age, where a new baby doll every year for Christmas was just expected. But she loved to play electronic games with older brother, too. Davis was sitting in front of the television directing battleships to ward off aliens. Once Townsend had showed off her new doll to Kyle, she sat next to her brother and grabbed a remote.

Kyle patted Davis on the back and said hello. He was a great kid. Even though he wanted to keep his attention on his game, he looked away and said a proper hello to their guest.

Jana came in and gave Pops a hug first before she reached Kyle. "Hi Sweetie. Merry Christmas. This pie looks absolutely perfect. We'll have dinner in just a few minutes. I hope you're hungry."

"I've been hungry since last week when you told me everything we're having today. Can I help you with anything?"

"No, thank you. Just enjoy yourself. I'm sure Towne and Davis will let you destroy a few aliens with them, if you'd like."

Jana disappeared with Pops back into the kitchen. Kyle walked over to the decorated Christmas tree by the picture window.

She studied all the ornaments, carefully hung on the tree. Most of them were handmade by the kids, and Kyle couldn't look away. Tiny hand prints and gingerbread men with little fingerprints as buttons. A homesickness she'd never experienced suddenly hit her hard. A homesickness for a home she never had. Her childhood tree was made of store bought

36

ornaments, glass angels she wasn't permitted to touch, lights that held no imagination.

She looked back at Towne and Davis, playing so well together. Chandler was taking a close up of Townsend in concentration. What Kyle couldn't figure out was if God was giving her a glimpse to what she might have one day, or God was punishing her by showing her what she wouldn't.

✝

School began the week after the first of the year. Kyle arrived earlier than Paige and went into her room to set up. Her nerves were setting in and the cup of coffee she drank an hour before was making her feel shaky. She had twenty sixth-graders arriving in a half hour and student teaching was going to feel years in the past.

Paige knocked and bound in with typical Paige style. She reached Kyle in record time and gave her a big hug. "Friend! I'm so excited to have you here. We're going to have so much fun together. I can't believe I haven't seen you since in over two weeks. How was your Christmas?"

Kyle laughed, as she usually did when greeting Paige. "I had a beautiful Christmas. How about you? How was Florida?"

"It was gorgeous, girl. I can't wait to go back. My grandparents told me to bring you over Spring Break. Just us girls. They'll spoil us rotten. They have to, it's what I'm used to."

"That sounds like so much fun. My family vacationed there once when I was a little girl, but I'm sure there's so much I don't remember."

"I have tons to tell you about, but I better let you get adjusted. How are you feeling?"

"Scared to death, to be honest." Kyle lifted her hand to show how it shook.

"You'll be fine. They might be little boogers for a day or two, but hold tough. Once they know you mean business and demand respect, you'll be gold."

Paige proved to be right. It was a difficult few days, but once Kyle laid the ground rules, the students got in line. By Thursday afternoon, Kyle was so excited to go for a run with Paige that even the forty degree weather didn't dampen her desire.

The girls started out in a slow jog. It was obvious that Paige had a lot to say. "Okay. So, I have some news. My little brother called last night and told us that he has officially accepted a position for a new job. It appears that he's moving home."

Kyle could tell Paige was waiting for a response. "Really?"

"Really? That's all you have to say? I saw you two go googly-eyed over each other when you met. He won't say boo to me about it, and believe me, I grilled him on our vacation. He's so stubborn. Not so stubborn that you shouldn't date him, mind you. But, brotherly stubborn. Anyway, he was offered the head coaching position at the high school next year. And just like that, he's coming back."

"That's great for him. He's seems so young to be a head coach. Is that what he does now?"

"He's the assistant coach about two hours north of us. But, he's going to build his house on our property, so now he'll only be a minute away. I can't wait. For as obnoxious as he was growing up, he's pretty neat to be around now. You should find out."

Kyle shook her head and tried to speed up their gait. "I have to admit, he seems like a wonderful person. And he's a great looking guy. But, I just got out of my last relationship seven months ago. And you know how horrible that was. As much as I would love to be ready to date your brother, if he would be interested in dating me, I'm just not ready yet."

Paige's tone tendered. "I'm sorry. I'm such an idiot. I know you were hurt. I push and push, but I don't mean any harm."

Kyle turned her head to look at Paige and slowed to a walk. "I know that. I promise I would never be upset with you for caring about me. And, like I said, your brother is obviously very special. Too special. Maybe that's a big part of why I'm so afraid."

Paige shook her head. "Please don't ever say anything like that again. It really upsets me. You deserve the most awesome guy out there. You do. Why do you think I'm pushing so hard for Callin? That should tell you something."

Kyle nodded. "Thank you. You're a wonderful friend."

They picked up and started running. Kyle, slightly lighter in her step.

CHAPTER 6

Callin hadn't stepped foot onto his former football field since that final night. It was just as difficult as he had always imagined.

He was about to become the youngest head football coach Greenville High School had ever had. Getting the head position was a mixture of talent and timing. He was the best quarterback the school had every known before or since, and his college grades were exemplary. He had been the assistant coach near Augusta when he learned that the head coach at his hometown school was retiring.

He inhaled deeply. The smell of cut grass mixed with chalk took his mind back six years.

The opposing team had been playing dirty all night. The defensive end had a late hit and took Callin out. He felt his knee buckle beneath him and knew in that instant that his football career was over. The smell of sweat mingled with the pain until the three hundred pound guy pushed off him. He heard the sounds of his coaches calling for the paramedics. And then the stands, filled to overflowing, went completely silent. His breath came in spurts and he hit his good leg over and over to keep his focus off his destroyed knee.

The paramedics were there in seconds, and Cal stared into the lights while they worked on him. Lights that he'd never see again in the same way. As a player.

He was placed on a stretcher and as they began to wheel him toward the ambulance, the crowd erupted in cheers and applause. And their hometown hero wept.

Cal looked up at the lights where he stood, remembering. It was the middle of the day, and the lights wouldn't come on until dusk. He couldn't believe he was back. It was just like God to bring him full circle. The place where his dreams were shattered would be the same place his dreams would come true. He was going to be the head coach of the team he would always love.

Sutton Cassaday was going home. She had spent five years at the greatest party university in the country. There were many tears shed in front of her professors to get her grades up to where she could graduate. She promised her parents she would finish college with a Bachelor's degree. They didn't say what her grades had to be.

The movers had arrived an hour before she did and had already started to haul her things back into her room in her parents mansion. She had partied early into the morning and slept as long as she could before making her journey home.

The only good thing about coming home was Callin Jennings. She had heard from an old high school friend that he was moving back home, too. Perfect timing. Of course he would go to the same church his family went to, which meant she would, too.

She'd had a crush on Callin since she first saw him in high school her freshman year. He was the best looking guy she had ever seen and just picturing him in her mind had her heart fluttering. He wasn't good looking in the same way as the models she dated, but he was a rugged handsome. He didn't care if his hair was unruly, and cut it short when it was hot out. His hands weren't smooth like her last boyfriends, but spoke of hard work and tough labor. But even in his cowboy ways, he had style. It wasn't a surprise that he had an older sister with a great fashion sense and a mom that came from old money.

But it was his eyes that she remembered most. A green that changed with his mood. But when he smiled, they seemed to grow a shade brighter. He had been a year ahead of her in school. He was a fallen star, the football cliché that busted his knee in the last game of his high school career and ended his future in football. But, even when he fell, he didn't burn out. He was just as bright, in her eyes. In every girls eyes, as much as she could remember.

Back then, Sutton followed him around the best she could. The problem was that he didn't go to parties and he didn't date. She had to get creative, and found out where he attended church. She had no interest in listening to some guy drone on and on about everything she was doing wrong from a hypocritical pulpit. But, she sacrificed for three years of her high school life. It seemed like they were right back where they started.

✝

Callin left the field and made his way to his property. Coming home was hurting more than he'd envisioned. He'd stayed away as long as the Lord would let him. When the head coaching position became available and the school had wanted only him, he knew it was time to face his ghosts.

Dust kicked up in his rear view mirror, a sign they needed rain. His parent's home came into view, and he continued on a quarter mile until he reached his parcel of land. A cluster of trees had been cleared and the contractors had prepped to begin laying the foundation. The house was a great design. Not overly large, but big enough to start a family with room to grow.

Kyle's face brushed up against his mind. He felt like a fool. They'd met once and he knew virtually nothing about her other than what Paige let slip out on purpose from time to time. He'd heard around town that she had just appeared one day at Hayfields, completely destitute, bruises on her face. He didn't listen to rumors, but he couldn't help but think there must be some truth to them. As much as he'd like to question Paige about her sudden appearance in town, that just wasn't him. God would lead him where he needed to go, as long as he had the patience to listen and follow.

Cal stood outside his truck and took it all in. His house was going to be built, starting in just a few short hours. There was no turning back now. He was home.

✝

The school year ended as quickly as it began, and Kyle found herself working alongside Pops once again. As much as she loved spending time with him again, she was missing Paige.

42

Sunday mornings had become her time to catch up. They would have a few minutes after church to sit on the bench and chat before Kyle met up with Pops for lunch.

Kyle was anxious to talk with Paige Sunday morning. She was prepared to catch up with her friend. She wasn't prepared to see Callin sitting next to his sister. She knew he was coming home, but she didn't know when. Now she did.

Her nervousness irritated her, but it clung to her, refusing to ease it's grip. When service ended, she waited inside with Jana and Chandler hoping Cal would leave before she walked out to her car. She knew she was being ridiculous. Even if she decided she was ready to date, it didn't mean his feelings were the same. And even if she wanted to be ready to date, she just knew she wasn't. Her heart hadn't healed, and there was no way to tell when it would.

Jana and Chandler led Townsend and Davis out front and Kyle walked with them. She was relieved and disappointed when she realized that Callin had left with his parents. Kyle said her goodbyes to Jana and the kids while Andy lagged behind to talk to Pastor Jeremy. When she made it to her car, she saw Paige leaning up against the trunk.

"Hey, friend." Something in Paige's voice frightened Kyle.

"What's wrong?" Kyle couldn't hide her fear. There was a pain surrounding Paige that was almost palpable.

When Kyle tried to find Paige's smile with one of her own, Paige broke. Tears created a steady path down her cheeks and she didn't hold back. Kyle embraced her and rubbed her back until she could talk.

Paige wiped her face and tried to find the words.

"I miscarried last week."

"Oh, Paige. I'm so sorry. Why didn't you call me? I would have been there for you in a heartbeat, you know that."

"I do know, but I was being angry and stubborn. I wanted to have my pity party all alone for a couple days."

"How are you feeling? Are you in pain?"

Paige wiped her face again. "No, I'm fine. Physically, anyway. I feel like sleeping all the time, but it might just be because I'm sad. I feel like I'm in this hole and I don't even know how to begin to crawl out. I didn't know I could hurt this bad." A sob escaped and Kyle grabbed her hand so she could continue.

"Gray's working constantly. They asked him if he would take over as Chief of Police. Crazy timing, right. I want so much to be happy for him, but it's hard. He's working so many hours, and I don't have school to occupy my mind. I'm just having a rotten time."

"Can you do coffee tomorrow morning?"

"I would love that. Are you sure you can do that? I know how busy you are at the store." Paige sniffed, and brightened a shade.

"Mondays aren't too bad, and Pops won't mind."

Kyle squeezed Paige's hand and they talked a few minutes more before they set a time for their morning get-together.

✝

The aroma of coffee beans and steamed milk permeating every inch of the Java House would have made Kyle smile if it were any other day. She was seated in an overstuffed chair, sipping her latte when she looked up to see Paige walk in. They gave a quick embrace hello, like it was any other day. But, it wasn't just any other day. Kyle couldn't help but feel inept in her understanding of what Paige was going through.

Paige waited for her coffee, then sat opposite Kyle.

Kyle didn't know exactly what to say, so she spoke from her heart. "How are you feeling today?"

Color had returned to Paige's face, though her smile faltered. "I feel a bit better. I think I needed to cry and vent. Thank you for being there yesterday. I didn't want to talk to my mom, for some reason. I can't really explain why. And Gray's dealing with it in his own way."

"Are you two alright?" Kyle thought of Gray and the look in his eye when he spoke to his wife, when he spoke *of* his wife. His love was evident in the way he grabbed her hand, held it close, and whispered in her ear. Kyle wanted them to be okay.

"We will be. We're just both really sad right now. We do best in the trials of our marriage when only one of us is depressed at a time. We don't have much experience with both of us being upset at the same time. It's usually me being crazy and unreasonable and he's my strong, solid rock. My rock kind of crumbled on me for a couple days."

"Well, I'm here for you, day or night. Just call me, okay? And you know I'm praying for you both every time I think of you, which has been quite often. I love you both."

"Thank you. I appreciate you so much." Paige smiled and their conversation moved to other topics. "Gray's new job is going to keep him busier than ever, but he's going to be so great at it. It's what he's always wanted. He has a wonderful team of officers, too. That's going to be really important in the transition."

Kyle nodded, knowing she was right. "He's going to be so amazing as Chief, and everyone seems to really respect him."

Paige smiled, thinking of her husband. "We'll be fine. And having Callin back in town will be good for me. We love to ride the horses up at my parents. I haven't ridden much since he's been away. I'm really looking forward to it."

Cal's face invaded Kyle's thoughts. His smile, his eyes, his shoulders. Paige spoke and Kyle's face reddened. "Callin started building his house last week. I can't believe how much I've missed him."

"Is he happy to be home?" Kyle didn't want to seem obvious

and hoped her face had returned to its natural shade.

"I'm really not sure. He's not one to show his feelings much. It's so annoying. I never could figure him out, and I'm usually really good at that sort of thing. I think he's dealing with some tough memories, but it's time to face them and move on."

Kyle wasn't sure what Callin's difficult memories were, but she assumed they involved some girl from high school. She was happy when Paige changed subjects again. Two hours later, Kyle and Paige said good-bye and promised to get together at least once a week to catch up. It was simply what friends did.

✝

The following Sunday, Kyle worked to prepare her heart for when she'd see Callin, seated with his family. She was caught off guard, once again, when a girl she'd never seen came in and gushed over how long it had been since she and Cal had gotten together. She gave him her full attention and was determined that she'd have his. She was a gorgeous girl. Long, blond hair, perfectly highlighted. She was slender and looked like she worked hard to wear clothes that accentuated her shape.

Kyle was furious with herself that she was so completely overwhelmed with jealousy. Her past had welcomed fear, disgust, anger. Even hatred. Her life given over to God had replaced those feelings with love, compassion, gentleness, forgiveness.

Jealousy was a new emotion altogether. And she didn't like it one bit.

✝

Kyle had vowed to protect her battered heart by keeping too busy to think of Callin Jennings. Keeping Cal out of her head might have been easier if she would have declined the invitation to the church picnic. But Kyle wanted the fellowship, craved the conversation.

The picnic was held at the mission house in the middle of town.

The building was a nineteenth century hotel converted to house several missionary families. Dark wood, intricately carved and highly polished, ruled the décor. It would have felt dreary if not for the large windows welcoming the sunlight. The property was large with an enormous deck in the back overlooking a tranquil lake that pushed up against a line of trees. Kyle was enjoying the view when Cal quietly walked up and stood next to her.

"Hi there."

Kyle blushed immediately and was so angry that she couldn't control the many colors of her face. "Hello. Welcome home."

"Thank you." Callin leaned up against the railing and looked out over the water. "It's beautiful, isn't it?"

Kyle nodded her agreement. "It's majestic. It looks so serene until you look closer at all those tiny bugs. I've always loved to watch them land and make ripples. Something so little setting off so much action."

Cal smiled. "I've lived on a lake my whole life and never thought about that."

They looked back at each other and Kyle felt her face heat again. His eyes were so clear they startled her. She paused in them for a moment before realizing she should speak. "How's your house coming along?"

"Great. Thank you for asking. I think my dad's working extra fast to make sure I move out of their house as soon as possible."

Kyle laughed "I know for a fact that they're thrilled you're home. So is your sister."

"Me, too. I wasn't so sure I would be, but I'm getting used to it." He hesitated to study her face. She was striking to look on. Skin so smooth, hair he wanted to run through his fingers. Perfect lips. He could imagine looking at her face a lot more often.

Kyle was still curious what his past hurt could have been when the blond girl from church walked up behind Cal and put her hands over his eyes.

Cal took her hands away and turned to see her. "Hi, Sutton."

The jealousy Kyle felt when she saw Sutton talking to Cal was replaced with an oppressive feeling of insignificance. She wanted to run away. She didn't see that Cal was just as embarrassed as she was.

"Hey, Cal. I was hoping you'd be here." Sutton moved in close and Cal inched away.

"Sutton Cassaday, this is Kyle Evans. Kyle moved here last year. She teaches with Paige. Sutton and I went to high school to together."

Sutton held out her hand. "Nice to meet you."

Even as they shook hands, Kyle knew Sutton's words were as insincere as her smile. Kyle was in her way and she was making it very apparent.

"Nice to meet you, too. Cal, it was good talking to you." Kyle excused herself and walked away as quickly as she could before Cal could respond.

Cal spoke with Sutton for a few minutes before excusing himself. He saw Kyle across the room talking with Paige. The next time he tried to find her, she was gone.

CHAPTER 7

The summer seemed even shorter than the previous year, but Kyle figured it had to be her schedule. She worked at the store Monday through Saturday and spent Sunday afternoons turning her little home into her little castle. She'd painted the main room and was making plans for the kitchen make-over.

Every time she accomplished something she hadn't done before, she mentally patted herself on the back. When she hung her curtains by herself, she was almost giddy. For most people, it probably wouldn't have been something to celebrate. But, for her, it meant another step away from what and who she had once been. She was getting stronger, more independent. Her proof was all around her. Painted walls and straight curtains, school books and a full pantry. She was making it, something a year before she had seriously doubted could ever happen.

Callin spent every spare moment building layer upon layer until his vision began to take shape. He'd worked construction with his dad from a very young age, and was so grateful that he was taught as he grew. His dad had been patient in explaining how and why things were done, and his patience was reaping its benefits through his son's hard work. Cal just couldn't help but wonder what the hard work would be for. Or who. He thought of Kyle and her smile made him smile.

Martin Jennings walked through the framed door and called out for Cal. He was surprised by the progress his crew and his son had made in just a few short months

When Martin discovered his youngest child was coming home to stay, he made the decision to go into semi-retirement from his building and remodeling company to help Cal build his home. And his wife had him nearly full time and up to his neck in renovating their own home. He was just happy he loved it, or he figured he'd be close to mad crazy by now.

When Callin didn't answer, Martin made his way to the back of the house where the kitchen was being prepped for dry wall. He found Callin, hammer in hand, staring out the window into the copse of trees beyond.

"Hey son. Exactly what are you working on at this exact moment?"

"Hey, Dad. Got lost for a second. I guess I have a lot on my mind."

"Best stay focused, or that girl's liable to give you a flat thumb."

Cal smiled, and figured there was no use denying it. "Yeah, but she's worth it."

Kyle was proud of herself that she had let go of her emotions for Callin. She couldn't live her life hoping for something she wasn't ready for, and jealous for someone she had no attachment to. She'd learned a very important lesson that life is just too short to be anything but grateful. Grateful for her salvation, for her life, for her friends, for her job. It was her choice, and she chose gratitude. And with gratitude, it was easy to choose happiness.

It took all of Saturday for Kyle to complete her painting project in her kitchen. But by late Saturday evening she was able to clean up the mess and step back to observe her work. She was excited to be finished so quickly with such drastic results. And best of all, she had her Sunday afternoon free. Kyle ate her normal Sunday lunch with Pops after service As soon as they returned to the property, Pops and Kyle changed into their work clothes and met up in the garden.

"Thanks for helping me today, Sweet Girl. I'm sure you have better things to do than hang out with this old man. All those young gentlemen at your church wantin' to go out with you and you're stuck here with me." Kyle smiled at Pops. How many times he'd said the exact same thing. The truth was that Kyle enjoyed Pops more than anyone else she ever known. He made her feel safe with her past and her secrets. He never questioned her, he just loved her.

"Well, believe it or not, you're fun to be around. And I love getting my hands in the dirt. Plus, there aren't any young men at church that I'm interested in spending time with," Callin Jennings face appeared in her mind, but just as quickly Sutton Cassaday was standing next to him. "Nope, I'm happy right where I am."

Pops took his pruning shears and began cutting away dead branches while Kyle pulled weeds. "It's funny how everything beautiful is so hard to maintain, but weeds never seem to have a problem thriving."

Pops cut another branch, "A lot like our hearts, don't you think. God has to do His pruning to make our dead hearts flourish. It takes love and care and time. But those nasty weeds in our minds grow out of control sometimes with no help at all. All you can do is keep pulling 'em up."

That night before bed, Pops words replayed through Kyle's mind. The weeds of her heart were wild and out of control. Salvation had done some heavy pruning and she continued to grow in her faith. But the guilt and shame of her past nearly blotted out the light. She slipped into sleep, wanting the Gardener to produce a great harvest in her. And she prayed for the weeds of her past to dry up and fly away in the wind.

He looked in her eyes handed her a gift wrapped in gold, "You are the most beautiful girl I've ever seen. You should really be a model." Other guys had said that to her before, but they only wanted to use her. This was different, she was sure.

She reached for the gift and opened a diamond necklace. She threw her arms around him and then let him clasp it around her neck, completely unaware that it would be ripped from her throat in just a few short weeks. He turned her around for her to look at it shining in the mirrored glass.

She had no idea at that moment just how much that gift would cost her.

Kyle woke from her nightmare, drops of sweat dotting her brow. "Oh, Lord. I'm such a mess."

No, Baby. You were lost, now you're found. My precious daughter, live like you've been found.

Callin had always felt a deep love for his church. He and his family had been members of Life Way since he was an infant. Jeremy took over for his dad when Callin was a sophomore in high school. A few families had a difficult time with a new pastor, even if he was their former pastor's son. They were used to being taught a certain way and any change was going to be a difficult adjustment.

Several members left, which never made sense to Cal. Either way they were getting a different pastor. But, his parents never said a word. They had watched Jeremy grow up and saw him through seminary. He had new ideas and in a matter of a few years, grew the church to nearly double the size.

His church was one of the things Cal missed the most once he moved away. They were a family, sure as if they were blood. He didn't find that at any other church while he'd been gone. He couldn't wait to get back and see everyone again. He was excited to get involved again and be a part of something to grow him closer to God.

All that made his frustration even greater when Sutton Cassaday seemed to want to dig her talons into him. He was uncomfortable and her presence was making it tough to focus.

And she made it harder to talk to Kyle.

CHAPTER 8

School started in a rush and Kyle was more than ready. The past semester had given her a confidence that she needed to gain respect and be better able to teach the way she'd always intended.

Her students seemed eager to learn and willing to listen. Maybe they sensed her enthusiasm, she wasn't quite sure. But, she was loving it all the same.

The Friday night at the end of her first week, she found herself over at the James' for dinner. After they had eaten, the kids scattered and Jana and Kyle went out back, as they had started a tradition of doing.

Jana couldn't hold back any longer. "So, what's going on with Callin Jennings?"

Kyle was trying so hard not to think about him, that she wasn't prepared to answer right away. "I don't know, really. I've been so busy. And I know I'm still not ready for a relationship. I know I sound like a broken record, but I still don't feel like a guy like him should settle for someone like me."

"I know you think that, but who is someone like you? What have you done that's so bad you think no one should love you?"

"I was such a horrible sinner, Jana. More than anyone I know. I still am. I did things that make me cringe when I think about them." To prove she was right, Kyle felt herself shake.

Jana repositioned herself to get more comfortable "I never told you about how we got Townsend, did I?"

Kyle shook her head and Jana continued. "Davis was two years old when I was diagnosed with breast cancer. At the time, it was suggested that I have a double mastectomy. I listened to my doctors and had the surgery, along with chemo and radiation.

After the diagnosis, I was a bitter, angry mess. I railed at God. I had lost a part of my body. I was unable to have more children. I wasn't sure I was even going to live through it and I couldn't understand how a God that was supposed to be loving might possibly kill me when my baby boy was so small and my children needed me the most.

I turned away from Him. Not for long, but long enough to make me see what life, and death, would be like without Him. I apologized. I repented and I felt His mercy and grace completely envelop me. I thought I had it all together again. I went into remission and completely recovered. When I had been cancer free for a bit, Andy and I decided we wanted to adopt.

We traveled overseas to get Towne. She had been within days of dying from malnutrition when she was found in a tapioca field in Thailand. We expected her to be small. We expected her to be scared. We even expected that she'd have a very difficult time adjusting to life in America. But, we didn't expect her to be deaf. We were completely taken by surprise. And I found myself angry, again, at God. This time my anger only lasted a few days. I guess I had learned a very important lesson.

We brought her home and met with specialists that recommended a cochlear implant. Eight years later, Towne is a hearing, speaking testament to the power of God and his healing hand.

I made it through, again, but those times in my life will always make me angry with myself when I look back. In the end, Townsend is the best gift I could have asked for, and it came from something I was nearly willing to give up my faith for.

So, what's worse. Sinning when you don't know Christ. Or turning away from Him when you do know Him?"

Kyle thought it over and felt something stir inside. She was going to feel that forgiveness to her core one day. It might not be right then, but she would believe it.

✝

The last bell sounded and Kyle hurried to get her papers in order for the following day. She wanted to get home to start on dinner. She had plans to walk a pan of lasagna over to the main house for Pops, Jana and Andy by five-thirty. Chandler had started a new job at the local convenience store and Davis and Townsend were staying over with friends.

She grabbed her bag and hurried out the classroom door. She locked up and searched for her car keys when she heard Callin's voice.

"Hi, Kyle."

Kyle smiled up at him. His nearness made her heart twist and she immediately noticed how handsome he looked with his new haircut. "Hi, Callin. I'm surprised they let you leave the field this time of year."

"I just ran over to talk to Paige for a few minutes before she left." He was hoping his motives weren't too obvious, but running into Kyle made it all worth it. He wanted to be able to at least see her to say hi, but having a conversation was an unexpected surprise.

"She's still in her classroom, working hard. How's the team coming along?" Kyle forgot she was in a hurry and began to relax.

"They're a great group of kids. Real hard workers. I want them to do well because it's my first year, but I'll be proud of them either way. How's your class this year?"

"They're good kids, too, so I can't complain. Paige told me you're moving right along with your house. How's it coming?"

"I'm planning on spending Christmas there, so I'm hoping it's finished by then."

Kyle laughed and found herself not wanting their conversation to end.

Callin was feeling the same way, but when Paige came from her room, he realized how long he'd been away from practice.

"Hey, Paige. It was great to see you, Kyle."

Kyle blushed red and responded. "It was nice to see you, too."

"See ya, Paige." Cal waved and started back toward the high school.

Paige and Kyle walked slowly out to their cars when Paige asked "Why did he come by?"

"To talk to you."

Paige rolled her eyes and they both giggled.

Football season overtook the entire town with the colors of Greenville High. The hometown team was dearly loved and strongly supported. Kyle remembered football as one of the few things she and her Dad enjoyed together when she was growing up. When Chandler invited Kyle to go with her and the rest of the James family, Kyle couldn't wait.

The air was crisp as darkness settled in and the game lights surrounding the field jolted on. Kyle inhaled the scents of fall and found herself craving chili dogs and nachos. Townsend wanted to sit next to Kyle and Kyle put her arm around her to keep her warm.

Paige had asked Kyle to join her and her parents after Kyle had already accepted Chandler's invitation, but she saved Paige and the elder Jennings couple three seats. Gray was working again, and Kyle kept wanting to talk to Paige alone to see how she was doing. Paige arrived ten minutes before kick off and her parents followed within a few minutes. Their excitement was contagious. They'd seen Cal as a player and then as an assistant coach, but this was something completely different. Their pride was obvious and theirs was the loudest section in the stands.

Kyle watched Cal on the field. He was passionate with his team and solely focused on the game. On the way off the field for half time, Kyle saw him look into the stands for his family. Her heart raced to look at him. His baseball cap made him look like a kid, and his smile lit up the field. He was so handsome.

When Kyle noticed Sutton walking down toward the field with a couple of friends, Kyle's heart ached. Why did she keep doing this over and over again?

By the time she made it home, she felt like she hurt all over. It was a physical pain to be so emotionally stuck and unable to move. It was obvious to her that for her heart's sake, she would have to avoid the Friday night games.

She had joined a Bible study that met early on Saturday mornings, and saw that as a good reason to skip the games and call it an early night on Fridays from then on. It was a good excuse, but it didn't help her heart one bit.

Saturday morning, Sutton had a pounding head ache and had already thrown up twice. She was sure she had a couple pain relievers in her purse, but she couldn't find the bottle.

She had waited around after the game for Callin to come out of the locker room, but after a half hour, her friends were becoming impatient. She left with them in a huff, angry at them that they wouldn't wait for her, angry at Callin for taking so long. They went to the local hang-out where she drank too much and stayed out too late. It was so easy to go back to home town old times.

She made her way slowly to her parent's room. She'd seen her mother only three times since she'd been home. Three times in four months. She'd seen her father once.

The door to her mother's room was closed and Sutton felt anger eating her alive. How was it possible that a mother couldn't love her own child? It didn't make sense to her as a child and it didn't make sense to her as an adult. She knocked hard on the door, determined to drive the question from her mind, but the knocking sent a wave of nausea through her punished stomach.

She didn't hear anything and opened the double door. She saw a lifeless form in a lump in the middle of the four poster bed. Sutton didn't look at her, but went directly to the drawer where her mother kept her medicine in the master bathroom.

Sutton picked up bottle after bottle and read the labels. Antidepressants, sleep medication, muscle relaxers. It was a wonder her mother was ever awake.

Sutton found the pain reliever and swallowed three without water. She left the room and resisted a strong urge to slam the doors. She knew it would only make her head worse.

She returned to her room and laid down face first into her pillow. A silent tear slid down her nose and hit her pillow. She wiped it away and pretended it never happened.

Football season ended with a winning season. The team didn't go to a championship game, but they were strong and poised. Cal knew that building a championship team could take a few years, and he had the dedication to get it done. He was proud of the boys and let them know every chance he got.

The Jennings family spent Thanksgiving in Florida with Martin's parents, which meant they'd be home for Christmas. Cal was excited to see his Gram and Paw, but was ready to spend his first Christmas in his new house. He cut down a tree for his living room as soon as he got back home from their trip. He didn't have decorations to hang on the tree, but that didn't matter a bit.

The scent of pine mingled with the new home smell and Callin couldn't help but smile every time he walked through the front door. The following week, he bought some lights and a few boxed ornaments and placed them on the tree with Christmas music playing in the background. He'd never cared to help his mom with their family tree, but he was lost in the moment. This house held so much promise, such an amazing future.

When he was finished, he went to his fridge and pulled out a carton of eggnog his mom had dropped off. He went back to look at his tree and drank out of the carton, just because he could.

✝

Grayson had taken time off to travel to Florida with Paige and had to return to work immediately, once they arrived home. They'd purchased an artificial tree a few years before that looked just like a Douglas fir. It's lights were already in place and all Paige had to do was hang ornaments. It was her favorite job. She'd received enough decorations from students over the years to fill the entire tree, but all she could think about was the ornaments her children would make for her one day.

She had a host of tests scheduled for the first of the year to see why she and Gray were having so many problems getting and staying pregnant. The sooner she made it through the holidays, the sooner they could move on with their lives.

When she miscarried, everyone told her it was one of life's normal events. She would get pregnant again soon and have a house full of children. But there was one question she couldn't get out of her mind.

What if they were wrong?

CHAPTER 9

Life Way Church held a Christmas Eve social and the entire congregation showed up, along with extended family and out of town guests.

Pops went with Kyle and found himself, again, being so grateful for this little girl in his life. It had been a year and a half. He had seen her change from a terrified child to a self-confident young woman. He'd seen her saved, baptized and watched her grow closer to the Lord. And he felt privileged for the front row seat to the show.

The candle light service was poignant and everyone laughed when the children put on their manger scene play. One of the little shepherd girls had two pacifiers in her mouth, a mother's attempt to keep her from being the loudest little actress. She was quiet, but covered baby Jesus with straw until another little girl became upset that Jesus wouldn't be able to breathe.

Chandler was in charge of the children and handled the problem with expertise. She was able to laugh along with the rest of the church when things didn't go perfectly and Kyle marveled at who Chandler would one day grow into. Most of the children followed her lead and motions during the songs. She was a natural with the kids, and Kyle was so excited for her to become a teacher. She found herself choking up when thinking about losing Chandler the next year, but it would only be for a little while.

Service ended and the group walked over to the building beside the sanctuary. A buffet of every type of food imaginable was lined up along the back wall. The aroma was enough to ensure people kept their conversations short until Pastor Jeremy prayed and lines were formed.

Pops and Kyle sat at a round table with the James' family. The Jennings sat next to their table along with Martin's parents who'd flown into town two days earlier. Kyle was anxious to meet Paige's grandparents that she'd heard so much about. But when she looked over and found Callin looking at her, her nervousness intensified. How he could do that to her continued to make her angry with herself. Especially when every time she saw him, Sutton seemed to be standing by his side.

Blake Stark walked over from where he was seated with his family and sat down in an empty chair next to Kyle. Blake was three years older than Kyle and had gone to high school with Paige. His family owned quite a bit of land in town and had Greenville's only real estate office. Blake was preparing to take over when his parents retired, and Kyle knew he was a very eligible bachelor in the church.

"How's everyone doing tonight?" Blake was smooth with a salesman's personality. He could talk to anyone about anything and leave them feeling like it was the best conversation of their lives.

"Well, hello there, Blake. We're having a great time, how about you?" Jana had known Blake since his dad sold her and Andy their first and only home twenty years back.

"Beautiful service, wonderful food. Can't get much better than that." He smiled easily and turned his attention to Kyle.

"How's teaching going, Kyle?"

"Really well, thank you. It's been a great year so far. How's the real estate business?" Kyle returned as politely as she could.

It wasn't that she didn't like Blake. He seemed like the perfect guy on paper. He was successful, wealthy and good-looking. But there was something about him that she couldn't quite place. She didn't want to judge, but she couldn't help but feel like his faith was disingenuous. It was something in how he spoke or maybe it was his actions.

Or maybe it had everything to do with the boy at the table behind him. Kyle was finding it difficult to concentrate on Blake's words. The volume had grown to a din as people were finishing their food and starting on their talking.

Kyle watched Paige walk out toward the restroom and excused herself from Blake. She didn't want to appear rude, but was so relieved to be away from him that she audibly exhaled.

✝

Blake watched Kyle walk away and kept his eyes on her. She was the most beautiful girl he'd seen in all his years growing up in this sleepy, boring town. He was destined to live his days out here, he might as well live them out with someone as gorgeous as Kyle Evans.

Callin tried not to watch as Blake made a move on Kyle. He saw when Kyle got up and left the table. And he watched Blake stare after her until she disappeared. Jealousy was a very uncommon feeling in his heart and he disliked it immensely.

He saw Sutton walking toward him from the other side of the room, and he quickly got up from his seat and left the building. The cold air slapped his face but did nothing to calm his frustration. He pulled his keys from his pants pocket and grabbed his cell on his way to his truck. He phoned his mom and told her he'd left and would meet them back at the house.

When he hung up, he knew he'd be grilled on why he left so suddenly. But it was worth it if he didn't have to watch while Blake Stark tried to win over the only girl Cal could see when he closed his eyes.

✝

Christmas passed and Kyle felt that she appreciated it even more this year than the last. She was understanding the heart of Christ more intimately, with a deeper love, and her closeness to Him made everything about Him more real and special. His birthday was one of those times.

January's frigid temperatures were harsh, but she felt desperate to go for a long run. Paige had a month full of doctor's appointments so Kyle drove over to the James house to grab Chandler for a jog.

Chandler was thrilled to see Kyle and was easily talked into a freezing cold work out. She bundled up and they started out from the house.

Kyle put her gloves on as they started out in a slow gait. "I'm so glad you were able to come with me. I've been wanting to catch up with you about your life. How's work going?"

"I love it. Mr. Tate is so sweet to me. I couldn't ask for a better boss. I'm trying to earn as much money as I can before I leave for school. My parents are paying for my tuition, so I want to be able to help them out as much as I can with spending money." Chandler had a way of making everything seem so exciting with the tone of her voice.

"It helps when you like what you're doing. It makes earning money much easier," Dodging a patch of ice on the road, Kyle asked. "Do you have a boy at school you're interested in?" Kyle had never heard Chandler mention a boy, but was curious just the same.

"I don't. I figure I'm leaving anyway. Why get attached. My parents decided a long time ago that we aren't allowed to date in high school, so that makes it a little easier to say 'no' when someone asks me out."

Kyle thought about that and wondered how her life would have been different with the same rules. The boys she dated in high school led her down the path straight toward Paul. What would her world have been if Paul had never had a place in it?

"Did you hear back from Carson College yet?"

Chandler slowed a bit back to a jog to continue talking. "Nope. But, I think I'll get in. My grades are good and both my parents went there. That's how they met. Did you know that?"

"No, I didn't. That's sweet. So your mom didn't grow up here?"

"She lived here when she was small, but she spent most of her childhood in Alabama with my grandma's family. Then they moved back when she was in high school. My dad was born and raised here. They knew each other in high school, but didn't fall in love until they saw each other on campus at C.C. They moved here after they graduated and were married.

I know mom misses her family back home, but I think she's happy here. We're not too far. My Aunt moved back to Alabama after she graduated, so we stay with her every summer for a few weeks. She has seven horses, so we ride the entire time we're there. I wanted to be a horse trainer the first time we visited, but I thought it meant teaching the horses with a chalk board and school books. So, I changed my plans to involve kids, instead."

"That's great you all are so close. I don't know any of my extended family. It feels so foreign when people are close to their parents, let alone their aunts and uncles." Kyle laughed, but then realized it wasn't funny.

Talking and the cold air began to burn their lungs and they slowed to a walk. Kyle enjoyed Chandler so much. She was grateful she had decided to talk her into this madness.

By the time they got back to the house, their feet were frozen and they couldn't feel their noses.

Jana made them hot chocolate with marshmallows and Kyle drank it down knowing that the cocoa's calories just canceled out their run.

CHAPTER 10

Kyle tipped her face to the sun and smiled at its warmth. She slammed the door of her old car and stepped onto the curb. Gazing down the tree-lined road, she sighed. *Freedom.* She'd never get used to what this place symbolized. Deliverance. Salvation. This town, this street, this life. She was so very blessed.

The warming February day was a confusing contrast to the month before. The warmth was promising an early Spring, soon to be ushered in as March quickly approached. It wouldn't be long before flowers of every color and fragrance would adorn the streets and fill her senses. Spring would always be Kyle's favorite time. It meant rebirth and new beginnings. It was Kyle's life being vibrantly lived out.

Kyle pushed the door open to the feed store and heard the familiar bell that would summon Pops. She inhaled the mixture of saw dust and hay as he entered from the back of the store as quickly as he could, which was slower than the day before. Kyle had begun to worry about him, but whenever she mentioned he go get a physical at the doctor's office, he always told her the same thing, "When Jesus comes for me, ain't nothing more I want to do than follow Him home."

Kyle still liked to check in on him, but didn't want him knowing it. She would bake him one of her cakes or pies and deliver it when she knew he was at the main house. And she would drop in at the store to say hello whenever she came to town.

"Well, hello there, Sweet Girl. What are you doing in here this morning? Shouldn't you be teachin' those younguns?" He shuffled over and met Kyle in an embrace.

Kyle returned the hug and patted his back before she released him. "It's Saturday! Please don't make me work more than I have to."

"Well, you know, those kids are lucky to have you. There's

nothing you can do wrong."

Kyle blushed and glanced down. She couldn't help but wonder if Pops would feel the same if he knew the entire story. She understood forgiveness. Jesus loved her, no matter her past. But, some of her secrets she vowed to keep buried, even from those closest to her.

"I came into town to get some paint and drop cloths. I'm working on the bedroom this weekend while I have the chance." Kyle smiled at the prospect of change.

Pops was always so encouraging of her choices. "Well, well. You know if I ever sell my farm, that old barn is going to be the reason. You've done a beautiful job fixing her up.

"So, what color paint did you pick out?" Pops turned and rounded back toward the cash register when a couple of customers looked like they were close to needing to check out.

Kyle pulled a paint sample from her bag and handed it to Pops. Pops took it from her while sliding on his glasses he kept in his front shirt pocket. "Well, ain't that purty! It's got some yellow in it, don't it?"

Kyle's smile broadened, "Yep. I think it will brighten up the room quite a bit. Plus it makes me feel happy."

"I can see that." Pops smiled back. Kyle didn't know that her smile was all he needed some days.

"So when do we get to start working together again?" Pops had been asking the same question for a month, but she knew he hadn't forgotten.

"April third, as soon as Spring Break starts. We have a few weeks yet." Kyle was excited for her time at the feed store. It reminded her of when she moved to this town, and all it meant.

"Well, okay, Honey. I'm sure you have more to do than talk to an old man like me."

Kyle squeezed his hand before turning to leave, "Never, Pops. But, I'll see you later."

✝

Callin glanced across the street and saw Kyle let the door close at Hayfields and head down the sidewalk toward the hardware store. She stopped to talk to two young girls and Cal realized they must be her students. Even from a distance he could feel her love for them, see in her motions how much she cared. The sunshine reflected off her hair, turning it golden and illuminating her smile.

His heart clenched, like it normally did. Kyle filled his mind more these days than he liked. He wanted to spend time with her and get to know her. He'd talk to her as much as he could at church and he'd see her running with his sister. But, he wanted to ask her out on a real date. So much it nearly hurt.

But, if it wasn't Sutton or Blake getting in his way, it was the look in her eyes that always stopped him short. Just when he felt he had the courage, she would look at him like she was seeing a memory. He just knew he couldn't compete with an unforgotten past.

He debated whether or not to get her attention, but decided against it. He tugged his baseball cap tighter down on his head and tried to refocus on his plans for Monday's lessons. He had a life he had to push forward, no matter how heavy it felt.

✝

The smell of coffee still lingered in the air from her early morning cup when Kyle closed the front door of her home with her foot. The renovated barn still looked the same on the exterior, but was brand new inside. Just like her. At least that's what she kept telling herself.

She knew she was saved. She knew she was forgiven. She knew it in her mind and she believed. So, why couldn't her heart believe it, too? Maybe because even though Jesus could forget, she couldn't. With every step forward, she'd take one step back into the drudge and muck of the past. It would splatter onto her present, cloud her future.

Kyle sighed and set the paint cans on the kitchen counter.

"I'm sorry, Lord. I keep trying and I keep failing. I know You love me."

With the paint stirred, brushes ready and drop cloths down, Kyle rolled the fresh color onto the scarred walls, covering the stains.

She kept doubting and He kept reminding.

"Yes, Jesus. I know how much You love me."

✝

Kyle didn't enjoy grocery shopping any day of the week, and it was much harder after a long day at school than on a Saturday. But her painting project had given her no choice.

She had just put the last of her items in her shopping cart when she turned the corner and found herself nearly colliding with Callin Jennings.

She was flustered and immediately reprimanded herself. "Hi, Callin."

Cal looked equally surprised and responded, "Hey, Kyle. How are you?"

"Great, thank you. How about yourself?"

Cal leaned against his cart and willed himself to think clearly, "I'm doing great, too. It's been a really good week so far. The kids have been unnaturally quiet this week, for some reason. Maybe they're growing up."

Kyle smiled. She was grateful that they had teaching in common. "I've noticed that with my class this whole year. They seem very mature for some reason. It's a big stretch since last year, that's for sure."

"Sixth grade is a tough grade to teach. I'm not sure I'd have any hair left on my head. I'd either pull it all out or it would fall out. I really admire you for taking on the challenge and being so great at it."

Kyle felt her face begin to warm, "That's sweet. I don't think tenth grade is a whole lot easier, if I remember correctly. In fact, growing up, I thought every grade was horrible."

Callin laughed and agreed, "I definitely remember Paige having a harder time than I did. I had one best friend and sports to keep me busy, so I didn't have much conflict."

Kyle noticed how much she liked the deep baritone in his laughter, and how his smile was just the slightest bit crooked. "Yep, guys seem to have an easier time of it. But, it all works out in the end for us all, I guess."

Cal shifted feet, "Thankfully, I think you're right.

"I'm usually always here on Tuesday nights. This isn't your normal night, huh?" Cal was enjoying watching her expressions. Her eyes told a story, like they were learning how to dance.

"No, I usually shop on Saturdays, but I was painting this past weekend and didn't have time."

Callin realized he could have talked to her all night long right there in the bread aisle, "Did you paint your house, or are you an artist?"

Kyle laughed, "Ha, definitely not an artist. I'm pretty sure I made my art teacher cry in high school. A couple times. No, I painted my room. It was the last room that needed painting in my little home, so I can say I'm finally all finished. Or I can start all over again."

Cal grinned. "That's how it works, according to my mom."

"Aw, I love your mom. Your parents are so cute. They're really such great people." Kyle thought of Anne and Martin Jennings with admiration.

"They are. And they love each other more than anyone I know."

"That's really neat. That kind of love seems really hard to come by in today's world." Kyle was starting to see that it might be hard to come by, but it wasn't impossible.

"Hard, but not impossible." Callin echoed her thoughts and she had to smile.

"It's been really great talking to you. I don't mean to hurry off, but I'm afraid my ice cream's going to melt to milk." Kyle reluctantly ended their conversation.

"I've enjoyed talking with you, too. We should do it more often." Callin nervously watched Kyle's response, but she smiled.

"I agree. I'll start shopping on Tuesdays from now on." She teased.

"That, or you're always welcome over to the main house. Friday nights are our family nights. My parents would love to have you over anytime." And so would he.

"I'd love that. Thank you.

Cal was grateful for the opened door. "Have a great night, Kyle."

"You, too. I'll see you soon."

Callin studied Kyle's eyes and wanted to memorize her smile, even under the fluorescent lights of the local grocery store.

As she walked over to the check out line to purchase her items, Callin turned slightly and stole another glimpse of her one last time. Kyle looked back at him and they both smiled.

As Callin walked away he muttered to himself, "Okay heart. Settle down."

✝

Paige sat in the doctor's office with Grayson and willed herself not to cry. This was their third round of testing and they all said the same thing. It was highly unlikely that Paige would ever carry a baby of her own.

The doctor's words jumbled once she'd heard the results. Gray held her hand and then put his arm around her. She was crumbling and couldn't stop. When she couldn't hold back her tears, the doctor left them alone in his office. Her cries turned to weeping and Gray felt helpless by her side.

She knew there was purpose in her pain. She knew there was a plan in her suffering far greater than anything that could happen without it. But, as they walked from the office and made their way to their car, Paige wasn't thinking about any of that. She was thinking of the baby she'd never hold.

✝

Chandler heard the mail truck pull up in front of her house right after she had applied her second coat of toe nail polish.

"Aw, man." She blew on her toes and then grabbed a piece of paper to fan them dry. She was expecting something life-changing in the mail, and wet nail polish was about to drive her mad.

"Hey, Baby. Pretty color." Jana came into the kitchen from putting away laundry.

"Hey, Mom. Miss Tara just dropped the mail in the box and I have to wait until my toes dry."

Jana laughed, remembering the excitement of college acceptance letters. Like her daughter, Jana had only one school she had dreamed of attending. "Do you want me to go out and look for you?"

"Oh, no thanks, Mom. I think they're dry enough for flip flops." Chandler carefully put her feet in her sandals and gingerly walked down the gravel road to the mail box at the end of the drive. She pulled out several letters and quickly leafed through the envelopes.

Just as she closed the door of the box, she heard a rustle in the wooded area next to the house. She turned her head toward the noise and stared into the forest. The trees were mostly bare, usually making it easy to spot an animal running away. She kept her eyes trained on the place she heard the noise, but saw nothing. As she hurried back to the house, she thought to herself that whatever animal made the sound she'd just heard must have been very large. And it rattled her.

Once inside the house, she looked out the window and then closed the blinds before she found the letter she'd been waiting for and tore it open.

"Yay! Mom! I got in."

Jana came back into the kitchen and wrapped her arms around her oldest child. "Congratulations, Baby. But, can I tell you that I had no doubts whatsoever."

Not long after, Davis came through the door followed by Townsend and Andy. Tennis and soccer practices were over and the evening routine was about to begin.

Chandler held the letter up for her dad to see. "Chan, honey, congratulations." Andy was so grateful that his daughter's dreams were coming true, but he was having a difficult time letting her go. But, if she had to leave him to go anywhere, his and Jana's Alma mater was the place he wanted her to be.

Townsend stood beside her dad and read the letter. "This means you're going to Carson College?"

Chandler knew how hard this was going to be on her little sister, "It does, Towne, but you know I'll see you as much as I can. And I'll never be far. You've heard it before, all you have to do is think of me and you'll have me with you."

Townsend teared up, "No, it's not the same. I don't want you to leave me."

Chandler put her arms around Townsend, "I'd never leave you. I'm just going away for a little while. I'll see you every chance I get. And I'll always, always love you with all my heart."

Townsend wiped her eyes and seemed to feel better. Chandler was going to miss Townsend, too. She nearly broke down thinking of the day she'd say 'good-bye'.

Davis bounced the soccer ball on his head until his mom grabbed it and ushered him toward the bathroom to wash hands before dinner, and life resumed as normal. At fourteen years old, Davis might realize how much he would miss his sister when she was far from home, but it was harder for him to express.

Seated around the dinner table, Jana looked around at her little family. Her babies weren't babies anymore. Life was changing so rapidly, sometimes she felt like she would do anything to slow it down. She had always tried so hard to live out every second, enjoy every moment. But, they grew up anyway. And she sat, helpless, as she watched time continue to devour their childhood.

CHAPTER 11

Grayson left for work and Paige wrapped herself up in a blanket. She had just grabbed the box of tissues when her phone rang. Kyle's name ran across the screen.

"Hey, Ky. Feel like coming over and listening to me cry?"

Kyle felt the tears rush to her eyes. She didn't have to ask. The results were the same.

Kyle made it to Paige's house in a matter of minutes. Paige met her at the door and they cried together. There had been countless hours of laughter during their friendship. Now it was time for tears.

Kyle brewed some coffee and sat by Paige's side in silence. They didn't speak for a long time when Paige finally interrupted the silence.

"The baby was due this Friday. I wonder if he would have been late like his daddy was." Paige continued to stare ahead, lost in mourning.

"Why don't we hold a memorial?" Kyle spoke. Paige hadn't thought of that. Maybe remembering would hold some closure.

"What would we do?"

"Well, when my grandma died, my mom told me to write her a letter and then we attached it to a balloon. We let the balloon go and watched it disappear. You could write a letter to the baby. Tell him how much you love him, how you can't wait to see him someday in heaven. Tell him how much you miss him. Then we can let it fly away to heaven."

Paige nodded, "I'd like that. Maybe it could be just you and me, right after school lets out on Friday? I don't think Gray would understand why I need to do something like this. And then I'd get frustrated."

Kyle understood. Sometimes pain was easier to handle when less people are involved.

They sat a few more minutes surrounded in stillness before Paige spoke again. "I'm mad. I don't think I'm mad at God. I'm just mad. And really, really sad. Today is almost worse than the miscarriage. At least when I lost my baby, I still had hope to have another. There's no more hope. What a horrible feeling."

Kyle thought a moment. "There's always hope. God's bigger than any test result."

Paige knew it was true. But, she also knew that she might never totally understand all of God's ways. His will for her life might not make sense to her, but it might simply just be.

Kyle didn't think before she said the words. They flowed out before she could reel them back in. "Jesus was adopted."

The words hung in the air while neither one responded.

Paige ran over the words again and again. And for the first time in twenty-four hours, she smiled.

Thursday afternoon, Sutton parked her sporty red Porsche next to Callin's jet black Ram pickup truck and checked her makeup in the rear view mirror. It took her a while to come up with a legitimate reason for why she would be at the High School, but she always thought herself to be highly resourceful. Thankfully, her mother was acquaintances with one of the ninth grade Math teachers, and it had been a very long time since Sutton had seen her to say hello.

She opened her car door and was careful to maneuver herself to standing without showing too much. She was enjoying the sun and the cute outfits she was able to wear in the warmer weather. Her skirt was awfully short, she knew, but why waste what God had given her. Sutton walked into the front office and asked to see Mrs. Brown. When the secretary informed her that Mrs.

Brown had gone home for the day, Sutton thanked her and walked straight toward the football field. She had timed it to ensure that track practice would be close to ending and Callin would have plenty of time to talk to her.

She walked to the bottom seat of the bleachers and scanned the field. She saw Callin watching some of his players as they ran sprints. He stood next to his two assistant coaches, nodding with satisfaction on how fast his guys were running. Track season would collide with Spring football practice and Callin was pleased to see how fast his star player was running the one hundred.

Sutton studied how he held his clip board, how he stood with confidence. She could see how white his teeth when he laughed, even from so far away. Yes, Sutton would be so proud to be his girlfriend. She envisioned herself sitting in the stands, running up to him at the end of the games and giving him a huge kiss for all the world to see.

The track team continued to practice and the boy's eyes drifted to Sutton. She smiled at them all and started walking toward Coach Jennings.

"Hey Cal." Sutton beamed at Cal as she moved toward him.

"Hi, Sutton." Callin's surprise was impossible to mask.

"I was here to say hello to Mrs. Brown, but she's already left for the day."

Cal relaxed slightly, knowing that Sutton hadn't been there just to see him. She carried the conversation, "I didn't know you practiced this time of year."

Cal waved to the other coaches and began to walk toward the weight room, Sutton falling in step with him, "We don't. Quite a few of my guys are in the weight room lifting, but we have some of our best players running track to stay in shape and gain speed. Our QB runs one of the fastest one hundreds this year."

Callin noticed several runners gawking at him with Sutton and suddenly became very aware of how it might appear. "I'm sorry to shove off so quickly, but I have to go check on how weight training's coming."

Callin felt rude, but couldn't think of what else to do. Sutton slowed and then grabbed his arm and her hand lingered, "Maybe we can meet up for dinner sometime? We never see each other. Well, other than on Sundays."

Callin dropped his arm and did what he could to not shrug her off. "That's kind, Sutton. But, it's probably not a good idea."

Her face fell and Callin didn't know what to do. Girls weren't typically so forward with him, and he didn't want to hurt her feelings. He tried to soften the rejection, "I'm really busy right now. Ya know."

Sutton's face broke into a smile, "Of course. Well, I'm always available." She touched his arm again and he had no doubts of what she had intended with her words.

Then he heard a whisper, as clear as if the Lord bent down and cupped His hand over his ear.

Flee.

"Okay, I'll see you later, then. Have a great week." Cal felt like he was practically running toward the school. He looked to see onlookers continue to stare and knew Sutton was hoping he'd watch her and her short skirt walk away.

Once inside the building, he locked himself in his office. He knew most men would consider him crazy for turning away someone like Sutton Cassaday.

But alone at his desk, he wasn't thinking of Sutton or her advances.

He was thinking of Kyle.

"Dear Lord, I guess I just pray that if Kyle and I are meant to be, that you heal her. I don't know what happened to her, but I know she seems so fragile. Please help me know what to do.

"Because I really, really like her."

Friday's bell sounded and Paige remained at her desk, motionless. The excitement of the weekend had the kids laughing and squealing, but Paige let them pass without notice. She held the letter to her first child gingerly in her hands. She'd worked on exactly what to say for two days. The envelope felt so heavy that she wondered if the balloons would lift.

She knew that God wouldn't grab the balloon and show her baby the letter. But, then she questioned if maybe He would. He certainly could. Heaven wasn't something she could put her mind around, so she had rarely tried. Now that she had a part of herself living there, she'd been thinking a lot more about it.

Kyle walked in holding three helium balloons. She looked at Paige holding the letter and waited.

Paige finally looked up, eyes dry. "I'm ready."

The two walked to the P.E. track where they were alone. Kyle tied the letter to the balloons and held Paige's hand. "Do you want to pray, or would you like me to?"

Paige had written everything she had inside of her heart onto those pages. She didn't feel like she could say another word. "It would mean a lot if you would."

They bowed their heads and Kyle began. "Dear Lord, we know that Baby is safe. We know he's loved and happy and that we'll see him someday. But, the pain is still here for Paige and Gray. It's real and it's raw and it hasn't gone away. So, I pray that you heal their hearts, Lord. Comfort them now. Help them to move on, and grow them closer to You.

"We don't know how heaven works. Your timing is so different from ours, that Baby might never have known a moment without his Momma. Or You might be able to show him how much his

Momma adores him. We don't know. But, we do know that you can use him for something amazing on this earth. And I pray that whatever you have in store for Paige and Gray, that they will see Your fingerprints all over it.

"We pray these things in Your name. Amen."

Paige kept her eyes closed in silent prayer for another few moments, then let her love letter fly. Then they stood and watched the balloons dip and bounce until they were out of sight.

✝

Sunday morning, Kyle arrived at church with only minutes to spare before the worship team began their opening song. She sat in her usual place and gave hugs to Jana, Chandler and Townsend.   Davis and Andy sat on the other side of the girls so Kyle smiled at them and waved.

Pastor Jeremy began his sermon on Philippians 2:4-5

4 Let each of you look out not only for his own interests, but also for the interests of others. 5 Let this mind be in you which was also in Christ Jesus.

These verses inspired Kyle to look outside herself and strive for the mind of Christ. She could see how her pain and fear colored every decision she made, every thought she had.

She walked out of the sanctuary and into the cloudless day. She knew that she would ensure her perspective on things would line up with how Jesus saw things. As she was making plans in her mind on how to accomplish this, she looked up to see Sutton and Callin standing near a cluster of trees just a few feet away. Sutton was moving closer to Callin with every laugh, every smile. Disappointment crushed her, making it hard to breathe. Cal had awoken a dormant part of her heart, that part she continued to try to push down.

Kyle looked away and asked herself how God would look at the situation. It didn't take long to find the answer. He would remind her that He had chosen her husband for her from before she was created. She just needed to be patient.

Paige walked up to Kyle and grabbed her arms, "Hey friend. Are we running tomorrow?"

Kyle was thrilled to see that Paige was returning to her old self. She knew there were moments of sadness and doubt, but Paige's smile had returned. "Yes, I'll bring my stuff to change into."

Kyle and Paige walked to their cars and said good-bye.

Callin saw Kyle walk out of the sanctuary and he wanted so much to go talk with her. He was agitated with Sutton, but didn't know how to get away without hurting her feelings. She kept touching him and he was beginning to feel uncomfortable. The last thing he wanted was for Kyle to think he was interested in Sutton. Callin finally broke free from her and watched Kyle drive away. Kyle did something to him that was foreign. She made him want more than the life he was leading.

"Okay, Lord. I have to hand this over to You. The timing is all Yours."

CHAPTER 12

Paige poked her head into Kyle's classroom on Monday afternoon. Paige had a white visor over her dark hair. She removed it and ran her fingers through her short hair. She'd just gotten a pixie cut and was getting used to the feel of it. "Hey, Ky. You ready?"

Kyle looked up to Paige's smiling face. If Kyle had ever wanted a sister, she would be just like Paige. "Ready as I'll ever be. Let me get these last couple of papers graded and I'll go get changed."

Paige and Kyle had been running together so long that they knew when to slow it down and when to kick it up. Their love for the outdoors and the ability to laugh while working out made it fun and interesting. Winter had disappeared in silence and Spring had gladly taken its place. The flowers Kyle had been longing for hadn't disappointed. Their fragrance during the girls' long runs kept them moving.

Kyle finished her last paper and hurried into the restroom down the outside walkway to change into her running gear. She tied her shoe laces and then pulled her hair back in a ponytail. She grabbed her bag and closed the bathroom door behind her with her hip.

Something caught her eye to her right in the woods beyond the school. She thought she saw a figure moving into the brush and fear shot through her. His face, his eyes. It had been over two years without a word, but his promises to find her shrieked through her mind. Feeling like she was being paranoid, Kyle looked away and trotted over to where Paige was stretching on the bench outside their classrooms.

Kyle threw her bag in her room and went to stand next to Paige, "I thought I just saw someone in the trees by the restroom.

"Maybe it was a kid passing through. What are you thinking?"

"No, I'm sure you're right. I'm so paranoid sometimes. I'll stretch when we get back. Let's do this."

They took off in a slow jog and like every other day, they passed the high school football stadium within minutes. Three coaches stood with their backs to them, clipboards in hand, watching the runners.

Paige cupped her hands around her mouth and hollered, "Hey! Coach Jennings! They're looking good, Brother!"

Callin turned around and waved. He caught Kyle's eye and smiled. Kyle's heart flip-flopped and she smiled back, gave a wave and then quickly looked away.

Paige saw the exchange and asked Kyle, "Why don't you go out with my brother?"

"Because your brother has never asked me out."

"Well, I know he invited you over to my parents. I know it might be difficult to start dating again, at first. But don't you think it's time to start living?"

Kyle sighed, but Paige pressed on, "It's been two years, Ky. And you know God's going to protect you. If it's not God's will for you and Callin to be together, than He'll close that door. But, you'll never know unless you give it a chance."

Kyle remained silent.

"Sweetie, he likes you and you like him. Everyone knows it. Come over for dinner Friday night. I'll help things along." Paige looked over at her friend and grinned.

Kyle laughed and side-stepped a frog in the path, "Okay. I'll come to dinner, but only to get a home-cooked meal. Cal and I don't need any help. I thought he liked Sutton Cassaday anyway."

"No, he doesn't. She likes him. He likes you." Rolling her eyes, Paige said sarcastically, "And you said you don't need help."

✝

Chief Grayson Williams was sitting at his desk when a young girl and her mother walked through the front door of the station. At thirty years old, Grayson knew he was extremely young to be the Chief of police. The fact that he looked twenty-five made shock the normal response of people who met him for the first time.

The mother walked her daughter over to the front desk and asked to file a complaint. The front desk officer directed them back to Grayson's office.

Grayson stood and extended his hand as the mother approached, "Hello Sir, I'm Joy Roig and this is my daughter, Megan. We needed to talk to someone about a man who was watching Meg at the school."

Gray, a former linebacker at Greenfield High, still knew most of the teachers and coaches. He had other reports of a man being seen in the area and had already placed additional officers near the school grounds to patrol the area.

"I'm Chief Williams. I really appreciate you coming in. You're the third complaint this month.

Can you tell me what happened, Megan?"

Gray invited them to sit as Megan pulled her blond hair away from her face and bit her lip while deciding where to begin. "Well, I was running the track yesterday and walked back by the concession stand to get some water. I saw this man across the street and he was looking at me. When I went back to the track, I saw that he could still see me and that he was watching me. It felt creepy 'cuz he was older and not supposed to be there. I could see a young guy acting like that, but he was like, a grown up. I'm only sixteen years old. There's something wrong with that."

Grayson typed as she talked and then looked up from his

83

computer screen, "Can you describe him for me? His age, hair color, height. Could you see any tattoos?"

"No, he was pretty far away. I didn't really get a great look at him. He was wearing a skull cap, so I didn't see his hair. He didn't look real tall and he didn't look skinny or fat. He was just pretty normal looking. Except creepy."

Grayson went on to ask Megan and her mother a few more questions before having them sign the statement and walking them to his office door.

Grayson rubbed his hand over his blond, short-cropped hair and felt a tremor of dread breeze over him. He didn't have anything concrete, but something was going to happen. No one watched girls like that without a motive and intent. He had to find this guy. As soon as Megan and her mother left with the artist to try to compose a sketch, he turned to his deputy and voiced his fear, "We need a break soon or someone's going to get hurt."

Kyle knocked on the front door to the Jennings' old white farmhouse and waited. This house could have been on the cover of a home and garden magazine. It had the charm of days gone by mixed with the class and elegance of modern style. Black shutters adorned the windows and a red door welcomed its guests. A black porch swing hung to the left and black rockers invited a sit in the shade. She could almost see the lemonade resting on the small tables placed between the chairs. Two ferns rested on either side of the door in tall planters. It was similar to Pops home, but had a woman's touch that Pops didn't possess. The thought that maybe she should work on the house, not just the barn, flitted through her mind.

Kyle refocused while she balanced the strawberry pie she'd made for the dessert in her right hand. With her left hand, she pushed her hair behind her ear and straightened her t-shirt beneath her jacket. Her jeans were worn, and suddenly she became self-conscious. At least she would be comfortable.

Martin Jennings opened the door with a broad smile and quickly extended his hand, "Well, Hello, Kyle! So glad you could join us tonight."

Kyle shook his hand and he led her inside.

Kyle was mesmerized with so much to admire on the inside. The interior was spacious and homey. Anne and Martin had done a beautiful job renovating the house the year before, and it was like a brand new home. Martin led Kyle through the great room to the back of the house where the kitchen was located.

Martin moved aside and let Kyle walk past him, "Anne's in the kitchen making things smell good and I have no idea where anyone else is. Just go on in and make yourself at home."

The kitchen was larger than anything Kyle had seen and was perfectly ideal for entertaining.

"Hi, Miss Anne." Kyle called to Anne who was occupied with taking a ham from the oven.

"Hello, Kyle! I'm so happy you were able to come tonight. Why in the world haven't we done this before?" Anne took off her flowered oven mitts, took the pie from Kyle and then gave her a warm hug. "Callin's out in the barn and Paige and Grayson should be here any minute."

Kyle hung her jacket on the coat rack. "Is there anything I can do to help?" Kyle looked around to find something to do, and noticed the table was already set and the glasses were topped with ice.

"Thank you, Sweetie, but I think everything is under control. We just need to wait for the mouths to get here."

At that moment, the back door opened and a very dirty Callin Jennings walked into the kitchen. He held a bridle in his hands and didn't look up when he entered, "Mom, this bit's tearing off…" He looked up to see Kyle and shock registered in his eyes. Kyle knew immediately that no one had informed him of her attendance at dinner.

"Hey, Kyle." Callin raked his fingers through his dark brown hair, messing it up all the more.

Kyle smiled at the look of him. How he could be such a mess and so handsome at the same time gave her pause. "Hey, Cal. You look like you've been working hard."

"Always." He grinned and then looked down at his sweaty t-shirt clinging to his chest. "Okay. I'm off to get cleaned up. I'll tell you about the bridle later." He dodged by Kyle and headed to the stairs.

"Sometimes I think that boy should just move back in with us. He's here more than he's at his house, that's for sure."

Kyle smiled and asked, "That's so nice that he built his house on the property, too. I know he loves it."

"Yes, it is wonderful. I really missed him when he was gone. His place is gorgeous. He and Martin did an amazing job building it."

Anne placed the green beans on the table and turned back to Kyle. "Paige and Gray moved into our old house on the East and Cal built on the West. This will all be their property some day, so it's easier to have them here already. Martin's parents left the ranch to us before they retired to Florida.

"I'll tell you, the day Martin's rough old cowboy of a dad told us they were going to move to Florida to live in a retirement village was the day we realized that anything can happen and probably will. Martin and I moved in here and remodeled the whole house. It was a crazy time. We were redoing this house and starting to build Cal's at the same time. It took a while, but I feel like it's really ours now."

Kyle looked around at the off-white wood and glass cabinets, granite countertops and ornate woodwork above the doors before replying, "It's a dream home, no doubt about it. You have wonderful taste."

"Well, thank you very much. Do you still enjoy living out in

Pops barn? Paige told me you've really been fixing it up." Anne sat down across from Kyle, giving up that her family would be on time.

"Yes, I love it. I'm still getting used to living by myself. It can be pretty scary out so far from our neighbors. It just feels so secluded and can get so dark. But, it's comfortable."

"Pops is quite a doll, isn't he? Our whole town absolutely adores that man." Anne stood up when she heard a car door and walked to where she could see out the front windows.

"Paige and Gray are here. I'll start filling the glasses." Anne said while reaching for the pitcher of sweet tea.

Kyle was making her way to the front door when it opened and her best friend walked through with her husband.

"Hey there! I'm so glad you came." Paige gave Kyle a quick hug and put her arm around her to head back to the kitchen. "Has Callin finished up with the horses yet?"

"Yes, he has." Kyle nudged her friend. "He apparently didn't know y'all were having a guest tonight."

Paige shrugged and said, "I must have forgotten to tell him."

Grayson grabbed his wife's shoulders from behind and squeezed, "She does convenient stuff like that all the time."

Kyle smiled and watched the family as they united around the kitchen. Martin had reappeared from his study and Callin had come back scrubbed clean and dressed in fresh clothes.

Once they were seated around the table, Kyle began to feel her nerves. She glanced at Callin and realized that he was feeling his, as well. Somehow that was comforting.

The table was made of a rich mahogany and extended throughout much of the expansive dining room. Kyle and Callin were seated across from each other, making it obviously easier for conversing.

After Martin blessed the meal, he said, "So, Kyle, tell us your story," Martin's innocent question startled Kyle for a moment and it showed on her face. Paige noticed it immediately and asked, "Tell us where you were born." That should be an easy enough start.

Kyle recovered quickly and began to speak. She couldn't remember ever feeling comfortable talking openly about herself. Other people were her focus because they were interesting, and because that kept the spotlight off of her. But, there she sat with her best friend, the boy she realized she was falling for and their family. It came to her in an instant that it was time to move forward.

"I was born in a small town in southern Indiana. I'm not very close with what family I have there and I needed a change. God led me right to Pop's front door. I got a job at the feed store that day and moved into the barn that night. Thankfully, he'd already had it set up for a guest house. I only had a few classes left of my internship, then started working with Paige."

Martin smiled at her and commented, "It's pretty obvious you were meant to be here."

Kyle cleared her throat, and pressed on, "Yes, it is. God's constant provision made me realize pretty quickly that there's no such thing as coincidence. I wasn't saved until after I came here. I left a pretty difficult life behind. There's no doubt, I'm very blessed."

Paige expertly changed the subject and Kyle felt the relief. She'd done it. She'd opened up publicly and survived. It wasn't much, but it was a start.

Anne asked about Jana, Andy and the kids. "You usually spend Fridays with the James family, don't you, Kyle?"

Kyle finished her bite before responding. "I do. Chandler was working tonight, though. And Jana and I see each other quite a bit during the week. They won't miss me tonight."

Callin looked down at his plate and wondered if they'd miss her the next Friday. Or the next.

Laughter sounded around the table when Paige told of her student's stories. She had some characters in her class and always enjoyed being able to out-craze them. Her students loved her zany ways and her ability to make school fun. Many of her kids were from tough backgrounds and she made it her life's goal to make school a place of safety and refuge.

Callin talked with passion about his football team. He was the type of coach who treated his team like family. They knew Coach Jennings was on their side and they showed their loyalty to him in every game. Even though he had only been their coach for a year, he felt the boys coming up through the next few years would lead them to state title.

"The guys are already stronger than they were in the fall. They're such hard workers. We have a lot of seniors graduating this year, but the guys coming up are really solid." Cal looked at Kyle and smiled before looking back at his plate. She tried as hard as she could not to blush, but it was just impossible. While everyone noticed, everyone pretended not to. But, their hearts smiled.

Dishes were cleared and Kyle's strawberry pie was served with fresh whip cream. Kyle had offered a store bought brand, but in the country real whip cream wasn't hard to come by. It was absolutely perfect on top of the berries and all taste buds were satisfied.

Grayson finished first and directed his question toward Paige and Kyle, "Have you had any reports of a strange man watching the school? "

Paige replied with her mouth full, 'Maybe, why?"

Gray continued, "A girl came in and filed a complaint. There have been several sightings at the High School, but I wasn't sure if the guy had been to the middle school, as well. Why do you say maybe?"

"Kyle thought she saw someone on Wednesday. Do you think he's dangerous?" Paige asked Grayson before looking back at Kyle.

"Well, you know, I'm always cautious. I believe that people escalate from bad to worse. If this guy's watching girls, then I don't think it's unreasonable to assume that he's going to act at some point. What did you see, Kyle?"

Kyle's thoughts flew to the figure she thought she saw days before. "I'm not really sure. I heard a noise, a rustling in the tree line next to the girl's restroom. It all happened so fast. I was looking down toward the ground, thinking maybe it was an animal, but instead I thought I saw a brown hiking boot. Afterward, I realized the noise sounded like something too large to be a raccoon or even a dog. I don't know. It was more like I felt someone there, than saw him."

While Gray nodded and seemed to try to think of additional questions, the man's face from Kyle's past flooded her mind. He said there was no place she could hide where he wouldn't find her.

As conversation turned light once again and the coffee and dessert had disappeared, Kyle refocused on the present. By ten o'clock, she was beginning to feel sleepy. She didn't want to leave, but knew she couldn't stay. She never knew there were families like this one. Families that loved each other so easily. Families that laughed together and truly cared for one another's feelings.

No, she really didn't want to leave.

"I better be getting home." Kyle stood and found her jacket. She turned to Anne and Martin, "Thank you so much for everything. I had such a wonderful time and dinner was delicious."

The others stood to walk her to the door. Paige and Anne gave her a quick hug and welcomed her back anytime. Callin held the door open for her and followed her out to her car. He could almost hear his sister giggling like a little girl.

As they stepped off the front porch steps, Callin spoke, "I'm really glad you came over tonight. I only seem to see you at church and never get much of a chance to talk. I really enjoyed tonight."

Kyle stopped by the door of her car and turned toward Cal, completely unaware of the cool breeze touching her cheeks. "I really enjoyed tonight, too. You have an amazing family."

"Thank you. They seem to think you're pretty okay, too." Cal smiled. He reached in front her and opened her car door. "I hope I see you again soon. Other than at church. Oh, and the grocery store."

Kyle smiled up at him and felt her heart rate speeding. "Thank you. I hope so, too."

Once Kyle was behind the wheel, Cal closed her door and she started up the engine. She began to pull out down the drive and they waved. As she drove away toward the main road, she looked in her rear view mirror to see him illuminated by the porch light, still standing there looking after her.

When Callin returned to the kitchen, he found his mom wiping down the table.

"How are you doing?" Anne asked without looking at him.

"I like her, Mom. I like her a lot."

"She is precious. And smart. And beautiful. But, that look in her eye, it worries me. She's broken, Cal." Anne moved the cut crystal vase filled with red roses from the island and placed it in the center of the table.

"And God can put her back together." Cal stated, as the matter of fact that it was.

She turned to face him, "I just don't think you should keep pining over her when you don't know if she'll ever be ready for a relationship."

"I'm not *pining*. I'm waiting. There's a big difference." Cal pulled out a chair and sat down with a thud.

"Well, lately it seems a lot like pining to me."

"Please don't say *pining* again. It's my new most hated word. *Losing* used to by my most hated word, but now it's *pining*."

Anne leaned on the chair opposite Cal and looked into his eyes, "Well, Beau, I'm afraid your doing both."

✝

Kyle bolted the door behind her and did a quick search of all the rooms. Fear. Her unwanted companion that refused to leave her side.

"Lord, please take this from me tonight. Please put Your legions of angels around me, inter-locking arms, and surround my home. You are my strength and my refuge." Peace enveloped her as she changed for bed and brushed her teeth.

"I love You, Lord." Her heart warmed and she smiled as she immersed herself in her comforter. She picked up her Bible and study book from her end table and set them on her lap. She had one page of homework to do before Bible study the following morning. As she opened her Bible, it immediately flipped to that well worn page in Jeremiah. Chapter twenty-nine, verse eleven.

"For I know the plans I have for you," declares the LORD, "plans to prosper you, not to harm you. Plans for a hope and a future."

She smiled and ran her fingers over the verse. Plans. Hope. Future. She thought of Cal's face. His eyes, his smile. "I really like him, Lord. He's so special. He's kind and gentle. But mostly, he loves You. So why am I so afraid?"

It was nearly eleven-thirty by the time Kyle finished her lesson and turned out the light beside her bed. As she faded to her dreams, all she saw was Cal smiling at her. And for at least a moment, she wasn't afraid at all.

She couldn't breathe. His knee was on her chest and she thought she was going to die. He held her shoulders down and released one to cover her mouth. When he moved his knee, she screamed and tried to break free.

He stood up on the bed and kicked her. She flew off the edge and hit the end table, knocking over the lamp and landing with a thump on her side. She covered her face and wept. 'Why! Why!'' She felt the blood trickle down her arm and felt the bedspread move as he jumped off the bed, over her and turned around. He reached down and grabbed her hair, pulling her up...

Kyle woke with a start, bathed in sweat. She thought she saw the figure, again, standing in her doorway. When the haze lifted and she realized she was safe, she hugged her knees to her chest, rocking back and forth.

I'm right here, my Child. I'll never leave your side. Not for one second.

"Thank you, Jesus. Thank you."

CHAPTER 13

Sutton was sick and tired of this dull and dreary town. If Callin wasn't going to take her up on her offer to show him a good time, then she'd find someone that would. She deserved to be treated like a queen; regarded like she was somebody because she was somebody. There was no shortage of men that would love her.

Sutton called a few of her old sorority sisters to meet them out in the city at one of the most popular dance clubs. Most of her old friends were busy and declined, but two of the girls she used to party with agreed to meet up with her.

The club was dark and loud, blaring music that made a body want to move. The rhythm set the three girls in motion as soon as they were carded and entered the door.

Sutton immediately spotted a guy that had spotted her. He nodded his head at her and she nodded back.

"He's hot, Sutton. Go for it, girl." Liz shouted at her friend.

"No, I want to get some free drinks first. Right, girls?"

Emily giggled and took a shot that the bartender had just handed her. 'Whew! Things are starting out just about right."

The girls danced together, aware that every male in the room was gaping at them. Sutton loved the spotlight. She felt important, wanted. Desired.

Guys bought them drinks, one right after the other, and soon the girls were dancing provocatively with random men. Faces and bodies melted together and Sutton lost track of her friends.

Someone took Sutton and held her close and began kissing her. She couldn't remember if she knew him and kissed him back. He bought her drinks and more drinks until she staggered to the bathroom and threw up.

A girl in the next stall was crying and vomiting, saying to no one that she wanted to go home. Sutton got up from the floor and made it to the sink. A couple girls around her, too sober in her opinion, were staring.

"What are you looking at?" She spat at them. Who did they think they were? She was Sutton Cassaday. Her daddy was the richest man they would ever dream to meet and she was his heir. "Quit looking at me." She was absently aware that she was slurring, and then became irate when one of the girls at the next sink asked her, "Do you need help? You don't look so good."

Sutton tried to roll her eyes and walked back out into the chaos and confusion of the raucous music and the mass of jumbled legs and arms.

Someone groped her as she walked aimlessly looking for someone. Liz? Or was Kristin there. No, Kristin wouldn't be here.

Strong hands swung her around and she stood face to face with another stranger. He was insistent and Sutton felt herself drawn to his confidence. He danced her over to the front door and led her outside into the blackest night.

She was unable to walk to his car, so he held her up as she stumbled forward. He put her in his front seat and slammed the door. She closed her eyes and wondered where they were going. She wondered what his name was.

The car smelled like pot smoke and vomit, and Sutton had to work at keeping the rest of her drinks down. She looked over at the stranger next to her, driving her somewhere, and saw through glazed eyes that he looked a lot like a turtle. She started to laugh, and he joined in, unaware that he was the joke. Or was she?

The guy parked the car and half carried Sutton up a flight of stairs to a small apartment. He didn't turn on the lights, but led her to a bedroom.

She began to lose consciousness as one thought reverberated through her mind…

She deserved to be treated like a queen.

✝

Sunday morning came quickly and Kyle dressed in a rush. She was not one to be late, but if she was, she preferred it not be to church.

She jumped in her car and waved to Pops as he was watering the flowers on his porch before putting on his tie for his church service.

By the time Kyle opened the heavy wooden doors of the sanctuary, the worship team had begun their opening song. She found her place next to Chandler and began to sing along with the rest of the congregation. Cal and his family were two rows up and one aisle over. In the past, Kyle refused to even glance in Callin's direction while she was focusing on worshiping. After Friday night's dinner, it was proving much more difficult to stay collected.

When they were dismissed, Chandler grabbed Kyle's arm and nearly jumped up and down in front of her. "Kyle! I got in to Carson College! I want to start in the summer, but I think I'm going to wait until fall. I wish I could intern with you when the time comes, but that would be a pretty long commute."

Kyle laughed at Chandler's excitement and gave her a hug. "I'm so happy for you, Chan. I really meant what I said before, you are going to be an awesome teacher. The kids in children's church sure love you. That's a wonderful school, too. I bet your parents are super excited."

"They are so happy. I just wish I could start teaching now. I don't want to wait four years. Well, hopefully three years, but either way. I'm ready now."

"You're going to be working your whole life. Enjoy college while you can." Kyle gave Chandler a hug goodbye and

96

congratulated her again before waving to the rest of the James family. Once outside, she immediately caught sight of Paige and Grayson. As she made her way over to talk to Paige, she noticed Sutton was at Callin's side once again, laughing as she touched his arm. A strong wave of jealousy stabbed at Kyle and it took all she had in her to continue forward.

"Hey, Ky." Paige put her arm around her shoulder. "What did you end up doing yesterday?"

Kyle fought to find the words to carry on a conversation when all she wanted to do was run. "Not too much. I read a little bit and got a head start on lesson plans. What about you?"

At that moment, Callin said something to Sutton and made his way to Kyle. Before Paige could answer, Callin interrupted by touching Kyle's shoulder.

"Hey, Sis. Can I interrupt?" Paige smiled and rejoined her husband.

"Hey, Kyle."

With two simple words, Kyle felt a weight lifted from her as she smiled up at him. In her peripheral, she saw Sutton staring at them, with arms crossed. As much as she knew that church wasn't the place for drama, the scene was playing out anyway.

"Hi, Cal. How are you?"

"Great, now. I've been wanting to talk to you."

Paige and Gray said their goodbyes and Cal walked Kyle toward the parking lot. Several pairs of eyes followed them the entire way. Chet Woods and Blake Stark both had their hearts set on Kyle.

"Bummer, dude." Chet said and turned toward his car. Blake continued to stare. Chet had a great view on life and on God's plans for him. Blake was just angry.

While Blake was angry, Sutton was livid. She had invested a lot of time on Callin Jennings. Every Sunday she made it to that sanctuary and set herself right in front of him, wanting to make sure he got a good look. It didn't matter how tired she was or how her head ached from the night before. She wanted Callin.

And she was used to getting what she wanted.

✝

Callin walked out of the weight room Monday morning and headed toward the Middle School. With only the library between the two schools, it would have been a quick jog. But with the way his heart was racing, he thought it would be a better idea to walk a bit slower to steady the beat.

He found Kyle sitting at her desk, finishing up lesson plans. He knocked on the open door and peered in.

"Hey, Kyle." Kyle looked up and smiled, heat rising to her face.

"Hi Cal. How are you doing today?"

Cal walked toward her and leaned against the desk opposite her. "Great, thanks. I should have asked you yesterday, but I thought this was a good excuse to see you today. "He grinned down at her, "I was wondering if you'd like to come to the main house for dinner again Friday night. If you don't have any plans."

"I'd love that." She smiled back, "What dessert should I bring this time? "

"Hmm. Maybe something chocolate? No, definitely something chocolate." His smile widened and Kyle's mirrored his.

"You got it. I'll surprise you."

"Okay. So, I'll see you Friday. I'll try to clean up before you get there this time." Cal stood to leave and looked back before walking through the doorway. "Have a great week."

"You, too."

When he was gone, Kyle leaned back in her chair and couldn't for the life of her wipe the smile from her face. She was happy, truly happy. And excited for the first time she could remember. Plans. Hope. Future. No wonder it was her favorite verse.

CHAPTER 14

Chandler was stocking the makeup shelves when the bell above the door sounded. Mr. Tate was in the back room finishing up inventory, so Chandler quickly made her way up to the front to see if she could be of assistance.

A man was standing at the cash register, waiting for her, when she positioned herself behind the counter.

"Good afternoon. Can I help you with anything?" Chandler smiled at the customer.

The look in his eye changed to something Chandler hadn't seen before. She couldn't quite place what it meant, but she became instantly uncomfortable. He looked vaguely familiar. Maybe he'd been in before, but she couldn't place him.

"You sure can help me with something, Chandler." The man rubbed the scruff of his days-old beard and looked her up and down. Chandler pulled her uniform jacket closer to her and shrunk back.

"I need some gum."

Chandler looked down and pointed to where he was standing, "It's right there in front of you."

"Oh, yeah. So it is." He didn't take his eyes off of Chandler when he spoke, "You're a very beautiful girl."

Chandler stuttered, "Thank you."

He bought his gum with cash, walked to the door and turned around, "Oh, and Chandler. You need to be careful taking out the garbage at night here all by yourself. It's dangerous out there alone."

He walked out and Chandler listened to the door clank shut. She started to shake and chided herself for making too much out of the situation. The man was gone. Everything was fine.

She went back to stocking and looked up at her reflection in the mirror above the lipsticks. She put her hand over the pocket of her uniform.

She wasn't wearing her name tag.

Sutton was angry and sulking when she pulled through her parents gate leading to their massive home. Most would call it a mansion, but Sutton had seen bigger. She parked her car beside her mother's Mercedes and threw it in park. She sat behind the wheel for a few minutes to compose herself.   Life seemed so out of control. And she was a girl who demanded control.

She suddenly felt emotional and felt a catch in her throat. She didn't get emotional. She prided herself on being strong and capable, just like her father. She didn't see him much when she was growing up. But when she did, she remembered a stoic man, always in complete control. She would get his attention, someday, by being just like him.

Her parents had bribed her with a house of her own if she graduated from college. So she did, barely. They kept their word and built her a home just a few miles from theirs that rivaled the best in the latest model homes. While Sutton loved the house, she had yet to move. It sat, furnished but without a resident, for a year.

If she was being honest with herself, she was afraid to be on her own. But she would never admit that to anyone else. Her parents never bothered her about moving, just like they never bothered her about getting a job. They didn't want to ever do anything that would hurt their friendship, so they lived together as they always had.

Sutton squeezed her eyes shut and willed away the tears. She was so angry about Callin that she could hardly see straight. She thought of telling her mother about what had happened with Cal, and how distraught she was, but she decided against it when she tried to imagine how her mom would react. Sutton knew her mom would become stressed and reach for the medicine cabinet, liquor bottle or both. No, she'd handle it like she handled everything else. Alone.

Sutton pushed on the rich mahogany doors with intricate beveled glass. The marble floors and wide, elaborate staircase greeted her. She grabbed her phone and threw her five hundred dollar purse on the table.

She dialed her mom's number. She just wasn't up for a search. "Hey, where are you."

Sutton listened to the voice on the other line, trying to gauge her mother's sobriety. "Oh, hi Darling. I'm out on the lanai."

Sutton ended the call and walked to the back of the house. The double doors were opened to the pool and gardens in the back of the estate. Her mom was lounging in a chaise, careful for the sun not to touch her skin. Her sunglasses covered her eyes, and Sutton couldn't tell if they were red and swollen, crazed or closed.

"Hey." Sutton stood over her mom and spoke with impatience.

"Hi, Darling. What are you up to today?" Her speech was slightly slurred and Sutton's impatience turned to disdain.

"I'm going shopping and out with friends tonight. My bank account is low. I need a deposit."

"Well, Daddy isn't here, so you'll have to call Janson." Sutton rolled her eyes. She couldn't stand dealing with her father's financial guy. For someone who essentially worked for her, he was rude, arrogant and gave her a difficult time every time she asked for the slightest bit of cash.

"Where's Daddy? I don't want to talk to Janson."

"How in the world would I know where Daddy is? You know he never tells me anything. Not that I want to know. Business here, business there. I go into a trance every time He mentions the word."

Sutton wasn't even trying to control her anger, "Do you at least know when he'll be back?"

"Sutton, why don't you just call him, for pity sake?"

Sutton turned away and stomped off to her room. She wasn't angry anymore, she was hurt and there wasn't any way her mom was going to know it.

The only reason she'd made an effort to talk to her mother at all was that she had tried to call her dad. Three times over the past two days.

He'd never called her back.

The week went as slowly as Callin had predicted. He'd always had a hard time sitting still, but movement this week was vital to get him through. School, practice and the horses kept him occupied during the day, but restlessness hit hard when darkness fell.

By Thursday night, Basketball on the television wasn't enough to keep the nervous excitement at bay. He was mentally preparing to spend the next evening with Kyle and he couldn't do a thing to help fade her face from his thoughts. It was obvious why Callin didn't date. This was torturous.

Callin turned the sound down on the game and picked up his phone.

The line rang three times before he heard a familiar voice on the other end, "Callin! My precious angel. How are you, baby?"

"Hi Gram. I'm missing you and Paw. Did I wake you?"

"Darlin', never. Is there something on your mind? You know I can always tell when something's bothering you."

Callin had always been closest to his father's mother. Their move away from Greenville hit him especially hard, even though he wasn't living close by at the time. Callin and Gram had a connection that few people in the world possessed. It only made sense he'd be making this phone call to her.

"Well, I met a girl."

Even in the silence, he heard her smile.

"Tell me about her, baby."

Cal sunk back into the sofa and crossed his ankle over his knee. Where to start.

"I actually met her a while ago. She works with Paige and goes to our church. She's so beautiful, Gram. And she has the sweetest spirit."

"So, why are you calling your Gram at nine-thirty on a Thursday night?"

"I've never felt like this before. I feel like she's the one, but I couldn't tell that to anyone else because it would sound nuts. I don't even know why she moved to town. She had a bad time of it in her home town and found herself in Greenville. I feel like I barely even know her, but she's got a hold of my heart. She's coming over to Mom and Dad's tomorrow and I can't wait to see her, but I'm nervous to see her. I feel crazy. Am I crazy?" Cal didn't feel like he'd taken a breath, and inhaled deeply.

Gram's laugh caught him off guard, "Baby, I trust your judgment more than anyone I know. You are intelligent, wise and honorable. But mostly, you listen to what the Lord is speaking over your heart. Keep listening. Take it one step at a time, and keep on listening to what your Jesus is saying."

Cal sighed and nodded to himself when his Gram spoke again, "And Callin. You're not crazy."

✝

The week had trudged on just as slowly for Kyle as it did for Cal. Friday afternoon, Kyle made her favorite Ooey Gooey Caramel Chocolate bars and prepared for an evening with the Jennings family.

She dressed in her favorite jeans and sleeveless blouse. It was a new experience to care so much about what to wear. She used a straightener on her wavy hair and put on a touch of lip gloss. Her face was glowing from a recent run and she found herself ready to go twenty minutes early. She didn't have to think about what to do with the extra time. She got down on her knees and had a talk with her Father.

"Hi Jesus. This is so new for me. I know You understand. I'm so nervous. Please calm my heart and help me to follow You. Please help me to know what You want for Cal and me. I don't want anything that You haven't willed for me. He's so precious, though, Lord. I just don't want to mess up again. Thank You in advance for answering my prayers.

"I love You, Lord."

Conversation was even easier than it had been the Friday before. Kyle knew she'd never tire of hearing of Callin's antics as a child.

When Anne started into yet another story, Callin interrupted her to make a quick exit. "Kyle! Why don't we go out and meet the boys."

Anne laughed and winked at Kyle, "You can leave now, Callin Thomas, but I'm pretty sure Kyle will be back to hear more."

Cal opened the kitchen door for Kyle and led her out back to the red and white two-story barn.

"This is a great barn. And you know I've become quite the barn expert." Kyle laughed.

Cal opened the barn door and switched on the light. Dusk was settling in and the horses were already in their stalls for the night. The smell of horses and hay was heavy, but Kyle loved it and breathed in deeply. It reminded her of summer and sunshine and distant, happy memories.

Kyle walked immediately to the dapple gray on her right. "Hi big boy. You are a beauty." Kyle rubbed his soft nose and he nickered in response.

"That's Duke. He's the oldest of the bunch and sweet as can be. They all are really. My mom has turned them into great big dogs. If they're in the paddock and see her coming, they all start running to her. Spoiled rotten."

Cal led Kyle to each horse and introduced her. There were five total and he was right, they were all loving and lovable. Duke, Patches, Ace, Remington and Prescott. Each one of them was beautiful in their own rite.

"When Paw, my dad's father, retired, he sold off the cattle for a pretty nice nest egg. My mom had the horses on their old property and had this barn built once they moved into this house."

"They sure are just adorable. I went to camp every summer as a kid and horseback riding was my favorite activity. That and s'mores around the campfire." Kyle laughed and Cal found it difficult to look away from her.

Cal led Kyle out the barn door and called to the horses, "G'night boys. See you in the morning." He closed the heavy door behind and they walked slowly back to the house.

"We should go riding sometime." Cal asked hopefully.

"I'd really love that. My Bible study's almost over on Saturday mornings. Maybe after that?"

"Perfect." They smiled at each other before heading into the house for what would become tradition. Every Friday night, Kyle would arrive at the Jennings home for dinner and companionship, becoming more a part a family than she'd ever known.

✝

"What are you doing?" He sneered, staring at the sandwich on the counter.

"I'm eating lunch.'" She closed the bread bag and opened the fridge.

"The bread doesn't go in the fridge. How many times do I have to tell you that?"

"I'm sorry.'" She muttered, head down.

"There are way too many carbohydrates in that sandwich. Did you put mayo on it?"

She looked at the sandwich and back at him, "No, I didn't. I've lost two more pounds. And I'm hungry."

'That would put you at a hundred and five pounds. My trainer said that at your height, you should only weigh a hundred and one pounds at the very most.'

She looked at him and felt the heat rise in her cheeks, "You talked to your trainer about me?"

"Of course, I did. I'm just looking out for you. I'm not going to be seen with a pig, Kyle. Try harder."

He grabbed her sandwich and walked away, taking a bite as he left.

Kyle woke with a start and sat straight up. As soon as she realized where she was she would usually praise God for how far she'd come.

Tonight, she cried out to Him. "Lord, please. Make these nightmares stop. I'm so tired, God. I'm so tired."

Dinner with Cal and his family had been perfect. She thought that Callin in her life would help put her heart back together. Her nightmare pummeling her as she slept was proof that only God could cut and fit the pieces. And make her whole again.

CHAPTER 15

Wednesday afternoon, Kyle noticed one of her students doing her best not to cry. She had grown accustomed to pre-teen drama, but this was different. Once the last bell rang, Kyle asked her to stay back.

"Did I do something wrong, Miss Evans?" Brooke Henderson was a slight, quiet girl. With fair blond hair and big blue eyes, she reminded Kyle of a doe, ready to run.

"No, Sweetie. You didn't do anything wrong. I was just noticing that you've seemed really down lately. Is everything alright?"

Immediately, Brooke burst into tears and covered her face. Kyle put her arm around her shoulders and let her cry.

After a few moments, Brooke had composed herself and wiped her face. "I just feel so alone, Miss Evans. My friends talk behind my back and make fun of me. My parents hate me. I go to church and try to do what I'm supposed to. It just feels so worthless."

Kyle handed her a tissue and Brooke continued "What's wrong with me that no one can love me? I just want to be loved, ya know? "

Kyle did know.

"Well, I can tell you that this age is really difficult. Girls can be mean and, unfortunately, it probably won't get any better until you're out of high school," They both sighed and gave a small laugh. "And parents don't always understand what you're going through.

"But, I can tell you one thing that will never change. God has an amazing plan for your life. He loves you, Brooke. He loves you so much that he died for you. I know you know that in your mind, but you need to know it in your heart, too. You are so special, Sweetie." Kyle hugged her shoulders again and then sat facing her.

"When I was growing up, I didn't think my parents loved me, either. I'm starting to think that's kind of a normal feeling for sixth graders. What I've realized as an adult is that people love you as much as they know how. It doesn't mean they're bad or heartless or that you're not worth loving. Sometimes it just means they were never taught how to show their feelings.

"When I was your age, I wish someone would have told me that God had a purpose for my life. Today, you are my proof of what my purpose has always been. I'm here in this school, teaching this class, because God knew that today you would need to hear what I had to say. I hope that when you're grown, you'll look back on this conversation when you've discovered what God has planned for you. It's going to be awesome."

Kyle squeezed Brooke's hand. "Are you okay, now? Is there anything else you need to talk about?"

Brooke smiled and her shoulders relaxed. "No, Miss Evans. Thank you very much. I do feel a lot better."

Kyle smiled back at her and replied, "I'm glad."

As Brooke picked up her backpack, she walked a little bit lighter. And Kyle thought to herself, "Yes, that's why I'm here."

Grayson entered the station and immediately noticed two girls with their parents seated at Officer Nick Brown's desk. He didn't even have to ask why they were there.

Once the group was situated with the sketch artist, Gray walked over to Nick. "Same perp?"

"Yep. Only he wasn't at the school. The girls saw him over at Fit's Gym. He was behind some trees and didn't budge even when he realized they saw him. He's getting bold."

"Yes, he is. Too bold."

Betty Marx had met her husband twelve years earlier in a local honky-tonk bar. She thought she'd finally found someone to help her make it in life. Someone who would put food on the table and be a father to her two children. Her ex-boyfriend left her as soon as he found out she was pregnant with kid number two. Betty found herself stuck in a trailer home with two babies in diapers and no way to legitimately earn money.

She should have realized immediately that the man she thought she loved wasn't who he claimed to be. He moved in with her two weeks after they met and told her he'd just lost his job. Her small welfare checks were now being used to buy beer and vodka instead of diapers and milk. Any confrontation on her part would result in a beating that would leave her unable to care for her children for days at a time.

She quickly found hints of his girlfriends and cheating. When he finally went away to prison, Betty rejoiced in her good fortune. She was free, for life, so she'd been told. Then last year, he reappeared on her doorstep. She took him in. She had no choice.

 This morning she woke realizing that she'd slept the entire night without being shaken awake, bothered or beaten. She had no idea where he'd been the night before and she knew to never ask.

A few weeks earlier, she'd found some woman's clothing in with his things. He was back to cheating and he wasn't even attempting to hide it.

When she'd found the clothes, she rushed to replace them and went to the tiny bathroom to cry. Her life had been reduced to hoping her husband had a girlfriend so he'd leave her alone. Of all the thousands of mistakes she'd made in her life, Earl Marx had been her greatest.

Sutton stood in front of the mirror and studied her outfit. Short running shorts and a tight t-shirt. She was ready to go work out. There were some guys at the gym that seemed interested in her. Maybe she'd find her prince there.

Fit's gym was the only gym in the small town. There were larger facilities a few miles into the next town over, but Sutton found that there were mostly single people at Fit's. The other gym was more family oriented. And she wasn't.

She parked and locked her car. She'd heard that some cars had been broken into, so she made sure she threw her purse into her gym bag and took it inside. There was no way she'd let someone take advantage of her.

As soon as she walked through the doors, she spotted a man by the free weights. He saw her, too, and didn't break eye contact. He was good looking, in a meat-head sort of way. His muscle shirt and work out shorts seemed a little dated, but Sutton knew she could fix any guy of his fashion flaws.

She put her bag down by the water station and filled her bottle. He stayed his distance, but continued to watch every move she made. Sutton topped her bottle and walked toward him. This was ridiculous. They were adults, after all.

"Hey." Sutton said as she casually walked by.

He looked her up and down and smiled, "Hey."

Sutton felt a wave of disgust, and kept walking. She wasn't the best at picking out winners, but she knew a player when she saw one. She went to the elliptical and punched in the distance and intensity. She felt his eyes on her and grew uncomfortable. She ended her work out early and went up to the girl seated at the front desk, "Hey. Don't look over, but there's a guy in a white shirt and navy shorts over by the weights. He's been watching me work out."

The girl didn't have to look, but smiled, "Yeah, that's Del. He likes the girls." The girl's voice shifted to a whisper, "Don't tell his wife, though. She gets pretty jealous."

Sutton nodded and felt relieved that she hadn't tried to talk to him.

Sutton walked back to her car and threw her bag in the front seat. She mumbled to herself, "Still no prince. Just another frog."

✝

Del Johnson had noticed Sutton months earlier, and continued to bide his time until he introduced himself. He felt triumphant today with the small exchange they'd had. And being able to watch her on the machines was an added bonus.

His wife had caught him with an old girlfriend a few weeks earlier and had really turned into a nag. She was following him and checking his phone. That was the main reason he chose to go to the gym while she was at work. There were some great looking woman that came into Fit's and he wasn't about to miss an opportunity if it presented itself.

He went to the window and watched Sutton walk to her car. He was really good with women and he knew she was as good as his. He just had to time it right. Until then, he had to finish his work out. He was a busy man.

✝

Chandler parked her car in its usual spot and headed into work. She used her key to open up and locked the door behind her. She liked to arrive a few minutes early to do a quick once-over.

Mr. Tate looked up from the cash register and smiled broadly at his favorite employee. "Good morning, Chan. Thank you for coming in so early. I appreciate you working a double. Are you sure you're going to be okay here by yourself today? I'll be back before it gets dark."

"I'll be fine, Mr. Tate. You go and have fun. You deserve it." Chandler usually worked Saturday afternoons, but didn't hesitate when Mr. Tate asked if she would take the extra hours while he went to the lake with his children.

Mr. Tate left the cash in the till to cover the day's purchases and gathered his things. He looked over his glasses and instructed Chandler, "Call me if you have any problems or questions. Anything at all, okay?"

"Thank you, Mr. Tate. I will."

Chandler heard the door chime just a few minutes after Mr. Tate had turned the sign to 'OPEN', and left her alone.

She looked up, with a smile on her face. The second she looked in his eyes, her smile vanished.

"Chandler. Chandler. That's quite an interesting name, Chandler. Where did you get a name that's as beautiful as you?" He walked toward her slowly, his gaze never wavering.

"Can I help you?" Chandler's heart raced and she prayed that someone would come in soon. A warning went off in her mind, but she'd never been in this situation before. She didn't want to do something foolish if this man was harmless. It was daytime, in a public place. Of course she was fine.

"I see you remember me. I'm downright flattered. What does a girl like you do on a Saturday night? Don't tell me, because I know. You work. That seems like a pretty boring life, Chandler. You need to get out more. Have a little fun. You know what fun is, don't you?" Chandler gaped at him as he moved closer.

The door opening behind him broke him from his progression. He turned abruptly to look at the couple entering the store and turned again toward Chandler. "I'll see you soon, Chandler."

As soon as he was gone, Chandler reprimanded herself. She didn't have experience with someone showing interest in her. No matter, she didn't want to be alone.

She dialed her mom. "Hey Mom. This man came in and he scared me a little bit. I'm fine. I'm sure he's harmless, but I don't want to be here by myself right now. I know it sounds silly, but I'm feeling kind of uncomfortable."

"Okay, Baby. I'll be there in a few minutes. Do you want to stay on the line until I get there?"

Chandler was beginning to feel ridiculous. The longer the time elapsed between her encounter, the more she felt that she was overreacting.

"Yeah. I'll stay on the phone with you..."

"Well, I'll let daddy know what I'm doing and head out. Is there anyone else there with you now?"

"Yeah, there are a couple customers and another one just walked in. I'm fine, really. But, if you're not doing anything else, we can at least spend some time together." Chandler smiled into the phone.

"I'll take as much time with you as I can, while I can. My baby's leaving me soon and then what am I going to do?"

Jana had been watching Townsend play her heart out in the second tennis match of the morning. Towne excelled in the sport and Jana enjoyed watching her excitement in a win and her calm spirit in the wake of a loss. Townsend's success in tennis was just one more thing that made her a miracle.

Jana smiled just to think about her little girl. Towne was maturing quickly in some areas and remaining ever innocent in others. It was that strange transition from childhood to becoming a woman. Jana had made it through with Chandler, but watching her youngest begin to show the signs was proving difficult for a mama to deal with.

Jana took the phone away from her ear momentarily to find Andy and let him know of her plans. Andy and Davis were across the park on the soccer field practicing before Davis's scrimmage. The sun was warming the brisk day quickly and it was turning into a spectacular morning.

"Hey, Babe." Jana called to her husband.

Andy hustled over to Jana, winded. "Hey. How's our little tennis pro doing?"

"Great. But, I'll need you to head over there now instead of her last match. Chandler needs me at the store." Even as she said it, an uneasiness rested on her heart.

"Is Chan alright?" Andy's concern worried Jana even more, but she knew her oldest daughter was in her Savior's arms. At all times.

"It sounds like she was harassed by a customer. She's fine, but she'll feel better if I'm there. Look at that, I'm still useful." Jana laughed to lighten her mood. But as she ran to the van and started it up, she couldn't shake the darkness.

✝

Tess Johnson was trying so hard to make her marriage work. She'd met Del in high school and was still waiting for him to grow up. He was the rebel her parents begged her not to date. But, she had a mind of her own back then and wanted what she wanted. That happened to be Del Johnson.

She had expected great things. He was smart, she knew he was. If only he would apply himself. He worked in a garage right out of school with promises of going to college to get his degree. It was on this promise that Tess agreed to marry him. Ten years later, he was still at the same garage. Still making about the same pay.

Tess knew he had cheated on her in school. He'd even had the audacity to cheat on her with her best friend. But, he had a hold over her that refused to loosen.

Her parents paid for her tuition, even though she had defied them by marrying Del. If it hadn't been for their generosity, there was no telling where they might be. She studied between shifts at the diner and got her nursing degree with honors. With the highest grades, Tess was the first in her class to get a job at the hospital's emergency room.

She was just coming off the night shift when she picked up Del's phone and ran her fingers over the worn buttons. She had caught him talking with an old girlfriend weeks before and as she stood there, she couldn't decide if it was worth it to find out, once again, that he was still unfaithful.

Six months earlier, she had gone to a small church just outside of town with her closest friend from the hospital. Del refused to go with her, and that was fine. But, then she was saved. Her entire view on her life had completely changed in the matter of a few days. She wanted to be more than what she was. She wanted to be the person God had called her to be. And she wanted her husband to come with her.

She placed his phone down and prayed. Until Del found the love that she did, he'd continue to be looking for it in the wrong places. She didn't have to see the proof to know that.

✝

Earl Marx checked his look in the rear view mirror and walked into the Handle Bar. Most everyone sitting with their beers and whiskey glasses turned to see him walk in. They knew him by name, but rarely said hello. Earl wasn't someone a person wanted to get close to.

The old timers at Handle's knew Earl's story. They knew what he'd been accused of doing. He'd been arrested right there by the old jukebox. Most of the patrons at Handle's had been up close and personal with the law at least a time or two. But none had been involved in a SWAT team breaking into their drinking establishment like Earl. That night, the cops had busted in with guns drawn. They made a bee-line straight for Earl and pushed him to the ground on his face. Earl fought off the officers until they finally had him cuffed. He wasn't quiet until after he'd been hauled to the police car and locked inside.

The conviction had been unanimous. The evidence didn't lie. It was during his second appeal that it came out a key piece of evidence had been compromised. He was free.

With no place to go, he headed straight back to Betty's. He'd
never loved her, barely even liked her, but he was a good liar.
When he'd first met her, he just needed a place to crash and
some spending money. Just like now.

He laughed out loud when he showed up on the doorstep of her
trailer the year before. He watched the color drain from her face
and her welcoming smile turn to a grimace of fear. She was so
easy to read. Fear. It's what he used to get what he wanted.

She let him in, she had no choice. Earl Marx was home to stay.

CHAPTER 16

Kyle's Bible study ended for the season and she and Cal made plans to go horseback riding the next Saturday.

Kyle woke early and read a chapter in John. One of her favorite moments in the Bible was when Mary stood weeping outside of the grave of her Lord. Then Jesus revealed Himself to her to comfort her.

Kyle felt like that's exactly what He'd done for her in her darkest hour. A Father that hurts so much when His child cries that He has to be by their side to make Himself known. How overwhelming that love.

Kyle opened the refrigerator to grab some yogurt. Even something as simple as a glance in her fridge opened her eyes to her blessings. Cupboards and a pantry filled with food reminded her of the times when she lived on a bagel a day. She'd come so far by His grace.

And it was by that grace that she was able to hope in her future.

"Okay, Lord. This is going to be the first time Callin and I will really be alone. No buffers. No family. No Paige. It feels like I'm going to need You more than ever today. Please calm my heart rate. That would be great."

Kyle dressed in her faded jeans, white tank top and cowboy boots. She pulled her long hair into two braids and took her old suede cowboy hat from the closet.

She drove with the windows down, the breeze caressing her face. She smiled as she thought of what the day held and her nerves dissipated.

Kyle parked out front and waved to Anne as she was sweeping off the front porch.

"Well, good morning, Kyle. Callin's already out in the barn."

"Good morning, Miss Anne. I'll go find him."

Kyle rounded the corner and stepped out of the sunlight, through the wide open doors of the barn. She heard a scraping sound and waited for her eyes to adjust to the darkness. She focused on Callin, turned away from her, shoveling hay into an open stall. He was already tan from his hours outside.

And he was shirtless. Kyle had to work hard at averting her eyes from staring at the muscles in his shoulders and back, but then put her focus on Duke.

She said with as much cool as she could muster, "Hey Cal."

Callin turned abruptly from his chores and smiled at Kyle. He saw her looking at the stall next to her and suddenly felt very exposed. He set down the rake and grabbed his t-shirt off the hook next to the stall, quickly pulling it over his head. Kyle looked at him and noticed that the shirt did very little to conceal what she'd just seen.

"I'm so sorry. I guess I'm running late."

'No, it's okay. I think I'm early. Taking care of the boys, I see." Kyle smiled back at Cal and took a few steps toward him.

"Yep. You look great." She was so beautiful, every time he saw her became more difficult than the time before. His heart tightened as he looked into her eyes. The brokenness that had seemed to be such a part of her was fading. He was sure of it. She was healing.

After readying Duke and Prescott, they climbed on their horses and slowly made their way behind the pastures toward the lake.

Cal could tell Kyle already had an attachment to Duke, and was happy to see her smile when he helped her up.

Kyle took in the scenery. Trees and land stretched as far as she could see, dotted with wild flowers of every color. "I can't believe how gorgeous it is back here. I'd be out here all the time if I could."

"Then I can't wait to show you the lake."

The trail was wide enough for the horses to ride side by side, making conversation easier. Callin pointed out where he and his dad would camp when he was a little boy, the tree he fell out of when he was ten, and the rope dangling over the lake that he still used on occasion.

The lake was as spectacular as promised. Lined with cattails and blueberry bushes, it reflected the trees that reached over its edge. Without a breeze, the water was glass, broken momentarily by a goose or family of ducks.

They made their way around the back half of the lake when Callin brought Prescott to a halt.

"I want to show you something. Are you alright to get down for a bit?"

Kyle had stopped Duke and waited for Cal to come over and steady him before she climbed down. While Cal tied the two horses to a nearby tree, Kyle walked over and marveled at the endless blueberries on the edge of the water.

"What I could bake with all these berries!" Kyle picked a few and ate them. "Wow. These are delicious."

"We'll have to come back again and bring some buckets. You can have as many as we can carry." Cal smiled.

"What I want to show you is over here." He led her to a boulder set on the edge of the water. "This is where I've always come to do my thinking. It's where I do most of my praying."

They sat on the rock, facing each other. It was already warming up from the sun as they sat looking into each others eyes a few heartbeats without speaking.

"What do you pray for?" Kyle asked.

"Everything, it seems like. I pray for my team, my decisions. I pray for my future.

"I pray for you." Cal looked away, unsure of how she would respond.

"I pray for you, too. For us." Kyle watched as his eyes met hers again.

Cal cleared his throat, "Can I ask you a question?"

"Sure."

"Can you tell me how you ended up in Greenville?"

Kyle's face clouded but then took on a strong resolve. Her mask was coming down quickly, and Callin felt her strength.

"It's a long story. This rock might start feeling pretty hard by the time I'm finished."

Cal readjusted himself and said, "I'm ready."

Kyle prayed quietly in her heart and then began "I guess you can tell by my name that my parents were hoping for a boy. My dad never got over his disappointment in seeing that pink baby blanket. I kind of felt like an unwanted stranger my whole life.

"I knew even as a child that my mom felt the same way as I did, like she didn't belong. It never seemed like my parents really knew each other. My dad would stay out all night sometimes, drinking. I remember once my mom left me alone and went to drag him home from a bar. She was in her pajamas, and I couldn't understand why she could go out in her pj's and I couldn't. It wasn't a great life for a little girl.

"And then she was diagnosed with breast cancer when I was in eighth grade. She died within months."

"I'm so sorry, Ky. I had no idea." Callin couldn't imagine how much that must have affected her life.

He took her hand and she continued on, "Once my mom passed away, my dad rarely bothered to come home. It didn't matter that I was there, alone. I think he just really wanted to forget the pain of failing to love my mom like he should have. I was the constant reminder.

"Middle School kind of tumbled into High School and that was an even worse nightmare. Friends I'd had since elementary school turned on me. I felt so alienated. I kept searching for someone to love me and I couldn't seem to find anyone. And then all of a sudden, I graduated and I thought I was starting a new life. I think I even felt hopeful for the first time.

"I was going to a local community college when I met Paul." At the mention of his name, Kyle stiffened and Callin held her hand tighter. She'd met him at a time in her life when she would have done anything to feel whole, the emptiness and loneliness had swallowed her.

"I was so lost and alone. Paul was a professor. He told me that I was somebody, and I believed him. I so badly needed to. I was with him for a couple weeks before he turned abusive. First it was verbal. It was his way of making me think that I couldn't make it on my own. And it was pretty successful. Soon, things got physically violent.'

She looked out over the water and into the trees, reliving something she wasn't going to voice. Cal didn't need to know. It made him so angry, he scared himself. What he would do if anyone tried to hurt her, he just couldn't say.

Kyle looked at him and gave a slight smile, 'But, then I heard a voice tell me to leave. That still small voice. I didn't recognize it until I came here. I got in my car and just drove. I had saved up a little money, even though at the time I didn't know what I was saving it for.

"The first day in town, I met Pops. He needed me as much as I needed him. I've said it before, but I truly believe that God's hand led me to his store. I had started going to church with Pops and finally the pain and loneliness overwhelmed me. It led to grief and despair, and I finally found myself on the floor weeping to the God I'd dismissed long ago. I got down on my face and begged for forgiveness. I asked Jesus into my life and haven't looked back."

She took in a deep breath and exhaled a lifetime of pain from her heart. It was out, it was over. "The good news is that I have a happy ending."

Cal took her in his arms for the first time and they held each other... He was somewhere between vowing he'd never let her have anything other than happy endings and wanting desperately to go back and change her entire life story.

"I'm so, so sorry you had to go through that." He whispered in her ear.

She released him and looked into his eyes once again, "I had to go through that to get here. Every trial is like gravel on a road. It can be loud, like the world. It can kick up stones and leave scars and it can make you slip and stumble. But, if you keep picking yourself up and walking forward, those pebbles will turn to stepping stones toward God's will for our lives.

"And they'll always lead you home. As much as I wish things could have been different, I'm grateful for where those stones have led."

He kissed her fingertips and whispered, "Me, too."

After a few silent breaths, Kyle smiled up at Cal, "So, Callin Jennings. Tell me your life story."

Cal smiled back, "Well, my story's so short, it's almost non-existent. I was raised in the church, I was saved when I was seven years old and baptized right here in this lake. I was the high school football hero until I blew out my knee. I guess that's a pretty common story for small town high school football. I lost my college scholarship, let go of my grip on faith for a time, then found my way back. Gravel roads." He looked back into her eyes and forgot what he was going to say next. Her eyes were the most unusual brown. Light, with flecks of gold. His eyes moved to her lips and back up to her eyes. That's when he

124

realized she was looking at his lips, too.

He put his forehead on hers and reluctantly sighed, "We should probably get back."

Kyle pulled away, closed her eyes and agreed with the nod of her head. Neither one could deny it now. They were falling fast and falling hard.

Cal stood and reached out his hand to help Kyle off the rock. She jumped down next to him and their hands remained entwined.

"You cut the tomatoes wrong again. Give me a break, Kyle! How can you not remember how to cut a TOMATO!" He held the knife in his right hand, half a tomato in his left. "Get over here! I'll show you again, real slow."

She balked and when he screamed his command again, she jumped and walked slowly toward him. When she was in reach, he slammed down the tomato and grabbed her right wrist. He forced the knife into her hand and repositioned the tomato on the cutting board. Standing behind her, he put his hand on hers and cut the tomato, the correct way. When he was done, he took the knife and threw it in the sink, while pushing her away.

"Seriously. You're so stupid. Why in the world would I be with such a stupid little girl? You know I have real women wanting me? Don't you know that? Real, smart women."

She stated to walk away the moment the tears began to streak down her face.

"Don't walk away from me!" He ran up behind her and punched her in the back. "You don't ever walk away from me!'" He swung her around and forced her to face him.

She didn't mean to say it, but it came out loud and clear, "Why are you with me if I'm so dumb!'"

He pushed her back toward the wall and then shoved her against the door, the door knob slamming into her lower back. "Stop it! Please! Just stop!" She screamed. He put his hand on her throat and squeezed to make her stop screaming.

"You want the cops to come? Is that it? The day I 'stop it', is the day you're not around anymore."

Kyle woke up into the blackness, then opened her eyes. If only she had listened when her heart told her to stay away from him, told her she was making a life-altering mistake by being with him.

But in the stillness of the night, she heard that same voice whispering over her heart right then.

Baby, you're sins have been forgiven... I remember them no more. Don't listen to the lies, Child. Listen to the Truth.

She reached for her Bible and held it against her heart as she lay back against her pillow. As the tears slid down her face and pooled in her ears, she sunk back into a fitful sleep.

✝

Kyle woke Sunday morning to gray clouds drifting in the skies and a chill in the air. Her head felt heavy from lack of a solid sleep and she prepared coffee to clear it up. A bowl of oatmeal seemed to be enough to erase the queasiness from her stomach. She had plans for today and an empty stomach coupled with a nervous stomach would be too much.

She grabbed her sweater and her Bible and headed to the church, her mind heavy on the dream from the night before.

She made sure she was early. She had some people to talk to. When she arrived, the James family was already seated. Chandler and Davis were laughing out loud about something, while Jana had her arms around Townsend. They were her family and they showed her she was loved. This conversation was going to be a difficult one.

"Hey there." Kyle said as she walked up to their pew.

Chandler gave her a hug hello and then Townsend threw her arms around Kyle's waist.

"How are you all this morning?" Kyle squeezed Townsend and gave her a kiss on the top of her head.

"Good morning, Ky. You look beautiful this morning. And you're very early." Jana laughed.

Kyle released Towne and sat down next to Chandler, facing the family. "I wanted to talk to you all."

She cleared her throat and continued. "I'm going to go sit up with the Jennings today and I wanted to let you know before I did. I know that's goofy to feel like you need to know, but I've been sitting with you all this time. You know I had to say something."

The adult's faces erupted in huge grins and Kyle knew she was making a public statement this morning, whether she wanted to or not. She couldn't help but smile back and blush.

"You're so sweet to let us know. I'm very happy for you, Sweetie." Jana winked.

Kyle continued to blush and stood up. "Thank you. I'll talk to you all after service." She stood to see Callin walking toward her.

"Hi there." Cal gave her a quick hug.

"Hi. I was going to sit with you and your family today, if that's okay."

Callin's surprise registered and it all of a sudden seemed so crazy that it was such a big event.

His face broke into a wide smile, "Yeah. That would be awesome."

They sat down and Kyle realized just how close they were. His arm touched hers and she studied his hands resting on his leg. They were strong hands that knew hard work. They were hands she wanted so badly to hold again.

From behind she heard Sutton and her friends come in, laughing loudly and making an entrance. Kyle could tell by the instant silence that Sutton had just noticed Kyle, sitting next to Callin.

"Kyle. Wow. It's so weird to see you out of your usual spot." Sutton spoke, trying to conceal her irritation. "How are you, Cal?" She purred. Kyle wasn't sure if she was trying to hide her disdain for Kyle and interest in Callin. If she was doing either, she wasn't doing it well.

"Good morning, ladies." Callin said politely while Sutton, Britt and Kristin seated themselves directly in front of them.

Kyle tried to ignore the frustration in her heart. Finally, she prayed. And just as quickly, she felt nothing but sadness for Sutton Cassaday.

With the mind of Christ, and the Holy Spirit, Kyle suddenly saw Sutton as her Father saw her. Sutton's heart was hardened by the blackest void that would never, ever be filled by anything other than the Creator of the world. Kyle had known that all consuming emptiness. She'd known that sin in the desperation to find something to fill the hole in her life, and the grief and anguish of not finding it.

She found she wasn't jealous of Sutton. She simply hurt for her.

Soon after, Anne and Martin, and Paige and Grayson arrived. They all gave Kyle a wave and a big smile and the worship team began. Kyle relaxed and was able to focus on the message. Just like her Jesus, He let Kyle know He was thinking of her always.

The message was on redemption.

✝

Service ended and Kyle and the Jennings walked slowly to the parking lot.

With Cal talking to Gray, Paige looped her arm through Kyle's and laughed loudly, "Well, you two caused quite a scene back there."

Kyle looked at Paige, "What do you mean?"

"You didn't notice the entire congregation staring at you? All the single people were hurling eye daggers. It was nuts."

Kyle hadn't noticed, and she doubted Callin had either, "That's so ridiculous, isn't it? It's not a big deal, I just changed seats."

"Yep. I agree. Most people stopped ogling pretty fast. But, you two have some serious admirers that were bound to be fairly upset."

Sutton and Britt reached Sutton's convertible and Sutton stared after Callin.

"Let it go, Sutton." Britt said.

"No way, I'm not going to just let it go, Britt. I don't get it. What does she have that I don't other than a sad puppy-dog life? Is that what I have to do, act all pathetic and lonely to get the guy? Maybe if I was poor and pitiful Callin would look at me."

"That's really unfair, Sutton." Britt stood in Sutton's line of vision and continued, "You know the right guy is out there. The problem is that if you keep your eyes on Callin and he's the wrong guy, you're not going to notice when the right one finally shows up."

Sutton pouted and let her anger course through her. No, Callin had to be the one for her. If he wasn't, then why did she want him so badly?

Paige released Kyle's arm and she and Gray said their goodbyes. Anne and Martin followed quickly and left Callin and Kyle, once again, by the side of her car.

"I know you always eat Sunday lunch with Pops, but do you think you'd be free this afternoon? "

Kyle's smile broadened, "Yes, I'm very free this afternoon. What do you have in mind?"

"I really don't have any plans. I just want to be with you." Callin took a hold of her hand and smiled back.

"Well, what would you think about blueberry picking and then giving me a tour of your house?"

"My house, huh? Sure. That sounds perfect."

"I'll call you when I'm on my way so I don't surprise you." Kyle teased.

Callin laughed and pulled her into a hug. "Great idea. I'll talk to you soon. Be safe."

Kyle drove to the diner to meet Pops and felt her heart warm her entire body. She had no idea she could have ever been this happy.

✝

Ma's Kitchen came into view and Kyle was upset with herself that she couldn't remember the drive there. So deep in thought. Pops' truck was already parked and Kyle found she was exceptionally hungry. Pancakes for lunch would be perfect.

"Hi, Pops." Kyle walked up behind him in his booth and gave him a side hug, then sat opposite him.

"Hi Sweet Girl. How was service this morning?"

"Wonderful, as usual. How about yours?"

Pops sipped his coffee and studied Kyle. "Fine. Fine. So, are you going to tell me why you're glowing brighter than a lightning bug on the blackest night of the year?"

Kyle's smile grew wide and she blushed uncontrollably. "I sat with the Jennings family today. It was nice."

"Nice, huh? Nice doesn't make a person look like that, Darlin'." Pops chuckled and looked at his Kyle. He knew that Callin Jennings, in particular, was the reason behind her smile. "You know I've known the Jennings family for the better part of my life. I went to school with Callin's grandfather and watched Martin grow up. That's a great family, I'm sure you know."

"I do. They have been very good to me." The waitress came and they placed their orders before Kyle continued. "I've been spending time with Callin lately."

"You like him." Pops didn't have to ask.

"Yes. I really do."

Their food arrived and Pops blessing on any relationship that might be beginning put Kyle's heart at ease in a way that surprised her. As she thought of the afternoon ahead, she couldn't help but pray silently with him, "Thank You, Lord. Thank you so much. I'll never stop saying it.'"

✝

When Kyle pulled off the main road and wound her way down the drive to the Jennings house, she immediately saw Callin waiting on the front porch. She had rushed home to change and phoned him as she was leaving to let him know she was on her way.

She cut the engine and noticed four pails stacked on the front step.

Cal stood as Kyle approached him and said. "You look pretty serious with all those buckets."

"I love my blueberry desserts, especially if you're going to be making them." Callin snatched the buckets and they fell in step toward the well-worn path.

Callin took Kyle's hand as they walked, like it was the most natural thing in the world. They walked to a patch of bushes where the sunshine wouldn't hit them directly. The sun had burned off the gray of the morning and they were left with a glorious afternoon.

Callin handed Kyle a bucket and they started picking, side by side, when Kyle asked, "You said your faith was shaken after you hurt your knee. How far did you wander?"

Cal loved to give his testimony. It had helped his players so much in the short time he'd been their coach, and he answered easily, "Not too far, thank Goodness. But far enough. I really just stopped praying. It's so funny how when we're angry with God we quit talking to Him like it's going to punish Him. But all we're doing is hurting ourselves.

"I pretty much just acted like a spoiled brat. My parents got fed up with my attitude and I left for school with a big chip on my shoulder. Maybe I felt like I had something to prove, I'm not sure. But, either way, once I was on my own I missed what I'd had. I missed having my God to lean on. I missed having my family nearby to listen to me and laugh with me.

"That year of my life without feeling His presence was the longest I've known before or since. But, it's like you said. That was my gravel on the road. I stumbled and I slipped, but then I used it to get me where I needed to go. I'm closer to Him now and my faith is stronger because of my failures. I'll always be grateful for that."

Kyle waited a few moments before she spoke, "I'm sorry about your knee. I can't imagine how you felt. But, I'm happy for the life you have now."

"Me, too. I'm happy you're in it." They paused from picking and stared into each other's eyes until they forced themselves to look away.

When the pails were mostly filled, they each carried two back to the house. Anne put them in freezer bags and handed them to Kyle before they left for Cal's house.

"Are you sure you don't want to keep some?" Kyle asked as Anne ushered them out the door.

"No, Sweetie. I have all I need with just a ten minute walk. You enjoy those. I'm looking forward to taste testing some of your creations. I'll see you Friday." She waved them off and closed the door once they were down the road toward Cal's home.

Cal's truck's tires crunched the rocks beneath and came to a stop under a cluster of poplars guarding the property. Kyle found herself staring at her dream. The two story house was a deep mustard color with black shutters. The wrap-around porch was dressed with a black swing and matching rocking chairs and the crisp white trim made it look clean and new.

"This is absolutely gorgeous, Cal." Kyle opened the door of the cab slowly and stepped down, keeping her eyes on the house. She climbed the porch stairs, feeling them solid beneath her feet. She reached the black front door and wished for all she'd thought she could never have. This home, this boy. This life.

Cal walked up behind Kyle and moved to her side to unlock the door. When the door pushed open, Kyle slowly crossed the threshold to take it all in. The walls in the front room were painted a chocolate brown, deep and rich. To the right was a small dining room with a rustic table and chairs, Flowers sat in the middle and Kyle smiled at the contradiction.

Cal followed her eyes and said, "They're fake. Mom bought them when I moved it to make it homey. I haven't had the heart to tell her that guys don't do flowers, so there they sit."

To the left was the living room and a staircase leading to the second floor. The banister was ornate, made of black wrought iron with intricate designs. There was pride in the building of this house. It shone in every inch.

Cal's boots echoed on the hardwood floors as he led Kyle into the great room. More to his personality, the great room held a big screen television, dark brown leather sofa and two coordinating recliners. The walls were a lighter shade of the brown from the entrance and there wasn't one thing girly. Nothing frilly in sight.

On the back wall was a large framed abstract that added just enough color to brighten the entire room. The fact that the decorating was done with so much artistic style hinted that Anne Jennings had a hand in this room as well.

"And here we have the most unused room in the house." Cal led Kyle to a spacious kitchen with deep brown walnut cupboards accentuated by a stone back splash. It was absolutely perfect, like every other room.

"I wouldn't use my kitchen either, if I could eat at your mom's every night." Kyle leaned against the black and brown speckled granite counter top and smiled up at him.

Cal joked, "Yeah, I'm kind of wondering when she's going to cut me off. I think my food consumption is the reason my dad hasn't been able to fully retire yet.

"I do have drinks in the fridge. And bologna. Are you hungry or thirsty?" Cal walked to the stainless steel refrigerator and opened it up to reveal very little.

"Hmm. I think I'll skip the snack, but a diet anything would be great."

Cal rummaged through the cans and pulled out two cold cans. 'It's fully loaded,. I hope that's OK. I kind of run on caffeine." He smiled.

"That's great. Thank you."

They walked back to the family room and sat facing each other.

Kyle sipped her drink and said, "So, tell me about your house. Paige said you built it yourself. That's amazing."

"I helped build it, but I had my dad next to me. I can't imagine what it would look like if it was just me." He laughed envisioning slanted walls and falling beams. He knew a lot about building, but not everything.

"When I got the job at the High School last year, I knew I'd need a place of my own. Dad had just handed over most of his responsibilities to his foreman at the company and they were nearly finished with their remodel, so the timing was great. When we needed someone from the construction site, we just contracted with them. It worked out really well."

Kyle looked at the expanse of the room, "Well, I absolutely love it."

"I was hoping you would." Cal looked down at his soda and cleared his throat. He felt like his feelings were in fast forward. He wanted this to be Kyle's house one day, too. He wanted to live out all his days with her by his side, with however many babies they were blessed with. He wanted to love her and protect her and sit on the front porch in the mornings drinking coffee and teasing each other. He wanted to hold her when she cried and laugh at her jokes.

He wanted what he'd prayed his whole life for. He wanted her.

They talked a few minutes more and finished off their drinks before they climbed back into Cal's truck so he could drive her back to her car.

They were almost back to the main house when Kyle spoke. "I had a wonderful time today. I loved your home and I can't wait to start baking with all my blueberries." Kyle looked at his profile as he drove. He was the most handsome man she'd ever seen. She took in his brow, his nose. And those lips. Her heart twisted to think of kissing them. She was suddenly feeling afraid of how she would handle it if things didn't work out. He was embedded in her heart in a way she hadn't expected. In a way that she thought was impossible.

He glanced over and caught her staring. He couldn't help but feel flustered, "I'm already looking forward to Friday. These weeks are seeming really long lately."

Cal parked his truck beneath the giant oak and went around to open Kyle's door. They stood silently for a few moments before Cal put his arms around her and held on tight.

"I'll talk to you soon." He kissed her on the cheek and said good night.

As Kyle drove home, she prayed fervently. "Please, God. Please. If my heart breaks this time, Lord, it's going to shatter."

I AM the mender of broken hearts, precious child. In love, there is no fear.

Peace settled over her soul and she sighed in relief. Because the thing about shattered hearts is that God knows every piece, every sliver. And when He collects the broken pieces to put it back together, He restores it to be stronger than it was before. And in its strength, it better resembles His own.

No matter how great the pain might be, Kyle knew God would bring her through it stronger. She had to hold on tight to that fact. She had no choice.

CHAPTER 17

Chandler grabbed her water bottle and towel. Spin class was starting in less than half an hour and it was always difficult to find a free bike. She had been going to Fit's gym for nearly six months and found that the classes were the best thing that had ever happened to her. She wasn't athletic like her brother and sister. She'd tried sport after sport and never found anything that she truly loved. Working out at the gym gave her what she needed and craved. Staying in shape without the competition. Chandler had never enjoyed competing, from a very early age. She enjoyed socializing, and the gym provided close relationships with the ability to stay healthy.

Her mom usually went with her. Spinning and the boot camp classes were their favorites. But Jana had committed to help out at the church and was going to have to miss today's class.

Chandler would much prefer to walk into places with her mom as opposed to being alone. She was friendly and always ready with a smile, but most would call her shy.

Fit's was just a few miles down the road, and Chandler made it to class in plenty of time. She set up her bike and went to the water fountain to fill her bottle.

Del saw Chandler and watched her from his place by the free weights. He was finishing his last set and was sorry to see that she was just getting there. He'd been watching Chandler since she started coming to the gym with her mother. Chandler was the type of girl that was beautiful without knowing it. Del saw that as an opportunity to draw her in. Her mom was great looking, too. At his age, he felt free to show his interest in mom or daughter. It was a good age to be, for sure. But, the mom seemed a little too invested in family. That wouldn't go anywhere.

But, Chandler. That just might.

✝

Sutton woke close to eleven o'clock Thursday morning and phoned her friends to make plans to go out dancing that night. She was mad at everyone in her life and needed to blow off some steam. Callin was an idiot, her mom was a lush and her dad was heartless.

She hung up with Liz and went into her parent's bedroom. Her mother was, once again, lying in her massive four poster bed with the shades drawn. Sutton stood next to her mom and studied her. She had once been beautiful, filled with promise. Her beauty contest awards hung in the trophy room, mocking what she had become.

The alcohol had helped to etch lines in her face. It didn't matter how much she did to erase them, lift them or fill them out, she was aging. Sutton picked up the flask next to the bed and the open bottle of prescription medication. She set the bottle down and held a family picture with both hands.

The family in the picture was composed of nothing but liars. Sutton smiled when she was told to. She couldn't remember a happy memory or a real laugh. She could remember vacations to France, voyages on yachts and cruises to Alaska. But the memories of laughter remained silent.

Sutton set the picture down and laughed to herself. She should have framed photographs of her with her nanny. That would be much more appropriate. She walked out of her mother's room and went to get dressed for the gym.

She dressed in her short work out skirt with a tight tank top and found herself regaining her confidence. She could have won every beauty contest, too, if her parents would have taken the time to enter her in the pageants and shows that were required. There was no telling who she could have been if they would have cared enough to give her a head start in life.

Once in the car, Sutton called a car service for that night. She wasn't going to have to call a cab again to come get her from some strange man's apartment. She wasn't going to have her father's do-boys go retrieve her car from the club the next morning. She had told herself that she was going to remain in control. And not go home with someone she'd never remember. But she dialed the number for the service anyway.

Just in case.

✝

Cal called Kyle every day that week, and she caught glimpses of him out on the field on her afternoon runs with Paige. Paige couldn't hide her excitement that Kyle and her brother were growing so close. Kyle didn't feel like she could confide her fears to Cal's sister, even if she happened to also be her best friend. Kyle knew it was God's way of making sure she relied solely on Him. He was all she needed. Isn't that what she told Brooke? Jesus was all she needed.

Friday night's dinner was fun and happy, and Kyle was excited when Callin asked if she wanted to go riding again on Saturday. It was getting more difficult for her to leave him these Friday nights, but knowing they would see each other the next morning, mercifully, made it a little bit easier.

✝

Kyle arrived early Saturday, before the heat of the day settled in. Callin had the horses saddled and ready so they could leave as soon as she arrived.

The horses knew where they were going without prodding and were happy for the leisurely pace. Kyle and Cal decided they could only talk in pig-latin until they stopped, and by the time they arrived at their destination, they were both laughing so hard their sides hurt. It felt so good to laugh.

They climbed down from the horses and Callin held Kyle's hand in his until they reached the rock.

Kyle sat cross-legged on the flat surface and faced Callin. "So, tell me how you became so proficient in pig-latin."

Callin laughed again, "Well, I grew up with Paige."

Kyle laughed, too, and Cal went on, "My Paw taught Paige the ancient language when she was really little. She used to walk around talking to herself in pig-latin and one day I begged her to teach me. We spent the whole day trying to get me to get it right. Finally, I perfected it and we vowed to only ever talk to each other in our 'secret code'. What we didn't know was that the code really wasn't so secret. We were scheming something in front of my mom who, of course, knew exactly what we were saying. It didn't end well."

Kyle laughed again at the picture in her mind, "Well, I'm highly impressed, really."

Cal looked into her eyes and their laughter faded. He touched her face and ran his thumb over her cheek. He loved her spirit. He loved her heart. He loved her laugh.

"I love you."

Tears instantly gathered in Kyle's eyes and when she smiled, they escaped down her cheeks, "I love you, too."

Callin sighed and pulled her into a hug. They held each other for a long time before they both realized they had to let go.

"I have an idea. Since we love each other and all, let's go celebrate tonight. I want to take you out to dinner. Somewhere fancy."

Kyle thought about and said, "Okay, how about burgers at Buck's."

"Buck's is fancy to you? I don't think I can stare lovingly into your eyes and whisper sweet nothings in your ear at Buck's."

"Wow, staring and whispering. You have a lot of plans for tonight." Kyle teased. "Hmm. Oh, what about Gio's. It's quaint and sophisticated and we can get a pizza. You can do all the staring and whispering you want."

"Deal." He hugged her again and let his arms linger for a few extra seconds. "We better get going if we're going to get all the way around the trail before the sun fries us. Eady-Ray?"

"Up-Yay."

Saturday morning was merciless on Sutton. Her head pounded and she was nauseous. She went to the same club Friday night as she had Thursday. Her friends turned her down for Friday. Sutton was feeling like they were pulling away. But she was used to that. Her mom had told her since she was a little girl that people would become jealous of her. Then they wouldn't want to be friends anymore.

Sutton had used the car service again and walked into the club alone. She figured Liz and Kate wouldn't have hung around her for long anyway.

Four drinks down and she was feeling ready to party. A good looking guy walked over to her and handed her a shot.

"Hey gorgeous. I noticed you came in by yourself."

Sutton was interested. He had the look of a cover model and the clothes that reeked of money. "I did come in alone. But that's no reason for me to leave alone."

By five o'clock in the morning, the car service had dropped her at her front door and she had the guy's name and phone number in her purse.

"The right guy. Maybe I've finally found him."

✝

This was the first date Kyle had been on in over two years. First she tried on a pencil skirt and button down blouse. "Too dressy."

Next she pulled on her jean shorts. She didn't even change shirts before she commented, "Not dressy enough."

141

She decided on a jean skirt and turquoise scoop neck shirt that showed off her golden skin. Before she could second guess that outfit, she heard Callin's truck pull into her drive. She glanced in the mirror and smoothed out her lip gloss before grabbing her purse and heading out the door.

He met her at her door as she was locking up and grabbed her hand.

"Hello." He walked with her the few steps to the truck. "You look amazing."

"So do you." Kyle took in Callin in his jeans and a fitted light blue button-down shirt, rolled up at the sleeves. For a cowboy, he sure knew how to dress.

The restaurant was dimly lit and filled with ambiance. It was classy and subdued, just as expected.

They sat across from each other and talked of the ending of another school year and what the summer held. They laughed at new inside jokes and ate their pizza by the candle's glow. When the pizza pan and plates were cleared away, they leaned in toward each other and held hands.

"You are so beautiful." Cal brought her hand to his lips and kissed it.

"So are you."

Callin looked at her lips and thought again how perfect they were. "You know I'm going to kiss you some day."

Kyle leaned in closer and whispered, "That's going to be one amazing kiss."

The evening ended after a movie and an ice cream cone. Cal walked Kyle to her door and waited while she unbolted the lock.

"I'm glad we had a reason to celebrate tonight." Kyle said, taking Cal's hand.

"So am I. I was thinking we should keep on celebrating. How about I take you to Buck's next week?"

Kyle laughed and agreed, "Sounds like my kind of celebration. Maybe we can throw in the end of the school year as a reason, too."

"Nope, I'm taking you out for tacos for our end of the year celebration. And then to Yuma's because I'm getting a new pair of boots. We can hit every restaurant all the way to Atlanta."

"Okay. And once we've gone to all the restaurants, we can work our way to all the mini golf courses." Kyle joined in the game.

"Okay, but I'm pretty lousy at golf."

"Perfect."

Kyle put her arms around Cal's waist and she was lost in his embrace. She listened as his heart beat accelerated and then he kissed the top of her head.

"I'll see you in the morning." He held onto her hand as he walked away and then broke away only when he had to.

Kyle turned on the lights and did her quick check, then sat down on the couch and bowed her head in her hands. "Oh, Lord. How did I ever doubt Your love for me? Ever."

Plans to prosper you, not to harm you. Plans to provide a hope and a future.

"Thank You, my Jesus. I believe You."

The guy's name was Shay Anthony. When he didn't call her by Sunday afternoon, Sutton sat out by the pool and phoned him.

"'Lo"

"Hey. Is this Shay?" Sutton was getting angry with herself for feeling nervous. He was lucky she was calling.

"Yeah, this is Shay. Who's this?" He sounded like she'd woken him up, but it was four o'clock in the afternoon. Even Sutton didn't sleep in that late.

"This is Sutton."

The pause on the other line was so long that Sutton pulled the phone away from her ear to see if the call had been disconnected. "Shay?"

"Yeah. Sutton who?"

Sutton's cheeks grew hot and she spoke with more attitude than she intended. "Sutton from Camio's. The dance club. I met you Friday night. And I was with you *all* night." Sutton heard her words and looked around to see if anyone was listening to her conversation.

"Oh, yeah. Sorry, you woke me up."

Sutton was slightly relieved by that fact. Maybe he just wasn't able to think clearly. "Well, I was just calling to see if you were going out clubbing this week. I thought I could meet up with you."

"Um. Yeah, no I'm not going out this week. I'm pretty busy all week."

The silence on the line was getting uncomfortable and Sutton was unsure of how to proceed. "Oh. Okay. Well, call me when things settle down."

"Sure. Talk to you later." The call ended and Sutton was left holding the phone to her cheek.

She stared out into the water and felt a deep wave of shame wash over her. Was this all there was in life? Her mom walked out and sat down next her, her sunglasses in place. She held a glass of wine in one hand and giggled when she splashed red onto her swimsuit. She didn't say a word to Sutton, but closed her eyes and slipped into another world. Sutton just looked at her.

She was the picture of the woman Sutton would one day become.

✝

The excitement for the end of the year permeated the halls of the school as Kyle made her way to class. The smell of chalk and the sound of children's laughter filled her senses and made her smile. It had been a great year.

What was prevalent in Kyle's mind this day was the full week off between the last day and summer school. She and Cal had made plans to be together as much as possible before the busyness of summer classes and the football team's off season work outs began.

The last bell rang and the kids burst out in shouts of celebration. Kyle gave her hugs and goodbyes to the children, knowing that she had done her best to love them as much as she could in the time she was given. They were good kids, every single one.

She closed her eyes, taking a deep breath. The smell of summer took her to a happy memory somewhere hidden far in the recesses of her mind. The rain mixed with the oils on the road, the jasmine and new flowers reminded her of freedom. Maybe this was the smell of every last day of school she had, but today it wasn't just the start of summer vacation. Today this smell represented her freedom to feel loved and be loved.

✝

The following day, Kyle waited for Cal on Pops front porch and leaned against the railing, taking in the beauty that was spoken into being. Giant oak trees controlled the perimeter of the property. Kyle loved to watch the birds flit and land, and rise up to do it again and again. Over the years, she had been witness to squirrels playing and eagles raising their young. She loved when Spring clothed every inch of the branches in green. Then when the green erupted into vibrant reds and oranges in the Fall, it was

145

like glimpsing heaven.

Her heart skipped when she heard Cal's truck come down the drive. He smiled at her through his open window and she picked up a small backpack she'd filled with snacks. Today they were hiking to a waterfall, something new for Kyle. Cal emerged from the truck and hurried to grab the backpack from Kyle. He was dressed in khaki shorts and a t-shirt that stretched to show well-worked biceps. His suntanned face highlighted the green in his eyes and Kyle couldn't wait until they were able to look at each other so she could study them again.

The ride to the falls wasn't as long as Kyle had anticipated. To be so close to this level of beauty without knowing it reminded her of all the days she was only a prayer away from salvation and didn't take the time.

They changed from their flip flops to hiking boots and started up the mountain. Tourists dotted the trail and kids ran past them to see who would be first. Cal took Kyle's hand and they let everyone fly by. There was no hurry, they wanted this day to last forever.

They heard the water crashing to the pool below well before they reached the fall. The smell of dirt and wood mingled with the scent of fresh water. When they finally made it to the top of the trail, the sight of God in motion left them speechless. The sun shone through the water, creating millions of diamonds shining just for them. A mist, like angel's breath, took over the end of the fall that lead to the peace of calm waters. Just like Jesus. Strong and mighty with a beauty that shines like precious stones, leading straight to peace.

They hiked back down the trail a bit and found a couple of sitting stones. Kyle pulled out two granola bars and a couple bottles of water when she found Callin staring at her.

"I know I keep saying this. But you are so beautiful."

Kyle blushed and looked down. "Thank you. I don't think I'll get tired of hearing that, so you can keep on if you'd like."

"I plan on it."

Kyle took a drink and asked, "So, how did your parents meet?"

Cal finished his bite of the bar, "They met at Greenville High. My mom's family moved to town when she was a Sophomore and my dad said it was love at first sight. Mom's a trust-fund baby, and her parents didn't approve of my dad. They didn't even go to the wedding. My mom's relationship with her parents was pretty strained for a while."

Kyle wondered if that was why she felt such a strong connection with Anne, they had so much in common.

"But, when Paige was born, my grandparents really softened up. And, of course, once I came along they couldn't stay away." Cal grinned.

"I love your modesty, Callin Jennings." Kyle teased. "You seem really close to your dad's parents, too."

"Oh, yeah. I really miss them. I was my Paw's little man. I followed him everywhere. And my Gram thought I could do no wrong. When I got in trouble at home with my parents, I'd hike over to the main house and she'd give me dessert and pretty much spoil me to death. I can't wait for you to meet them."

"They sound wonderful. I'm surprised your dad didn't follow in grandpa's footsteps and go into ranching."

"Yeah, my Paw was so wise to let his children follow their own dreams. He passed that on to my dad for me. I'm sure my dad would have loved for me to go into construction, but I just always wanted to play and coach football. He never made me feel guilty about it or tried to persuade me to go into the business. He taught me what he knew when I was younger, so I know how to use a hammer and a circular saw, but put a football in my hand any day."

"Were you and Paige close growing up?" Kyle had finished her water and gave Cal her full attention.

"We were close, but we didn't get along, if that makes any sense." Cal grinned. "I was really good at being a little brother. I put frogs in her bed, I chased her with snakes. I used to bug her to death when she had her friends over. And then when I figured out that she and Gray liked each other - that was a blast. I did everything I could think of to embarrass the tar out her."

"When did they start dating?" It was funny to Kyle that she had never asked Paige about this in all the time they'd spent together.

"I don't think you can really call it dating, but they started showing interest in high school. Gray's a year older than Paige, but he stayed at the community college to be near her. My parents didn't approve of us dating until we were out of high school, but Gray was over at our house every day that I can remember.

"You weren't allowed to date in High School? The James kids aren't, either."

"The majority of our church members went through a parenting class when I was in middle school, and that was one of the suggestions. Most followed through with it and it's been successful. It kept us more involved in sports and academics and out of trouble. The boys were taught that girls deserved to be treasured. We open doors and pay for meals. I learned so much just by watching my dad, so I've been blessed.

"The girls were taught that they deserved nothing less than total respect. Gray's parents went through the class with my parents, so he was brought up knowing how to treat my sister. He was welcomed over any time as long as my parents were there. You know our families are best friends, so we all grew up together."

"Oh, that's right. Gray's little brother was your best friend, right?"

"Justin. Yep. He still is. We were inseparable as kids. Man, the things we used to do. If my mom knew half of it she would die on the spot. We used to climb to the tip top of trees and rock them back and forth. We saw a bear in the woods once and followed it for hours. I have no idea what we would have done if we would have found it. We were crazy." Callin smiled at the memories. Kyle was just grateful the Lord protected him all those years.

"Justin and I were roommates at the University, too. He met his wife, Amy, our first day on campus, so it doesn't really seem like I saw him much during our college days. They were married less than two years later and moved into the married dorms. Their relationship was so inspirational to me. They followed God's will for their lives without question and were unshakable in their faith. The week after they graduated, they left for Indonesia and have been missionaries there ever since."

"Do you think you'll ever be called to missions?" Kyle asked.

"Definitely. In high school our families went to Louisiana and Kentucky for missions and my dad has worked with Habitat for Humanity for years. I love the missions, but so far I haven't felt that God's leading me to missions overseas. I don't know that He won't, but so far I feel like I'm exactly where I'm supposed to be."

"I love that perspective. There are so many people in need here, nearby. I've thought a lot about going to Haiti one day. I love the idea of adoption." She hadn't realized how it would sound, but the moment the subject of children came up, she was afraid she had scared him.

Cal wasn't scared. "How many kids do you want?"

"Right now, I guess I'd say two. But, for some reason I feel like it might be more. God has a way of making mince meat of my own plans. I try really hard to just stick with His."

"Do you want boys or girls?' Cal was having fun with this conversation. It had been on his mind for a few weeks.

"I don't think I care so I don't think it would matter. What about you?

"I think two, or more, sound perfect. I would love to have at least one little girl. Ryan, or maybe Evan for your maiden

149

name." Cal grinned

Kyle smiled up at him. "So, you like boy names for girls, huh?"

"I love your name. I seem to love everything about you."

"The feeling's mutual." Kyle warmed, feeling cherished.

Callin cleared his throat, "What's your best memory growing up?"

Kyle had to think for a few moments before answering, "When I was about ten years old, my parents took me to Disney World in Florida. What I remember most is being freezing cold in Indiana and then getting out of the car in Florida and feeling a warm breeze on my face. It surprised me. And I remember the palm trees and how strange they were to me. I went up to the tree trunk and felt the bark. I even took some home with me. It was the only time I remember feeling safe, for some reason. Maybe because it was one of the few memories that include my dad.

"Have you talked to him since you've moved here?"

"I called him when I first got settled. I was afraid to give him too much information, because I didn't want Paul to know where I was. I figured that he'd call me back when he wanted to talk to me. He never has. I just take that as my answer that he has nothing to say."

"Do you think that maybe he feels too ashamed to contact you?"

"I never thought of it like that before."

"It could be that he's afraid of being rejected. Maybe he needs you to call him again. I can imagine that would be hard for you, but I don't know any parent that doesn't love their child. And I don't know any child that doesn't need their parent."

Kyle brushed away a wisp of sun-streaked hair that had escaped her pony tail and thought about what Cal had just said. He was right, she knew it. Every girl needed her daddy, no matter what the past held. The problem was that she was afraid of rejection, too. She'd had enough to last a lifetime.

Kyle fell asleep that night thinking of the sound of her dad's laugh. One day. Maybe, one day. But, then her thoughts flew to Paul.

"I found something I thought you'd like to see." He had been waiting for her to come in the door and immediately yanked her arm. Bruises on bruises. Black on yellow.

He roughly led her to the guest room and grabbed her by the hair. "What's this?"

She cried out when he pulled so hard, strands of hair floated to the ground. Her packed suitcase she had hidden in the closet was opened on the bed in front of her. "I'm sorry. I'm sorry."

He pushed her on the ground and kicked her in the ribs, then got down next to her, his face next to hers. "Do you think you can leave me? No one leaves me. I will tell you when to go when I want you to leave." His spittle sprayed her face and she covered her eyes.

"You're such an idiot. I was this close to getting rid of you anyway. I've already found your replacement. Now, you might never leave."

He pulled her up by her hair and shoved her in the closet. "You think you had it so bad. Let's give you some perspective."

He locked her in and then she heard him bolt the bedroom door as well. Then all she heard were the echoes of her sobs.

CHAPTER 18

Sutton called some friends from high school and decided to meet them at a nightclub for a few drinks. She hadn't seen them in years and was grateful they agreed to meet her. She was feeling especially lonely. She'd never say it out loud, but she was feeling very unloved. It was a feeling she'd held close her entire life, but some days were worse than others.

She arrived at the club close to eleven o'clock and the reunited girls squealed as they hugged each other. Long lost friends. Although Sutton remembered clearly when Tamara stole her boyfriend and Pris told the whole eleventh grade that Sutton liked girls. It didn't matter tonight. They were there to build a new relationship.

The girls sat at the bar and had their drinks bought for them. It was rare they needed any cash. Men seemed to enjoy supplying them with as many drinks as they'd like.

Sutton wasn't feeling like dancing, but perched on her barstool like royalty for all the world to admire. A man approached her and extended his hand. "Hello. My name's Bret."

"Bret. It's nice to meet you. I'm Sutton." Bret took her hand and kissed it. She wasn't used to such chivalry and gave her full attention to him.

"I've never been to this club before, but I sure am glad I came tonight."

Sutton glowed with the compliment and responded, "We usually go to Camio's but I needed a change of scenery." And she wanted to be a little closer to home.

Bret had bronze skin and a touch of blond highlights in his hair. By his dress and mannerisms, he was accustomed to spending money. Sutton admired that in a man.

"It's pretty loud in here. I think I'd like to get to know you somewhere a little less noisy."

A warning sounded in Sutton's mind. It was the same warning she'd heard every other night she found herself in a bar or club. She was just too stubborn to listen. She was expecting him to invite her back to his place when he surprised her.

"I would love to take you out tomorrow evening. I have a great little restaurant I think you'd love." His smile was perfect. Sutton was guessing he had veneers, but she was never one to judge.

"That sounds great." Bret entered Sutton's number in his phone and kissed her hand good night.

By two o'clock, in the morning Sutton was ready to go home and have a good night's sleep. She had a date that night and she wanted to look her best.

Chandler opened the back door of the convenience store where she'd worked for months. The back alley had never bothered her before. But the encounter with that man who knew her name and issued a warning, kept her aware. Her eyes darted left and right. She hadn't seen him again since that Saturday she'd called her mom to come in, but she felt her nerves, all the same. Chandler prayed to Jesus to keep her protected under the shadow of His wing.

Chandler believed in angels with all that was in her. She had seen them twice as a little girl. Once she woke to find a mighty figure standing by her bed, another time one was standing outside guarding the driveway.

Chandler was only four years old when she saw Jesus face-to-face. Even at such a tender age, she realized that seeing Him was a sacred event. She really didn't think anyone would believe her, so she told only her parents. She never forgot that night, or any detail of the meeting. It had been pitch black outside. The only illumination in the room was her Cinderella night light. She didn't know what woke her, but she opened her eyes to see the God of the Universe standing at the foot of her bed. She wasn't frightened, she felt only peace. With a snow white beard and hair like cotton, He didn't look like any pictures she'd ever seen of Him in her children's Bible, yet she never once questioned who He was.

He didn't speak to her. He just looked at her with a love that was incomparable and smiled a smile that would put the sun to shame. She kept her eyes on His. And smiled back.

✝

Sutton woke on Saturday morning with shopping foremost on her agenda. She was going to make Bret drool. She had to travel a ways to find the perfect boutique and bought a slinky black dress and designer heels. She also found several additional outfits, a few extra pairs of shoes, and two purses. Shopping made her feel good.

She laid out by the pool for long enough to get that natural glow. By five o'clock, she was ready to start preparing for her seven o'clock date.

Bret asked her to meet him at a restaurant pretty far out of town. She was slightly irritated that he didn't offer to pick her up at her house, but she let it slide. Maybe it was better that she had her car with her. He might be a complete bore.

She straightened her thick, blond hair and applied her make up. Her eye shadow took the most time. She was going for smoky, sultry eyes and it took patience and precision.

By six o'clock she was ready for the forty-five minute drive to downtown.

She put the name of the restaurant into her GPS and arrived only a few minutes early. Sutton pulled up to the valet and watched him stare at her legs as she exited the car. She handed him her keys and walked inside. For a restaurant, the place didn't seem to focus much on food. Crowded tables were set in clusters with several girls dancing on strategically placed stages. Sutton scanned the room looking for Bret. She felt a pit in her stomach that nearly made her turn around, but then she remembered what a gentleman he had been the night before.

He saw her first and hurried to her side. He hugged her like he'd known her forever. "Sutton. I'm so glad to see you. Our table's over here."

He led her to a table that seated four people. Two men she hadn't seen before were already sitting down, eating their food and watching the girls taking off their clothes in front of them.

If Sutton wouldn't have been so embarrassed, she would have turned and ran. But she wasn't a baby. She was a woman and she could handle this. She'd just wait until dinner was over. She couldn't understand why Bret would want to watch such trashy girls, but so be it. She was hoping for a walk in one of the local gardens, or even a movie once they left this place. The sooner the better.

Bret pulled out her chair and introduced her to the men at the table. Sutton politely smiled and shook their hands. She still couldn't understand why she and Bret weren't seated at a table for two. Maybe these were business associates.

Sutton finished her meal and began to feel queasy from the grease and disgusting displays before her. She was ready to leave and told Bret just that.

"Sure. I need to meet with these guys first, somewhere more private."

The group moved to a back room where there were sofas and chairs set up. Bret and Sutton sat on a sofa and the other two men sat on one opposite theirs.

Sutton was shocked when Bret turned to her and she found herself the topic of the conversation.

"Sutton, I asked you here because I saw something special in you last night. You are gorgeous, confident and cultured. I'm sure you realize that girls like you are hard to find."

Girls like you. Sutton's mind was going over and over the events since the previous night. Bret continued, "These men are my associates. We travel to the smaller towns to find girls like you who are looking to live the life of luxury."

Sutton felt something in her heart warn her to run, warn her to get up and leave. "What exactly do you mean?"

Bret flashed his perfect teeth, "There are men all over the world that go through the airport in Atlanta. They are businessmen looking for a little company. All they want is for a pretty girl to accompany them to dinners, conventions and social gatherings. They pay top dollar for your time and you get a great dinner and fun night out."

Sutton thought for a second that it sounded like a good proposition, but then remembered something she'd seen about escorts. No way would they think she would sell her body. Would they? "What's the catch?"

The two men laughed, but Bret didn't flinch, "There's no catch. We just wanted to offer this to you because we have some clients coming in tonight and we were hoping you'd be interested in meeting with them."

Sutton felt something deep in her soul.

Child. Leave now. Come to Me.

She felt fear prickle the back of her neck and looked toward the door, "What if I decide this isn't something that I want to do?"

"Then you walk away. I believe you'll think it over and change your mind."

"Okay. I'll think about it." Sutton knew she was lying. She wanted out and she wasn't stupid.

She said goodbye and grabbed her purse. She didn't feel safe until she was in her car, driving home. She replayed the evening in her mind again and again. She wasn't sure what hurt more. The fact that Bret wasn't the right guy for her after all.

Or that he thought she would so easily prostitute herself.

CHAPTER 19

The Fourth of July was approaching and the town was splashed with the colors of freedom. It seemed that everyone in three counties was preparing for the dance at Skip's. Skip Walters held a party every year, ending the night with fireworks that could be seen for miles. He put it on for the town every year because his parents had before him. It was tradition that the townsfolk rarely missed. Kyle hadn't felt as much a part of the community the year before, but this year was different. In every way.

Kyle arrived as the sun was beginning its descent. The rows of cars sent a quick shiver to her stomach. She didn't want to be nervous, but she still didn't enjoy going to places by herself. Callin was already inside somewhere. He arrived early to bring in food and soft drinks for Skip and his wife, Nancy. The couple loved making their town happy and celebrating their country's independence, but they were getting up in years and it wasn't as easy as it had been when they were younger and the town was smaller. Callin and Martin, along with a few other long-standing citizens, offered to help.

Kyle had so wanted to arrive with Callin. But, she understood. She just wanted to be in there, next to him. She was so grateful that the moment she walked in through the barn doors, she spotted Paige and Anne. She made her way through the crowd and gave them both hugs that she needed so badly. Anne's welcoming smile and Paige's unique laugh made Kyle feel special and loved. Anne's cowboy boots and plaid shirt seemed out of place combined with her ever-stylish strawberry blond bob and manicured fingernails that accentuated her elegance. Paige's jean skirt and boots were paired with a flowing shirt with a wild pattern that matched her personality perfectly. Her pixie cut was covered with her cowboy hat and she wore her smile that seemed to be easier these days.

Kyle was settling in and having a good time when she looked across the room and saw Sutton and her friends looking around. Kyle could only guess who they were searching for. Sutton's blond hair was freshly high-lighted, long and beautiful. She knew it was an asset and she wore it well. Her tight dress was meant to show off her figure and it did. Kyle looked down at her yellow sundress and felt like Cinderella before the ball. Before the fairy godmother came and made everything magical. Before she was transformed into a princess.

Kyle excused herself and made her way to the bathroom near the back of the barn. She shut herself in and stared into the mirror. "I don't deserve him, God. I don't belong here." She closed her eyes and wanted to weep.

Lies, Child. Don't listen to the lies. You are My daughter, the daughter of the KING. Beloved, you are MY princess.

Kyle opened her eyes and tried to see the person her Savior saw.

Jana walked in and caught her staring in the mirror. "Hey, Sweetie. What are you doing in here? I think there's a boy out there somewhere waiting for you."

Kyle broke her gaze from the glass and looked down at her hands.

Jana gave her a hug and lifted her chin to make eye contact. "There's only one place you can look to find peace. If you look behind you, you'll find regret. If you look around, you'll find envy. If you look forward, you'll find worry. The only way you'll find contentment is by looking up."

Kyle smiled and nodded. "Thank you. I'm trying so hard. I really am."

"I know you are. Now go find that boy."

Kyle opened the door and held her head high. She might not always feel like a princess, but that didn't change the facts. That's exactly what she was.

Sutton knew she looked good. Every male eye had wandered in

her direction, many lingering. She went to the bathroom and checked her make up. Flawless. She applied more lipstick and went out again to look for Callin. She knew he was there. After her catastrophes with Shay and Bret, she refocused her energy on Cal. She arrived early, knowing that he had gone in the afternoon to help. But, somehow she kept missing him.

She was starting to get frustrated. She knew Kyle was there and she had really hoped to be able to talk to Callin before Kyle hung all over him. Even still, she would get him alone somehow. This was her last chance. She knew this was the only time she could show off her best assets. She sure couldn't go to church looking this good.

She sauntered back to her group of friends from church and picked up immediately in the conversation. She laughed and smiled, letting everyone know what a good time she was having and how much fun she must be to be around.

She saw him walk in the back door. He was so gorgeous. Enough to make her speechless. His cowboy hat made him look tough, even though she knew he was nothing but kind. His white button down shirt showed off his tan and hung loose over his faded blue jeans. Sutton's heart raced as she hurried over to meet him. She watched him from the second he walked in the door, and his eyes never moved from one direction. She followed his eyes and they landed across the room, directly on Kyle Evans. He didn't look anywhere other than at Kyle, including in Sutton's direction.

Callin saw Kyle the moment he walked in the door. She was the only one in the room. The lights overhead illuminated her smile, her hair, her skin. He walked toward her with purpose, dodging in and out of people dancing and laughing. Holding her was all he wanted and he didn't want to wait another second.

He swept her up in a hug and all of Kyle's fears and insecurities vanished.

Line dancing was in full swing and everyone seemed to be

having a great time. Children ran in and out of the adults, chasing and laughing. Older men sat in groups and talked about the parties of the past, while young mothers rocked their fussy babies that were ready for bed.

A slow song came on and couples paired off. Callin held his hand out to Kyle and she took it without speaking. There wasn't a need for words. She felt his hand on the small of her back as he took her in his arms and began to dance. She placed her cheek against his chest and kept in step with him. She smelled his scent of soap mixed with cologne and thought she could stay where she was for forever. Soon she let go of his hand and placed her arms around his neck. Song after song played, but they kept on without interruption. This was where they belonged.

 Martin and Anne danced across the dance floor from their son. "Well, Annie, it looks like our boy's lost his heart."

Anne smiled and looked up at the man she'd loved more than half her life, "No, Sweetheart. I think he's finally found it."

Sutton watched Kyle and Callin dance from where she sat at her table. A sadness overcame her that knocked the breath from her. Suddenly, it was quite obvious that Callin Jennings was in love and it wasn't with her.

She was so desperate to feel loved. For as long as she could remember, she took it in where she could like a vacuum. But it would just lie like dust in her heart. Sutton looked around the room and suddenly felt bared. She went to her chair and grabbed her sweater. Chet saw her and rushed over to help her put it on. Sutton turned around and smiled. "Thank you, Chet."

"You're welcome. Would you like to dance?"

Sutton studied him for a moment and discovered that she had never really seen him before. His blue eyes were filled with a gentleness that took her by surprise. Britt's words immediately came to her mind. Maybe if she quit looking at the wrong guy, she'd finally find the right one.

✝

Callin and Kyle continued to get closer as they danced. The
smell of her hair was intoxicating and Callin found himself
wanting to kiss her. It didn't matter who was in the room, who
was watching. Kyle felt the muscles in Cal's back and neck. If
she just looked up at him, she knew she wouldn't be able to stop
herself from finding his lips. She wasn't that strong, and the way
he was holding her, she didn't think he was that strong either.

At the same time, they broke apart and gave a quiet laugh. "I
think we need some air." Callin led her by the hand through the
crowd, out the back door.

The fireworks were nearly set up and ready. Another half hour
and it would be dark enough to start. Callin had set up chairs
and blankets for the whole family earlier that afternoon. Couples
and families were already gathering and finding their seats. He
and Kyle walked over and sat down on their blanket.

Callin started speaking once he was seated, facing Kyle, "I
always thought I was so strong. I think I prided myself on being
able to stay home on a Saturday night while my buddies were out
drinking and sleeping around." Callin took Kyle's hand and
kissed it. "I know now that I'm not strong at all. I'm thinking
things about you that I shouldn't be thinking. And it's driving
me crazy."

Kyle smiled and rubbed her thumb over his, "Me, too. So what
do we do?"

"Well, I know what we shouldn't do. We shouldn't be alone.
We'll just have to be smart and stay around other people for
now."

Kyle agreed and nodded.

"You know I'm going to marry you, Kyle Evans." Callin meant
it. He would marry her tonight if he felt like it was the right
time.

Kyle's heart jumped and her smile grew. "Well, when you decide to ask me, I promise I'll say 'yes'."

They put their foreheads together and touched noses.

"Okay, I think I'm going to need to ask you very soon." Cal laughed and broke away again.

The rest of the crowd from inside descended on them and found their places in time for the fireworks display to begin. Cal and Kyle held hands as the fireworks exploded overhead.

But it was nothing compared to the ones going off in their hearts.

Mr. Tate left Chandler up at the front counter while he retreated to the back for inventory. Chandler was beginning to dread inventory. That man always seemed to come in when Mr. Tate was in the back. Like he knew. As she stood thinking of her fear, he materialized in front of her.

"Chandler. Nice to see you, as always."

He was too old for her. Chandler couldn't understand his interest. She was barely out of high school.

Chandler stood up straight, pretending to be strong.

"I know you're lonely. We need to do something about that." He smiled at her, but something behind that smile was off.

"I'm not lonely at all, sir. I promise."

His smile instantly moved to a grimace. "I'm asking you out, is all."

"I understand. But, I don't even know you. And I'm leaving soon for college. There's no reason to start anything if I'm leaving." Chandler felt triumphant in her response. And when he turned to leave, she knew she had been.

As he reached the door, he turned back to her. "I'll come back. And I'll change your mind. You'll see."

✝

Sutton walked down the hall from her room to the stair case. She was so sick of seeing that closed door to her mother's room, she wanted to kick it in.

She spiraled down to the bottom floor and found the liquor cabinet. Vodka, whiskey, bourbon. They had it all. She chose the rum and poured the liquid into a crystal tumbler. She walked out to the lanai and stood over the edge of the pool. She'd never had a drink during the day. Somehow she prided herself on that. She'd drink until she was sick at night, but she never resorted to drinking in the middle of the day. It was the one small step that kept her from being just like her mother.

She stared at the liquid, gleaming in the sunlight. One sip and she'd be her mom. Just one sip. The ice clinked against the crystal and Sutton looked out over the water.

Why had they ever moved here? She never could understand. They'd had a beautiful home near Atlanta. Her dad had lived with them, she could remember that much. She thought back to her earliest memory, and she thought for a moment that she could remember smiles, laughter. She had to be mistaken. Her mom didn't smile. Laughter was a ghost.

She turned toward the house and looked up at her mother's window. The blinds were closed, like they'd been for Sutton's entire life.

She brought the glass to her lips and felt the tears fall to the rim.

Then she threw the glass and watched as it shattered against the slate, into a million shards of regret.

✝

Over the few weeks following the Fourth of July, Callin and

164

Kyle made sure they were never alone. Callin knew that he would ask her to marry him soon. He had the perfect ring in mind and planned to propose when summer school ended and their lives settled down.

Kyle fit into Cal's family perfectly. His mom adopted her into her heart and wanted the best for them both. She had given Callin ideas on that ring and made sure her son knew how important the wedding was to the bride.

Anne had lots of plans for the wedding in her mind, and hoped that her future daughter-in-law would welcome her opinions. Paige had married nearly five years before and Anne felt more than ready for another wedding. The early days of summer in the Jennings home were filled with laughter and love. Not one of them could feel more blessed.

And then the laughter stopped.

CHAPTER 20

Kyle was brushing her teeth before church service Sunday morning when she startled to a knock on her door. She rarely had visitors and suddenly a feeling of dread washed over her. Something was wrong. She peered out the side window before making her way to the door. Always cautious. Always careful.

Kyle opened the heavy door and smiled up at Pops. "Hi Pops. How are you doing this morning?"

Pops eyes filled with tears and he looked down as he cleared his throat. "Not so good, Sweet Girl. Not so good."

Kyle immediately gave him a strong hug, "What's wrong? What happened?"

Pops released her and put his arms on her shoulders, "I'm going to let Callin tell you, Honey. He's out front."

Kyle stepped outside and closed the door behind her and followed Pops around the side of the barn. Had something happened to Paige? Was there an accident? Fear settled in her stomach and held on.

Cal was standing on Pops front porch and turned toward Kyle as she hurried up the steps. His smile was missing and it seemed so unnatural. His face held a look of pain. Physical or emotional, Kyle couldn't tell.

"Hey, Cal. Sweetie, what's wrong?" Kyle noticed that Pops had disappeared and she looked around to see where he went.

Cal reached for her and held her, "I have some bad news and I don't know how to say it out loud." Tears now pooled in his eyes and Kyle absently thought that she couldn't remember ever seeing two men cry in one day.

"Okay. Who is it about?" Kyle tried to help.

"It's Chandler. She's missing. She disappeared last night after work." He paused again, searching for words, "She was kidnapped, Kyle." Cal looked into Kyle's eyes and tried to read her.

"Chandler? Okay. I don't understand. How do they know she was kidnapped?" Kyle turned away and placed her hands on her head trying to process what she'd just heard. Kidnappings didn't happen in Greenville. Petty theft and the occasional obnoxious party were fairly common, but serious crime was a non-issue.

"She didn't come home last night. When she was about an hour late, her parents called Mr. Tate at the store and he told them she had left on time. He usually walks her out to her car when it's dark, but a couple customers came in right as she was leaving. Chandler told him not to worry about it, she was parked fairly close."

Callin paused when he thought of how guilty Mr. Tate must be feeling right now. "Gray called me this morning. He's been at the store processing it as a crime scene. He realized that we would hear about it at church this morning. He didn't want us to be blindsided with the news."

Callin took her hand and brought her from her statue-like state. He led her to the porch swing and she sat down, looking straight ahead.

"I'm having a hard time understanding this. Has there been a ransom?' Kyle looked up at Cal and leaned forward, elbows on her knees.

"No. Her purse was found in the parking lot near her car." Cal paused again, trying to gauge what he should say. "There was quite a bit of blood, Ky. It doesn't look good."

"She's the sweetest girl I've ever met in all my life, Cal. There's not a soul that would want to hurt her. No one could hurt her!" The gravity of what had obviously happened was closing in and Kyle started shaking. Callin sat down next to her and put his arm around her shoulders.

"I'm so sorry, Ky. I know how much you love her and I wish I knew what to say… what to do."

Kyle sat up straighter, sniffed and wiped the tears off her cheeks, "We're going to pray. That's what we're going to do. We're going to go to church and be there for her family and pray that God will watch over her and keep her safe."

✝

Grayson had watched the surveillance tapes of Chandler's final hours before her disappearance until his eyes blurred. She had waited on several customers, but they all checked out. He watched her face in the moments before she left that night. She was smiling and happy. Grayson couldn't remember ever seeing her when she wasn't happy.

He watched as she gathered her keys and purse from behind the counter and said good-bye to Mr. Tate. She waved and then moved out of sight of the cameras.

The outside camera's picked her up until she walked out of range.

And then she was gone.

CHAPTER 21

Callin and Kyle rode with Pops to the church to be with family. Their church family. They had seen each other through births, baptisms, salvations, drug-addictions, cancer, wayward children. But, never this.

Word of Chandler's abduction traveled quickly and the parking lot was filled with people from churches all around the area to hold a prayer vigil. In a small town where everyone seemed to know everyone else, Chandler was a daughter, a sister, a friend to all. And she was loved so very much.

Jana and Andy were in the front row, holding tightly to Townsend and Davis. Townsend was sobbing, not fully understanding the implications of what was taking place. Jana and Andy held hands around their children and kept their eyes closed in constant prayer.

Cal, Kyle and Pops stood in the back of the sanctuary until Martin noticed them and gave his seat to Pops. The Jennings were there for the family when Chandler was born. Anne had taken a casserole to the new family all those years ago and held Chandler in her arms when she was only days old. Paige was old enough to be excited about holding the new baby and babysat a number of times, until Grayson caught her eye.

Kyle loved Chandler and her contagious laughter. She loved Jana and Andy, Davis and Townsend. Kyle wanted to go to them and be near them. Her heart was breaking for this family. Like every other person in the packed church, Kyle wished there was something, anything, she could do or say to undo it all. But she remained where she stood.

Prayers went up to the God that saves. Tears flowed without end and when people finally started to disperse, the James family didn't move. What else could they do but stay? Beg. Plead. Kyle felt helpless as they stood to leave.

"What should we do? I want to be there for them. I want them to know I'm here." Kyle asked Anne as they made their way to the door.

"They know you're there for them, Sweetie. What we can do is go back to the house and continue to pray. We can try to give them a call later and leave a message if we have to."

Kyle nodded and they walked to their cars. She had felt hopeless before, but nothing like this. As Callin drove to the main house, she put her head in her hands and silently wept.

✝

Gray looked at the man in front of him. Del Johnson returned Grayson's stare with contempt.

Gray leaned forward and began to speak, "So, I've had several reports that you've been harassing girls at the gym for a few months now. And then Chandler James goes missing. Chandler goes to your gym. So, you can see why you're here and why we're talking to you, can't you?"

"I have no idea who this Chandler person is. I date the ladies, I don't kill them." Del jerked back and the chairs legs scraped along the floor.

"Well, Del. No one said Chandler was dead. Except you." Johns stood behind Grayson and warnings went up for them both.

"Man, you don't have to say she's dead. If she's really been kidnapped, then you know she's dead. No one lives when they've been kidnapped. Don't you watch TV?" Del's smirk was enough to force Grayson to leave the room for fear of losing his temper. Johns followed him out, leaving Del to stew in the interrogation room.

"So, what do you think?" Johns asked immediately once the door closed.

"Hopefully we'll have more to go on when we verify his alibi for Saturday night. My gut is saying it's not him. He's a scumbag, but he doesn't seem the type. Plus with a wife that keeps such close tabs, I'm not sure how he would have gotten away with it. Being a low life cheater might just save him."

Johns nodded his head and tried to think of their next move when Nick came up to them with a message. "I got a hold of Del's wife. According to her, he was at home all night with her."

The officers knew not to always trust the alibi of a spouse, but they didn't have much choice. "Okay. We'll release him and ask around to the neighbors and extended family to see if anyone else saw him near his home to corroborate what Mrs. Johnson says. We need forensics to give us some help. Any word on when they'll be in touch with us?"

Nick shook his head, "It could take a while with so much to process." The footprints and scuff marks they had found at the store led them to believe that there were at least three perpetrators. That was going to slow things down.

Grayson returned to his desk and had just positioned himself in front of his computer when his phone buzzed. "Gray here."

"Gray, it's Chief Chapple over here in Chesterfield. Listen, I've had reports of some men in the area looking for girls to work for them as high end call girls. They've been in scouting our town for a few weeks now." Gray thought of how that could go bad, if Chandler had somehow turned them down and they became angry.

"How many men were there?"

Before Chapple even answered, Grayson had guessed.

"Three."

CHAPTER 22

Bradley Hudson was the best foreman in the surrounding area, it was a well-known fact. He was a tough boss, and required things to be done well and done as quickly as possible. But he was fair and honest and the men that worked for him respected him a great deal. Bradley insisted that his workers take Sundays off so they could go to church and be with their families. That's how he was raised.

Bradley had walked through the house on Manchester Road countless times before this Monday morning. He made sure the floors were swept from debris, codes were enforced and that nothing was missing or had been tampered with. He loved this house and all its character. He put his heart into his projects and this home was no different.

Bradley opened the back door and stepped out onto the covered lanai. He closed the door behind him and surveyed the surrounding woods. It was such a peaceful lot. There wasn't another house within a quarter mile and back in this area, all that could be heard was music of nature.

He stepped off the back porch and rounded the corner of the house. He walked a few steps before he felt something was wrong. The nature he loved so much was silent. His head swung to his left and it took him a few heartbeats to process what he was seeing. He realized after a few moments what it was, but his brain couldn't comprehend the scene.

He walked toward her until he was twenty feet from her body. He knew it was a girl from her painted toenails and auburn hair. Nothing else was recognizable.

Bradley ran to the back of the house, falling once then regaining his footing. He stopped at the corner of the house and vomited all he had eaten that morning. He crawled the few feet until his sight was clear from the carnage, and frantically called 911.

✝

Grayson and Johns turned on their lights and rushed to the scene as soon as the dispatcher came on the line to report Bradley Hudson's panicked phone call. The screech of his tires on the drive sent dirt floating to the skies. Grayson heard the call, knew in his heart this dead girl was Chandler, but prayed anyway, "Please no, Lord. Please, no."

Car doors slammed as the two officers found their way to the side of the house. Several additional patrol cars and crime scene vehicles pulled up behind. Soon, men and women were surrounding the area, taping off the crime scene and getting to work. The problem was that work this day was unlike any other day any of those present had ever seen.

Grayson stood staring down at what was left of Chandler James. He knew immediately it was her. The red hair identified her and the shock of what was before him nearly brought him down. No one spoke when they looked on her. It was too heinous, too personal.

A few officers turned away and went back toward the house. This wasn't supposed to happen in a small town, but this wasn't supposed to happen anywhere. In his wildest imagination, Grayson never could have pictured this. She didn't resemble a person anymore. Grayson could only pray that what made her look this way happened after she had been killed. But, deep in his heart, he knew better.

✝

Gray watched from a distance as the tent was constructed around Chandler, to preserve the crime scene and keep photographers from snapping pictures. He was running through his mind all the things that needed to be done when he heard the screech of tires behind him.

Andy ran toward the tent, slipping and falling before getting up again to reach his daughter. Grayson and two other officers held him back until he couldn't fight any longer and crumbled to the ground.

Jana had slowly walked to Andy and stood next to him where he had covered his head, weeping on the ground. She wrapped her arms around herself, staring toward her child.

"I need to see her, Gray. You know I need to see her." A sob broke her voice and she grabbed his arms, begging him to let them see their firstborn one more time, hold their baby girl one last time.

"Jana, you just can't. You just can't." Gray didn't know what else to say, and Jana broke down and tried to break free.

"No. No! I need to see her. I need to see her. I need to." She collapsed in Gray's arms until her hysteria wore her out. Gray began to feel his tears and let them fall.

"I'm so sorry, Jana." And then he prayed with all he had for God to pour down his supernatural peace and comfort that they wouldn't survive without.

✝

The pastor called his congregation together to be there for the family and to pray for the entire community. This was a fire no one ever expected to have to walk through. Pastor Jeremy only knew one thing to do.

Kyle and Paige heard the news while nursing coffees at the Java House. Paige called Callin and the three were going to drive to the church. It felt like a repeat of the day before, but hope was gone. Sadness settled on the tiny church and Kyle's lip trembled. There was no place to park in the lot behind the church building.

Kyle, Callin and Paige didn't know details, only that Chandler wasn't found alive. They walked in the front doors of the church and stood in the foyer, heads bowed. People were praying, crying, holding each other. Kyle looked to the front of the church and saw Chandler's family in the same pew, huddled together, as if they'd never left. They were sobbing and Kyle began to weep silent tears as she witnessed their pain. She simply couldn't believe it. She felt their anguish, she shared it.

After forty-five minutes, the trio walked back out the front doors. No one spoke on the way to the truck. There wasn't anything to say. Callin drove in silence for several minutes before he suggested they drive to his parents once again.

"I feel like we all need to be together right now. I feel like we need to appreciate having each other in our lives."

The girls agreed and Cal steered his truck toward the Jennings home.

The once quiet police station was now nearly overrun with officers and detectives from multiple surrounding departments. Grayson and Johns had scoured the tapes from the bars where the three suspects had been spotted and where several girls had been approached. Through facial recognition software, they easily identified the three men. Bret Redding was the ring leader and had several charges against him for abetting prostitution. He'd served time in prison in Atlanta and starting up business again almost immediately upon his release.

Grayson's heart and mind were in a constant battle since Chandler's discovery. He wanted to find this monster, but his emotions were making it nearly impossible to interview suspects. He felt himself wanting to punish them all, just for being disgusting human beings.

He entered the room that housed Bret Redding, ready to fight. "I'm Chief Grayson and I will tell you right now, I'm not in the mood to mess around. If you have anything you can give me to exonerate yourself, give it to me now. Otherwise I'm arresting you for the murder of Chandler James."

Bret's eyes grew round and he sat up straight, "What are you talking about? I don't even know a Chandler James."

"Tell me a little bit about your organization, Bret." Grayson didn't move a muscle as he stared Bret down.

"I don't force anyone to do anything! We pick girls that look like they might want to earn a little cash. We've never hurt anyone. You have to believe me!"

Bret's fear and outrage appeared genuine, but Gray was still ready to beat him to a pulp. "Where do you find these girls?"

"Bars, dance clubs, strip joints. Places that have the craziest girls. Our clients like that."

Gray's mind went to Chandler's sweet face. She would never have found herself in a place like that. "Where were you Saturday night?"

"I was in downtown Atlanta. Meeting with my associates. The two guys you have in the other rooms here and a couple of businessmen from New York."

When Grayson verified the alibi, three suspects were cleared and he was left where he started. With nothing.

CHAPTER 23

Grayson was watching the surveillance tape from the convenience store for what seemed like the hundredth time. He leaned back in his chair, rubbed his eyes and let the tape run.

As Grayson was lost in his thoughts, two boys appeared on the screen in front of him. Grayson hadn't let the tape run this far past when Chandler had left the store, and he hadn't seen these boys before. One looked familiar and it hit him in an instant who it was. Thoughts started forming too quickly as Grayson set into motion.

"Hey Bedford! I think I found something. "Grayson began to type furiously on his keyboard. Dan Bedford came over and sat down loudly in the chair opposite Grayson. Dan, the detective from the Sheriff's office, had been dispatched as soon as Chandler was discovered and was deeply embedded in the case. Gray wasn't going to be territorial. He was a big enough man to realize he needed all the help he could get.

"I saw Jimmy Aarons on the surveillance tapes from the convenience store right after Chandler left. I picked him up a few weeks back on shoplifting. Something's in my head from his story. Something about his dad."

Grayson had keyed in the boys name and pulled up his rap sheet. "Okay, it says here that he lives at 412 Wischler Lane with his mom and step-dad. His step-dad is Earl Marx"

Grayson switched screens and typed Marx's name into the database. "Earl was released from prison last year after serving only six years of a life sentence. A technicality led to an appeal that led to his parole. He's been a good parolee, checking in when he's supposed to, staying under the radar.

Well, here we go, buddy. Earl had been convicted of multiple charges of false imprisonment and first degree rape." Gray jumped up from his desk and called two of his officers to come with them. Gray didn't have any alternative than to get justice for Chandler. This was personal. This was way too personal.

Grayson and Dan, Johns and Nick jumped into their squad cars and peeled out of the parking lot. Grayson knew that seconds were precious with a psychopath on the run. Earl and Betty Marx lived five miles out of town in a mobile home at the foot of a small mountain. The shabby exterior appeared to be from lack of money, not lack of care. The surrounding yard was clutter free and flowers were blooming in every space possible.

Grayson knew Betty Marx from his run-ins with her son. She had only one son and protected him with all the venom the small lady could muster. He knew he was in for a fight when she realized why they were there.

Grayson didn't think that neither Earl nor Jimmy were at the house, but he and Johns drew their guns as protocol. Grayson rapped the door with the back of his knuckles and waited for a reply. Betty opened the door slowly and peeked out.

"What do you want?" Even as she asked, Grayson could tell she knew.

"Mrs. Marx, we need to talk to you about Jimmy and Earl. Can we come in?''

'What do you think they did?' Her sunken eyes looked like drugs had taken over her life, but after reading Earl's rap sheet, he figured it could be from fear and exhaustion.

"Please, Mrs. Marx. May we please come in? We want to help your son."

Betty opened the door and stepped away to the small kitchen on the left. "I noticed you didn't mention helping my husband. And why would you want to help my son? You didn't help him any by screwin' up Earl's arrest. Jimmy wasn't supposed to ever see Earl again. Neither was I.'

Grayson stood motionless in the small living room, watching Betty Marx busy herself with the dishes. The house was clean and maintained, but the holes in the walls and broken bedroom door didn't go unnoticed by Grayson or Dan.

"I haven't seen Earl since Saturday morning. Jimmy took off the same day with a friend and I haven't seen him either. He called yesterday, though. Said they're hanging out," Betty finished her last bowl and wiped her hands on her pants. "Will you tell me what you think they did?"

"Have you ever heard of Chandler James? Has either Jimmy or Earl ever mentioned that name?"

Betty paused and thought for a moment. "No, I've never heard that name before. Please tell me why. What does she have to do with Jimmy?"

Grayson didn't miss that Betty wasn't worrying about her husband and had her full attention on her son.

"Chandler was found murdered yesterday morning. Jimmy was spotted at the last place Chandler was seen before her disappearance at eleven o'clock that night. We don't know that he had anything to with the kidnapping or her murder, but he might have seen something that would help us."

"Was Earl with him in the store?" Betty's look became worried, not that Earl wouldn't have been with him, but that he would.

"No, Ma'am. On the surveillance tape, he looked to have been with another boy about his age. Do you know who that could have been?"

Betty visibly relaxed and answered, "Yes, that was Rob Tomlin. That's who he was supposed to have been staying with."

"Ma'am, are you afraid of your husband? Are you afraid for Jimmy's safety?"

"Officer, I married Earl. I chose this life. What else can I say?"

Grayson tried once more, "Here's my card. If I can help you in any way, I will. We can protect you and Jimmy."

"No, sir. I don't believe you can. Like I said, it didn't work before, why would it work now."

Grayson and Dan left the Marx house with Betty watching them out the front window. If they would have looked closely, they would have seen she was sobbing.

✝

Wednesday morning dawned with the haze of a nightmare. In the early hours of the morning, Grayson sat at his desk and raked his hands through his hair. He was exhausted and emotionally drained. Terry Johns hurried in and set a stack of papers in front of him.

"I've been searching the surrounding towns to see if we could find anything, like you asked. I think I hit the mother load."

Gray picked up the reports and leafed through the papers. Since the previous year, there had been a total of eight kidnappings and sexual assaults in three counties. All were young girls, kidnapped in dark parking lots.

"It says here that the girls didn't see their assailant's face and only have a vague description of the car he used." Gray read.

"I talked to the Chiefs in every town and they all said the girls were very traumatized. The perp wore a ski mask and covered their eyes until he got to the second location. They were put in the trunk. Carpet fibers show that the carpet was used in too many makes and models to narrow the search, but three of the girls said it was a white, older model car."

Gray set the reports down and tapped his desk. "Okay. We know Marx doesn't own a car, so let's check his family to see what they own. He has a mother in Bloomfield and an Uncle in Chesterfield. Check his jail roomies and any known friends or acquaintances. Anyone that has anything to do with him. I'll call on Betty again to see if she's seen him driving a white car and we'll go from there. There's no DNA anywhere on any of these girls? How is that even possible?" Grayson asked his rhetorical question and then answered himself.

"Since he's been caught before, he was making sure he wasn't going back to prison. He went to great lengths to make sure he wouldn't be tied to these kidnappings."

Grayson picked up the reports again and stopped abruptly on the last report from the month before. "Terry, look at this. The last victim reported that her assailant had someone else with him. A younger male. It could be Jimmy."

Terry took the report from Gray, "So, either he was looking for someone to brag to, or he was creating a successor. Either way, we need to go back to talk to Betty and get a hold of Jimmy. He's our key to finding Earl."

Grayson stood and holstered his gun. "The rage and level of brutality of what he did to Chandler indicates that it was personal. She must have rejected him in some way. "

"Right. If he knows we're on to him, there's no telling what he'll do."

"Then let's go find out if Betty's broken the news to him yet."

Kyle was numbly stocking bags of seed at Hayfields when Callin walked in. Life went on regardless of the pain that enveloped them. Callin walked through the door and straight to Kyle. When she looked up to see him, relief was evident on her face. Cal gave her a quick hug.

"I needed to see you." Cal held her hand lightly and stepped back. "Do you want to go for a walk?'

Kyle was so happy to see him, she would have gone anywhere. 'Sure, let me go tell Pops.'

They started down the main street and walked slowly, contemplating what to say. Cal knew how much Kyle cared for Chandler.

"Paige was over late last night. She told me some of what Gray had shared with her about Chan." Cal started.

Kyle's voice raised an octave, "What did he say?"

"That's why I'm here." Callin paused and words became difficult, "I know what they did to her, Kyle.'

"What do you mean, 'they'?" Kyle was trying to understand what he was saying. Even one murderer was more than she could imagine.

"The police have solid evidence now that there were three people that took Chandler, and Grayson said they think they know who they are. They just need to be found at this point. But, that's not what I wanted to tell you, either."

Kyle slowed and led him to a bench in the park. "Let's sit."

They angled so they could look at each other and Cal continued, "Grayson told me what the newspapers would be reporting. It's graphic and it's horrible and if you read it, the images will never leave your mind. Never. I needed to tell you before you read it without warning."

Kyle's brow wrinkled as she tried to imagine. "Can you give me a hint about what you mean?"

Callin shifted and began, trying to filter what was now embedded in his brain, "She was hurt before she died, Ky. I think that's all I should say."

Kyle crumpled and put her hands to her face, breaking down. "I feel sick. I don't understand, Cal. I just don't understand this at all."

Cal put his arm around her and drew her into a hug, "I know, Ky. I don't understand it either."

Grayson, Dan and Johns arrived again at the Marx home. The

officers outside made sure that neither Earl nor Jimmy had returned without them knowing. Officers were also stationed at Rob's house and his parents were beside themselves in fear. Their son had never been in trouble and now they might lose him forever.

Betty opened the door before Gray and Dan reached the steps, while Terry positioned himself outside the door.

Betty let them in and said, "They still aren't here, but I guess you know that."

"We do and we know they haven't called. There has to be some place they'd hide. Rob hasn't been home and his parents are worried sick. He's only fourteen years old, Betty. He might be in danger at this point, too. And Jimmy? Earl's hurt him before hasn't he?"

Betty turned and slumped onto the couch and fell into deep sobs. "He's still my little boy. He was so precious and sweet as a baby. He was only two when I met Earl. Earl didn't beat him too much. He mainly saved that for me." She gave a soft, melancholic laugh and continued.

"I have a daughter, too, you know. As soon as I found out Earl was getting out of prison, I gave her to my friend. I haven't seen her in a year. I've lost two babies now, officer. My babies." Betty wept again into her hands and wiped her hand across her face.

When she calmed down, she sniffed, "The boys built a tree house a few years ago in the woods a couple miles from Rob's house. It's near the water tower. I can't imagine they'd stay there for long, but I can't think of another place they'd be. Please, help my son, officer. You don't know what I've been through to make sure he was safe. It would all be for nothing if I failed."

Grayson put his hand on her shoulder, "Mrs. Marx, your daughter's safe. You've been a good mother to her, and you've protected her. And you'll love your son when he needs it most. I'll do what I can for Jimmy, but I can't make any promises. If he had a part in this, he's going to be punished."

Betty nodded and wiped her tears again as Gray and Dan turned to go find the tree house.

CHAPTER 24

The tree house was easier to locate than they thought. Garbage strewn about led right to the tree. The house was just a flimsy structure at the base of a large oak. The door was a blanket and the two windows were covered with towels. Gray had called for back up and the SWAT Team rushed in with guns drawn. Jimmy and Rob were inside, tired, hungry and covered with filth and grime. They didn't put up a fight, and within minutes the two boys were on their way to the police station. Earl was no where to be found.

Rob's parents met them at the station along with Betty Marx. They embraced their sons and wept tears of fear and relief. Rob was put in one room and Jimmy in another. Grayson decided to begin by talking to Jimmy. From what they gathered, he had been involved in two of his step-father's crimes. He probably knew much more than his friend. Gray greeted Mrs. Marx and sat down opposite her and her son.

"Jimmy, you know why you're here. You realize that you're in a lot of trouble."

Jimmy was slumped over and staring at the table. He hadn't looked up or acknowledged Gray. Any defiance Grayson might have expected simply wasn't there. Jimmy looked like he was in shock, not like he was evil. But, Grayson had seen the crime scene first hand.

"Can you tell me what happened this past Saturday night?"

Jimmy didn't move, but remained in his catatonic state.

"Jimmy, Honey, please. Tell Chief Williams what happened. Baby, please. He'll help you. He wants to find Earl. Help him find Earl, Baby." Betty Marx held her son's hands as she pleaded with him. His behavior was scaring her as well, and she was becoming distraught.

"Mrs. Marx, it's alright. We'll give him a few minutes."

Gray left the room and closed the door behind him. As he was approaching the room that held Rob and his parents, an officer that had processed the tree house location came up to him with bagged evidence.

"Chief, we found this in the structure in the woods."

Gray took the bag and looked through the plastic to see a checkbook with Chandler's name on it.

"We also found a wallet with Chandler's identification. Any money she might have had was gone. Marx probably only took what he could use."

Grayson returned the bag and thanked the officer. He knew that these three were the murderers, but even still, the proof hit him in the gut and took his breath.

With a renewed anger, Grayson swung the door opened and faced the Tomlin family. What he found was worse than in the room with Jimmy. Rob had his head down and was sobbing uncontrollably while his parents surrounded him. Mr. Tomlin sat quietly with tears streaming down his face, while his wife held nothing back.

Gray could see the fear on the faces of Rob's parents when they looked up at him in the doorway. Gray had fully expected to find the hearts of these boys hardened, filled with malice. Now, he was forced to take a different approach.

"Mr. and Mrs. Tomlin. I understand how hard this has to be for you."

Mr. Tomlin nodded slightly and continued to look at Gray. Mrs. Tomlin had her face buried in her son's hair while he continued to weep into his folded arms on the table.

Gray looked back at Mr. Tomlin and directed his questions at him, "Sir, do you have anything for me that can help us here?"

"Nothing but what I told you yesterday. Rob told me he was

camping with Jimmy for a few days. I didn't even know he wasn't where he was supposed to be until your officers came to find him Sunday afternoon. Jimmy spent most of his time at our house when the boys were together. I knew he didn't have the greatest home life, but I had no idea…"

Rob was beginning to quiet down, but kept his head down.

"Rob. I need some answers. We need to find Mr. Marx before he hurts someone else. We need your help."

Rob raised his head slightly and sniffed, wiping away the tears from his face. He was fourteen, but his thin build and tousled blond hair made him look twelve.

"I'm…I'm so sorry." Again his small body was racked with sobs and Gray remained seated until he composed himself.

"Tell me why you're sorry, Rob." Gray was going to get answers if he stayed all night. At least Rob was speaking. "Tell me what happened from the very beginning."

Rob covered his eyes, either trying to remember, or trying to forget.

"I met up with Jimmy on Saturday afternoon. He was so sick of his family. His step-dad was freaking him out, but he wouldn't tell me why. I told him to stay at my house, but he said he was sick of parents, mine included."

Mrs. Tomlin let out another sob and Rob continued, "I had my camping gear and walked over to Jimmy's house. We were meeting there and then taking off right away. He wanted to steal some beers from Earl and wanted me to hide it in my stuff."

"Okay, Rob. You're doing just fine. Keep going." Gray urged.

"So, we were headed to the tree house - that's where we were going to camp- but Earl saw us walking down the street and pulled up beside us."

Gray interrupted him, "What was he driving?"

"Some old car. I think he stole it, 'cuz he never drives it home."

"What color was it?" Gray asked, but he already knew the answer.

"White."

✝

Kyle had known fear. She had escaped evil before. But, knowing that there was a murderer somewhere in their little town had her looking over her shoulder, seemingly every second. When she reached the barn, she hurried to the door to unlock it and run inside. As soon as she opened her car door, she saw a figure to her right.

"Hey, Sweet Girl."

"Oh, Pops. I'm sorry. I'm so skittish these past couple days."

"Well, that's why I'm out here greetin' ya. I'd like for you to gather up some of your clothes and move on into the guest room in the house for a while. Until this crazy feller's caught. Would you do that to make an old man feel a little more secure? I'm worried about you out here, is all."

Relief flooded through Kyle and she beamed up at him, "I don't know why I hadn't thought of that. I just figured I'd have to tough it out alone and be brave. I'd feel so much better in your guest room. I'll get my stuff and head on up in a few minutes."

Pops smiled back at her and slowly walked back to the house. Kyle felt like God had answered a prayer she hadn't even prayed yet.

✝

Gray decided he didn't have a choice but to let the boys alone for a while. He sent them to booking and put them in separate cells. They were both a mess and desperately needed sleep. Jimmy still hadn't uttered his first word.

188

First thing the following morning, Gray brought Rob from his holding cell and met again with him and his parents in the same room as the afternoon before.

Rob seemed more composed and less frightened than he did just hours before. The rest and food had done him some good.

"Okay, Rob. Let's start from where we left off yesterday," Gray looked down at the typed notes in front of him. "Earl found you and Jimmy walking toward the tree house. He was driving a white car. What happened next?"

"He told us to get in. Jimmy looked around like he wanted to run. I couldn't figure out why he was so upset. He told me Earl beat him up every once in a while, but Earl didn't seem to be in a bad mood. Then I thought that maybe Jimmy was afraid he'd find the beers."

Rob shifted in his seat and looked down again at his hands. "We got in. He drove us around for awhile. We looked at girls. It felt weird with Earl with us, but Jimmy and I do that anyway. We did that for a couple hours until it got dark. Then Earl pulled out some beers of his own. He had them in the trunk."

When Rob mentioned the trunk, his face lost all color.

"Rob, Sweetie, do you need another break? Chief, do you mind?" Rob's mom was rubbing his back, but Rob interjected,

"No. I'm fine. I need to do this. I need it out of my head.

"When it was pretty dark outside, we went to that convenience store off of First Street. The Blue Star, I think?" We sat in the parking lot, drinking. Earl just sat in the driver's seat, staring inside. I saw he was watching a girl. She was really pretty." His mind started wandering off and the touch of his mom's hand brought him back.

"At about eleven o'clock, Earl told us to go inside and look around. He gave us some cash to buy something and told us to make sure that we stayed in there for a few minutes. We did.

We watched the girl leave and then we bought some candy bars."

Gray could tell he was losing Rob again quickly. Tears formed in his eyes and slid down both cheeks. "We got out to the car and then Earl drove to that house." Rob began to sob again, "We didn't know... He made us do it. He told us he'd kill us. He would have killed us."

Gray stood to leave. Fourteen years old and damaged for the rest of his life. What he saw would no doubt destroy his soul if it wasn't claimed by Christ. No one could survive seeing what he did without the power in the shield of God.

The sun would have seemed angry if not for a soft breeze calming the fury. Callin went by Hayfields again and found Kyle deep in thought. He startled her when he touched her arm and then quickly apologized.

"Hi."

"Hi. Are you okay?" Callin wrapped her in his arms.

"I am. How about you?"

"I think so. I wanted to take you away from this and go riding for a couple hours. Let's go escape for a while."

Kyle nearly jumped to where Pops was in the next room and grabbed her things. "Nothing could sound more perfect."

Kyle's walking shorts and gauzy blouse were going to have to do because she wasn't going to waste even the few minutes it would require to go home and change. Her boots were still in the back seat from the previous ride and what she looked like wasn't foremost on her mind.

It didn't take long to get the horses saddled and on the trail. They rode for nearly an hour in total silence. Both of them lost in their own thoughts. Both of them praying their own prayers. It was just what they needed.

After their ride through the canopy of the forest, they walked the horses up to the edge of the lake and jumped down. Kyle was becoming a great rider and her relationship with Duke was one of love and respect. She kissed and rubbed his nose before turning toward the water. The sun hit the surface of the water like a million tiny gemstones. The brilliance mesmerized Kyle as she sat down and took off her boots. Sweat was shining on Callin's face when he removed his hat, his dark hair plastered against his skull. He took off his boots and jumped in the cool water, fully clothed.

Kyle couldn't help but laugh out loud. He was just a big kid. He came out soaking wet and laid down next to Kyle, his eyes closed to the sun's intensity. "I'm going to regret that on the ride home, but it sure feels good right now."

He sat up and looked at Kyle, still looking at the water. "What are you thinking?"

"I'm thinking about Jeremiah 29:11. I've lived by that verse for more than two years now. It's the verse that's gotten me through every bad thing that's ever happened in my past. It's my promise from God that I have a hope and a future." Kyle swallowed her tears before she could continue.

"So, I keep thinking about Chandler. About her hope. What about her future?" Kyle looked away from the water and looked into Callin's eyes, searching.

Callin was silent for a few moments, "You don't think she has a future now?"

Kyle looked back at the water before answering, thinking how she hadn't considered that. "She does, doesn't she? Thank you for that, Cal."

"I wish I knew what to say to make everything alright, but there just isn't anything."

"No. I know. But, you're helping by being with me." She smiled at him and they lapsed into silence once again, both losing themselves in what had happened and what would happen next.

✝

Grayson Williams had never once questioned his decision to be in law enforcement. From his earliest memories, this was what he had gone after and fought for as his life's purpose. But, today, after hearing the full account of the last hours of Chandler James' life, all he wanted was to turn back time and choose a different career.

He was nauseated and completely wiped out. After the past days and all that he and his officers had seen and heard, he knew it was the right decision to pull in a psychiatrist to help them deal. It didn't mean weakness, it meant survival.

He picked up Earl's mug shot from seven years earlier. His eyes radiated evil through the paper. The feeling of dread continued to reach new heights each hour that passed without finding him. After being so careful with the other girls, Earl Marx had lost any rational thinking when it came to Chandler. According to Rob, she had rejected his advances to the point that rage overtook any coherent thinking. The police had evidence to convict and get a death penalty verdict, and he knew it.

Earl Marx was a sadistic killer with nothing to lose.

CHAPTER 25

Chandler's memorial was to be held one week after her mom and dad last hugged her goodbye. Her parents were in no way able to speak about their beloved daughter, but her Aunt Jean had flown in from Alabama. The church, once again, was packed to standing room only. It was a testament to how fully she lived and how loved she was.

An occasional sob was heard in the crowd, but mostly everyone kept a reverent silence. Chandler's aunt moved from her seat in the front pew and took her place behind the podium.

"Thank you all for coming today. It's very obvious that my niece was dearly loved." Jean's voice faltered for a moment before she went on, "Chandler was the first baby born into our family. I never had children, so she's always been like my little girl, too. When she was an infant, I spent all my spare money on frilly dresses and little shoes to send to my sister. I would take every vacation to come see her. I've loved her since before she was born. I'll love her always."

She wiped an errant tear and spoke on, "Chandler was the kind of person that made you want to be better. Her relationship with Jesus was strong and powerful from early on in her life. She saw angels and spoke with her Lord as she would a best friend. I remember when she was six years old thinking how I wanted a relationship with Christ like she had.

"She was such an amazing big sister. I remember the day Davis was born. She was three years old and she couldn't wait to hold him in her tiny little arms. She looked down into his face and said, 'His has small fingers.' Then she kissed his fingertips." Quiet laughter broke through the crowd.

"I came to stay with Chandler and Davis when Jana and Andy went to Thailand to bring Townsend home. Chandler was almost eight years old and was beside herself until her mommy and daddy walked in the house carrying this frail, scared, precious two year old baby girl. Chandler quietly took her hand

and just held it. It didn't take long before Townsend wouldn't leave Chan's side."

Jean paused before moving on. There was so much to say. "Jana and Andy couldn't have been more proud of her as their daughter. And for great reason. They made the decision when Chandler was just itty bitty that she wouldn't date until she was out of high school. I'm not sure if this was how she skipped all the pre-teen and teenage drama, but it never seemed to touch her. Chandler was self assured and knew who she was. She was loved and cherished, the child of the King.

"We can't understand why this happened. But, what I do know is that Chandler's story will go on. The memory of who she was will lead others to be better people. Her memory will lead others to the throne of the Savior."

Sutton Cassaday began to silently weep. She couldn't stop and for the first time she could remember, she didn't want to. She hadn't known Chandler well, but she did know enough to see that she was different. She was innocence. Sutton couldn't say that she'd ever known innocence. The lack of what should have been left her bitter, searching. As she sat in this church next to righteous and holy people, she felt her sin was obvious. Black and insidious, worn on her skin like a garment. The longer she wore it, the filthier it became.

But, in this moment, she was being called. She heard it in her heart. Her Savior had come to claim her soul. Her life was meant for more than this shame and guilt. She'd never felt so low, so desperate. She looked at Chandler's picture, framed next to her Aunt. Yes, Chandler's story would continue. Sutton would make sure her memory would carry on in her own testimony of salvation.

Sutton turned her heart toward the voice of her Savior and walked into the arms that had waited, opened, for so long. The day the world said goodbye to Chandler James' earthly body, heaven was rejoicing over Sutton Cassaday's soul.

Jean had paused again, trying so hard to compose herself. Her heart was breaking in front of a church filled with strangers. She sniffed and swiped another tear. "Most of you know through the newspapers how Chandler died. What you might not know is the reason for the level of brutality. The police were told that her murderer was enraged because after the kidnapping, she just stared into space. And every time he tried to harm her to get some type of reaction, she would smile. The more he hurt her, the more she smiled. Through the pain and torment that she went through those hours, that smile never left her face. While she was dying, her eyes never left the face of her Savior.

"Psalm 23:4 says 'Yea, though I walk through the valley of the shadow of death, I will fear no evil; For You are with me; Your rod and Your staff, they comfort me.' This passage means that even in death, God goes with us. Fear is overcome by His presence. I believe with all that's in me that Jesus Himself was next to Chandler that night. And her fear was overcome by His presence. He kept her focused on Him and on her home so that whatever happened to her physical body, her spiritual self was safe, protected.

"When someone we love dies, it's very easy to keep our thoughts on the pain that they endured, almost like they're trapped in those moments forever. But, Chandler isn't in those moments. She's not in pain, she's not hurting. So, in the days and weeks ahead, I don't want you to think of Chandler's death. I want you to think of her life. The life she led here on earth and the life she's living in heaven right now. And I want you to remember that smile. Because I promise you that at this exact second, and every second for the rest of eternity…that child is smiling."

Kyle's eyes were red and swollen when they left the church. She went in feeling hopeless and left with a renewed excitement about heaven. Chandler was whole and healthy, worshiping at the feet of Jesus. Hope. Future.

CHAPTER 26

Days crawled by without a hint to the location of Earl Marx. Gray was becoming anxious and angry. He hadn't taken a day off since Chandler's disappearance and Paige was beginning to worry. She decided to stay with her parents until Earl was captured. The women of the town were feeling vulnerable and Grayson was more than ready to finally put them at ease.

The stolen white car that Marx had been driving was found near the tree house two days after the boys were apprehended. The carpet fibers from the trunk matched the fibers on all eight of the kidnapping and assault cases in the nearby towns. Gray tried his hardest not to think of the countless lives ruined by one man's evil.

The call came around eight o'clock in the evening. Grayson and Bedford arrived first to the scene. Tyler Briggs had come home late from work to find that his house had been broken into. He didn't have much, but the money he left on the counter was gone and food from his refrigerator and pantry had been taken. Forensics arrived quickly after Grayson and began dusting for prints. It only took a minute. Earl Marx was still in the area and desperate enough to break into someone's home for food and a change of clothes. The fact that he wasn't worried about leaving evidence, again, sent a shockwave of fear through Gray. They tracked footprints in the backyard and had the direction he was heading. At least it was something.

✝

The breeze waltzed with the leaves overhead as Callin kissed Kyle's cheek and told her good-bye in front of the church. Kyle was keeping her scheduled lunch with Pops after church and promised she'd see Callin that afternoon. She was making her way to her car when Sutton called for her.

Kyle turned in surprise and braced herself for a dreaded

confrontation.

Sutton stood in front of her, "Hey. I know this might seem weird to you. I was hoping we could talk."

Kyle was still apprehensive but saw something in Sutton's eyes, "Sure. Let's go sit."

The girls went over to a bench beneath a great oak and sat down.

Sutton started, "I know how close you were to Chandler. I didn't know her very well, but her death really affected me. I wish I had known her. I wish I would have seen beyond myself to recognize someone so special. I've missed so much being so focused on myself."

Kyle waited in silence for her to go on, "During her memorial service, I felt like God was calling me. I've heard His voice before. I know I have. I just got really good at ignoring it," Kyle gave a small smile and acknowledged she understood. "I guess I never really felt like I deserved saving. I've gone to church much of life, but it never felt right."

Sutton's eyes brightened and her entire face lit up as she continued. "During Chandler's service, I finally listened to His voice. I accepted Him." Her excitement reached out and touched Kyle.

"I'm saved, Kyle." Kyle didn't think twice to embrace her and they broke down in tears. Kyle knew what salvation meant after years of a desolate heart. She understood the gratitude of being carried out of the depths of hell.

Sutton wiped her tears and said, "I'm so sorry for how I've treated you. I acted like such a jerk over Callin. It's so obvious he adores you. I hope someone feels that way about me some day."

"You don't have to just hope for it. Pray for it. God is crazy about you, Sutton. He's so crazy about you. He has amazing plans for you and a purpose that you can't even imagine. Your story is going to lead others to Christ, I just know it. There's nothing greater than that."

Sutton nodded and asked, "So, what do I do now? I know a little bit about your story, and since you haven't known me since toddlerhood, I thought you might be able to help me better than most."

Kyle replied, "Your baptism comes next. It will be an amazing day for you. After that, get involved in a Bible study or find a mentor. This is the time when Satan will really mess with you. He'll tell you lies, like you aren't really saved, or God can't love you because of your past. I've heard it all. And I've believed it a time or two. But, just get into the truth every day. Read your Bible every day and get scriptures in your head to prepare yourself.

"We can meet this week, if you'd like to. I can put together all the scriptures that helped me when I was first saved."

Sutton's excitement was evident again, "I'd love that. Any day would work for me."

Kyle mentally went over her schedule and they made plans to meet on Wednesday. Sutton knew she needed a plan. And with Kyle's help, she'd get one. She was saved and she couldn't wait to start living like it.

The steady drum of rain pelted Sutton as she ran from her parking spot to Hayfields to meet Kyle. She'd left her umbrella in the car and smiled up to the sky as the rain washed over her. It continued to surprise her how quickly things that used to be so important all of sudden just weren't anymore.

This afternoon couldn't have come sooner for Sutton. The past few days had been difficult and trying as well as thrilling and exhilarating. The conflicting emotions were exhausting. Sutton had her Bible with her at all times. It was her sword, her shield. The armor of her heart.

Kyle was waiting for Sutton in the back office with her own

Bible open. She had researched several scriptures and had written her favorite verses on index cards.

When Sutton came in out of the rain and found her behind the desk, Kyle jumped up to give her a hug. God was already giving her a sisterly love for Sutton that Kyle never would have guessed possible. They were a kindred spirit with the same beautiful death to their old selves.

"Wow. There's so much I don't know." Sutton shed her coat and sat down opposite of Kyle.

"I completely understand. I didn't know anything at all, so whatever you know is more than I did. It's a life process and it won't end until we're in heaven. The important thing is that we continue to try to get it all."

Kyle opened her Bible to Psalms. "Pretty much anything in the Psalms or Proverbs will speak to me at any given time. They are my two favorite go-to books. But, my favorite verses are these two," Kyle handed Sutton two index cards with 1 Corinthians 2:9 and her lifeline verse, Jeremiah 29:11. "Go ahead. Read them out loud and know that He's speaking right to your heart."

Sutton held the cards in her hand and first read the words to herself, then out loud, "Jeremiah 29:11, For I know the plans I have for you - plans to prosper you, not to harm you; plans for a hope and a future."

For as many times as Kyle had seen and heard those words, they never failed to touch her. Now, knowing that Sutton might be hearing them for the first time, relating to herself, it held something new.

Sutton smiled and stared at the words a moment longer and then switched cards, "1 Corinthians 2:9, No eye has seen, no ear has heard, no mind has conceived what God has planned for those who love Him."

Kyle smiled as she looked at the serene expression on the face of her friend, "They help me quite a bit when I'm in a bad place."

"You still get in bad places?" Sutton was surprised. Kyle seemed to have it all together. She never let on that she still had issues from her past.

Kyle sighed, "Sometimes I feel like I'll never quite get over the things I've done. I feel forgiven most of the time and then all of a sudden, my past sin is right in front of my face again. I feel like I've failed and all I did was have a thought or a nightmare."

"You have nightmares? I do, too. I've had them for as long as I can remember, but they're always the same."

Feeling the fragile pages of her Bible between her fingers, Kyle's thoughts went back to her last dream. "I believe that the devil can use many ways to torment us, even in our subconscious through dreams. But, when I wake up, I know Who's I am. I have His word right next to me and I'm protected. Our past is our past. Jesus doesn't condemn us."

Sutton groaned. "But, I've done such bad things. They're so horrible that I would never admit them to anyone," She looked down at her hands and cringed. "I believe that I'm forgiven. I believe that He died for my sins. But, my sins are just so huge."

Kyle felt like she could be saying the same words to Sutton, "It's grace. There's no explanation for His ability to forgive other than His all-encompassing grace. It's so easy for me to say to others and so hard to apply to myself."

Kyle ran her hand through her hair and started again, "I guess it's kind of like, if you think your sin is huge and my sin is small, but Christ forgave and forgot both, which was worse? They're forgotten, so it's like neither sin ever was."

"I wish my mind could forget." Sutton said quietly.

Kyle squeezed her hand, "But then we'd never learn."

"Can you tell me your story, Kyle?"

Kyle didn't want to open her wounds, but was prepared knowing she'd have to. Maybe that's how she'd finally heal.

"My dad was, is, an alcoholic. I don't remember ever having a conversation with him. My earliest memory was of my mom holding me, crying, while he walked out the door. I remember her tears on my face, his back as he left. It was like he wasn't really a part of our family. He came home for a couple hours to sleep off his buzz, then go to work. But, he was never really there."

"Did they divorce?" Sutton asked, while thinking of how similar their lives really were.

"No. My mom died of breast cancer when I was fourteen."

"Oh, Kyle. I'm so sorry." Sutton was shocked. All the times she was so ugly to Kyle and she had no idea what she'd been through.

"Thank you. It was the worst time of my life, but I was almost relieved for her. Jealous for me. I wanted to go with her more than I wanted her to stay. She was depressed most of my life. She loved me, I know that, but she spent most of her life in bed, crying. She was miserable. So was I. Once she died, I saw my dad less than I had before. I kept up my grades, but only to impress him.

I remember one year, it was his birthday and I bought him a cake and a small gift. He didn't come home that night, so I ate the whole cake by myself. I got sick and cried myself to sleep." Kyle surprised Sutton by smiling. It didn't seem like a happy memory, but it was nice to see she could smile all these years later.

"There's something that happens when a girl doesn't have her mom, but I think it's a lot worse when she doesn't have her dad. There are no guidelines on how to behave. There aren't instructions on how to act. We start looking for love anywhere we can find it. That includes college professors at small town schools."

"Or bars and nightclubs." Sutton nearly whispered her understanding. They were so much alike. "How was your professor wrong for you?"

"I was so tired of living in our big house completely alone that when he asked me to move in with him, I didn't think twice. Then he started getting violent. He beat me up. Emotionally and physically. But, I made my own choices and decisions. The life I led had been my choice."

"But, then you got saved?" Sutton was on the edge of her seat. She wanted to hear of Kyle's salvation.

"My ex was getting progressively more vicious. One night it was the worst it had been and I escaped. I just got in my car and drove. What's ironic is that I was so mentally abused that before I ran away, I was afraid to drive my car to the grocery store or the bank. I was so filled with fear of driving that I could only make right-hand turns. Then all of a sudden, I'm nearly 1000 miles away. I believe God carried me the whole way. I really do. I almost don't remember the drive. I was still afraid of Paul, but I wasn't afraid of the journey."

"And you found yourself here." Sutton carried on for her.

"Yes, I did. I found myself with a job at Hayfields and a home at Pops. I'd gone to church for a few weeks, just listening about God's love and forgiveness. That it was for me. My adrenaline was shot at that point, and I just laid down on the hard tile floor. I remember it was so cold on my cheek. I cried out to God. I didn't know much about Him other than what I learned as a child in the few Sunday School classes I'd been to. But I knew enough to know that He was the only One Who could bring me peace. I was right."

"I guess my question is, why can't the peace stay all the time?" Sutton showed slight frustration at herself.

"Because we're human." Kyle heard those words over her heart when she asked God the same question again and again. "We're going to feel down and sad and emotional. We're going to fail and sin, and all of that can affect our feelings of peace. But we have His word and we have the ability to immediately ask the Prince of Peace to bring it back into our hearts. My problem seems to always be remembering what to do when I'm feeling lost. I flounder and mope and then finally it hits me. I get on my knees and get it back."

"I guess this is just so new to me that I still feel like a hypocrite. Just a couple weeks ago, I was a completely different person. My friends don't even know that I've changed. How do I tell them that I can't go out with them anymore because I have Jesus in my life? I feel like I'm telling them that I was just like them and now I'm too good to hang out." Sutton looked exasperated.

"That is hard, I'm sure. I didn't have the same circumstances. No one knew me and I did my best to make sure that no one did. I think you start by telling them the truth. You were searching for something and you found Him. Tell them about Chandler. Tell them her story and how it led you to the throne. You don't have to condemn them. You don't have to tell them what horrible sinners they are. It's not like we're not sinners anymore, ya know? Be their friend, just be saved."

Sutton was nodding. She could do that. She knew it wouldn't be many more days before she would test her testimony.

CHAPTER 27

Kyle was still smiling from her meeting with Sutton when she steered her car into the driveway. The rain had slowed to a near stop by the time Kyle pulled in, but dark clouds persistently gripped the sky. She parked her car and killed the engine. She searched for a couple moments until she found her wallet and reached over to grab her purse and Bible. Slamming the car door with her hip, she searched through her ring of keys to open the front door.

She took the three steps up to the porch when she heard footfalls behind her. Thinking it was Pops, she turned to greet him. She took a step back as her purse and Bible crashed to the ground.

Forensics was already processing the Zachary household when Grayson arrived. He knew it had been Earl Marx. And just like the burglary at Tyler Briggs, he'd left again on foot. If the Zachary's had been home, Grayson would have been looking at more dead bodies and their suspect would have been long gone in the Zachary family car. They were running out of time. The next family might not be so lucky.

"What do you have, Jen?"

Jennifer Thorpe, lead forensic tech, looked up from her samples in the kitchen.

"Well, just like the murder scene and the Brigg's burglary, he's very sloppy. He's not trying to hide. Prints came back a match to Marx. He came in the back door by breaking the glass. He didn't seem to hurry. Made a sandwich, had some beer. It looks like he packed some snacks. Mrs. Zachary said that her jewelry is missing and they had some money in their bedroom that's gone. We do have an additional problem, though, Gray.

"He stole their gun."

"What do you want?" Kyle heard the dread in her voice, at the same time realizing that her question was ridiculous.

He had come from behind the barn and was now standing thirty feet from her. Kyle saw the gun, but didn't recognize the man holding it.

"I've been lookin' to get out of town and have a little fun. Looks like it's my lucky day.

Throw me those keys you're holding. We wouldn't want you doing nothing improper with 'em, now would we?"

Kyle processed her options, looking to her right and left, when his cackle interrupted her thoughts. He began closing in.

"You ain't gonna get away, girl. Don't you see this gun? I believe I told you to throw me those keys," His eyes were wild, "Now!"

Kyle threw the keys as far as she could in front of her and froze. She thought a thousand times what she would do in this situation, but her mind, her body, simply froze.

"Now I'm gonna drop this here bag," He spoke while maneuvering off the back pack from his shoulder. "Don't you worry none, we'll come back for this."

Kyle knew the man she was looking at had murdered Chandler. And she knew that if she didn't run, she'd die a much worse death than if she did. She'd heard time and time again that she was supposed to do whatever it took to ensure she wasn't taken to a second location if ever in a situation like this. Yet, she remained motionless.

Marx motioned with the gun for her to come to him. When she didn't move, he ran up the steps and grabbed her by the arm. All her nightmares, the life she used to live, came barreling back and assaulted her mind. He pushed her to the car, shoved her in the driver's seat and slammed the door. He kept the gun trained on her while walking to the other side to climb into the passenger seat.

While he was at the front of the car, she willed her body to move and made the decision to run. As she opened the door and ducked her head down, she heard a gun shot. And she heard herself scream.

✝

Grayson had just closed the door of his cruiser when the call came in to rush to the Hayfield farm.

Shots fired.

The words reverberated in his mind as Kyle's face came into focus. The Hayfield farm was a mile north of the Zachary house. Earl was there, he had no doubt. The idea of finding Kyle the same way he found Chandler would just be too much. He prayed, "Lord, I wouldn't be able to handle that. Please let her be safe."

Lights on and siren screaming, Grayson peeled into the long driveway leading up to the Hayfield farmhouse. Blood had pooled on the ground a few feet from where he parked his car. Drag marks led to a body just a yard beyond that.

Earl Marx was lying crumpled in a heap, stained through with a bullet hole in his right shoulder. Pops stood just past him, holding a shot gun over his head. Kyle was seated on the porch steps, leaning into the railing, hands cupped over her mouth and nose.

Grayson approached Pops, who stepped back and lowered his gun. "Hey, Pops," Grayson patted Pops on the shoulder, "I do believe you're a hero. Is he dead?"

"Nope. Just passed out." Pops walked over to the porch and laid his gun down. "I wanted to shoot to kill, Grayson. I did. I saw him going to take my Kyle and all I wanted to do was aim for his head. But, I ain't no judge and I ain't no jury."

"That took a lot of strength, Pops. I don't know if I could have been that strong," Grayson checked Earl's pulse and cuffed him in front, careful of his shoulder wound. "Paramedics will be here shortly."

Kyle didn't move, she stared ahead, past Earl's body to the barn beyond. Her greatest fear almost came to be, but she was safe. Adrenaline had surged through her body when she first saw Earl, heard his voice, realized his threats. It was now gone, leaving her drained, weak and exhausted. She wanted to sleep, but knew that her dreams would take on a new face now. Or maybe they'd just merge into one.

Grayson came and knelt in front of her, "Are you okay?"

Kyle dropped her hands in her lap and nodded her head, a tear falling down her cheek.

"You did great, Kyle. You're alive and you did great," Grayson patted her knee and then gave her quick hug. "I'll get your statement in a bit."

Kyle suddenly noticed Pops standing next to her. She stood up quickly and grabbed him in a fierce embrace. "Thank you. Thank you so much. I would have died if you hadn't been here."

"Shh now. I wouldn't have let that happen Darlin'."

The paramedics were parked next to Grayson's cruiser in a matter of minutes. Kyle heard bits and pieces of their conversation, 'massive blood loss, permanent damage, murderer.'

She moved in slow motion to the porch swing and watched as Marx was placed on a stretcher, IV inserted, and finally ushered away. Grayson was on the opposite side of the porch, leaning against the railing, taking Pops statement while he rocked in his chair. Kyle listened as the events were played out again in words.

"Well, I had pulled up to my mailbox, and of course I always go real slow on that road out there. I don't like them stones hitting my truck. I guess I was far enough away that he didn't hear me."

Pops shook his head, "I ain't never been so scared as when I saw him turning the corner around the barn, and then seeing Kyle's car at the same time. I knew what he was doing. And I knew who he was. I don't know how I knew for sure, but I did. His mind is evil. I read the papers. I knew what he wanted to do to Kyle and I wanted to kill him."

Anger flashed in Pops eyes and it occurred to Kyle that she'd never seen it there before. He continued on, "I keep a shot gun in the bed of my truck. Sure, I'm sure I shouldn't, but I'm old and set in my ways. It's what I've always done. I stopped the truck and got out, didn't shut my door or even turn off the engine, just went to the bed and pulled out my old twelve gauge."

Pops looked over at Kyle who was looking into nothing. He loved that child something powerful. He really, truly did.

"I snuck up behind the tree line and kept my eye on him. He was a good distance away, but I heard his voice. I saw his gun, aimed right at my girl. He's filth, Grayson. "

Pops swallowed hard and tried to ignore the choking in his voice, "I saw him make her get in her own car. I knew if she tried to run, he'd shoot her. If she didn't run, he'd take her in her car and I'd have a chase. I'm too old for that. I would have lost her. So, when he was going to the other side of the car to get in, I shot him."

She heard a car door, but didn't look up. She heard footsteps coming toward her, but still stared into nothingness. Cal knelt before her and pulled her into him, wrapping his arms around her. She took in his familiar scent, felt his embrace, and seized him with all she had. She broke down into deep sobs and she felt his tears mix with hers.

And they held on.

Kyle gave her statement to Nick while Grayson rode in the ambulance to the hospital with his prisoner. Kyle had to relive what had just happened, but this time Callin was a constant by her side. He kept his arm around her and gently squeezed her when she was having difficulty continuing. She leaned her head against him and wanted so much to just fall asleep in his arms.

Nick read her statement back to her and had her sign the electronic copy. She glanced up around the property and couldn't decide if she never wanted to leave or couldn't bear to stay. She knew she was safe. Marx was badly injured in the hospital. The two boys were locked away. Yet, fear gripped her, constricting her heart until she felt she'd pass out.

Hours passed and it was well into the night when the last of the forensics team departed. Martin, Anne and Paige had come as soon as they heard what had happened. They sat in the living room with Pops, Kyle and Callin. No one spoke more than a few words. It was a time when their presence was needed, but words weren't necessary. Silent prayers were lifted around the room and Kyle finally fell asleep.

The Jennings' left close to eleven that night and made sure Callin promised to call them if he received any news or if Kyle needed them. They said goodbye to Cal and Pops and Anne kissed her son's cheek.

Once the door closed, Cal looked at Pops and said, "Thank you, Pops." Callin's throat closed and tears threatened, "I don't know what I would have done without her. I just found her." He gently kissed her hair and looked back at Pops. His eyes were brimming, too.

"I'm not sure what I would have done, either, Callin. She's like my own blood. The little girl I never had."

"You mean a great deal to her, too." Cal said softly.

"Yes, I do know that. And she loves you with all her heart."

Kyle finally awoke close to two in the morning. Callin's sleeping face was the first thing she saw. It was a few seconds before she realized why he was there and what had happened. A few precious seconds when she wasn't thinking about Earl Marx.

When she moved, Callin stirred and found his arm was numb. They were sitting up, leaning on each other. Neither one wanted to leave each other, but Callin helped her up and walked her to the guest room. They held each other and after several minutes, forced themselves to separate. Knowing Cal was in the next room made it easier for Kyle to quickly fall back to sleep.

Cal grabbed the blanket off the back of the couch and lay on his back, staring up at the ceiling.

"Thank You, Jesus."

It was nearly an hour before Cal was able to sleep once more, and it was with praises on his tongue.

✝

Morning came abruptly and interrupted Kyle's nightmares. She was dreaming of being shoved in her car. She woke, startled, trying to get her bearings. Sunlight was streaming through the window, dancing with the dust. Kyle rubbed her face and then remembered that Cal had slept outside her room on the living room couch.

She had washed her face and brushed her teeth before she realized she was still in her clothes from the day before. She changed and brushed her hair before opening her door. She felt disappointment surge through her when she saw the couch was vacant, the blanket folded and back in its place.

She nearly cried when she went to the kitchen and saw him seated at the table, hands cupped around a mug of coffee. When he saw her, his face lit up and he jumped up, took her in his arms and rocked from side to side.

"How did you sleep?" Kyle asked him when he released her to pour her coffee.

"Not great, but I didn't really expect to." They sat across from each other at the small round table and Kyle blew on her drink before tasting it.

"Thank you for staying. It means a lot to me." Kyle took his hand. "Where's Pops?"

"He's out in the garden. I think that's how he's dealing."

Kyle knew he was right. He went there to pray, to miss Edith, to remember their good times. Today, it was where he coped.

They both looked at the door when the bell rang. Callin stood to answer it, and found a reporter wanting to interview Kyle and Pops. Cal politely declined and then broke the news to Kyle that her life had stopped being her own for a while. Earl Marx was national news. Kyle was going to be hounded and there was nothing they could do but wait it out.

Grayson sat outside the hospital room and tried to collect himself. He had barely slept and had spent hours with fellow officers and the DA to get Marx booked and indicted. He missed Paige and wanted to be at home, snuggled up next to her in their bed. Not here, keeping the press out, protecting this madman.

He looked at Marx, lying handcuffed to the bed. Surgery had saved his arm and he was in recovery. His shoulder would never work as it once did, but he would be well enough to stand trial for the brutal murder he committed. So, why was Grayson so sick to his stomach?

He returned to his seat and leaned his head back against the wall, thinking of Paige. They'd been through so much. He knew she was in pain. He was, too. But, he handled his. He didn't know how to help her handle hers. Right then, sitting a few feet from a madman, he finally understood that he just needed to be there. He needed to hold her. To kiss her. To tell her it would be alright. Someday. They had hope in their God. And they had each other.

Gray rubbed his eyes and sighed. Once Paige left his thoughts, he realized how much rage was burning inside him for Earl Marx.

He bowed his head and prayed out loud, "God. Father. Help me. I've never wanted someone dead before. I keep wishing Pops would have killed him. Please, take that from my heart. I can't do my job and be who You've called me to be with such anger and bitterness inside of me."

Gray squeezed his eyes shut, willing an answer. He didn't believe for a second that he was the only person praying that exact same prayer.

✝

Media from every news station and rag magazine camped out in the small town of Greenville. Kyle had given up trying to hide. If she was going to live her life, she was going to have to do it in front of a camera. She had spoken to God about her fears of Paul seeing her and trying to find her. In the midst of the traumatic time of her life, she was filled with His peace that surpassed all understanding.

Kyle had emerged from her car to find a man with a camera walking toward her. Hayfield's was just a few steps away, but he was next to her before she could move.

"Miss Evans, can I ask you a couple questions?"

Kyle felt her face heat and wanted to run. But, somewhere inside of her, she felt the power to speak her mind.

"I really don't want to be rude, sir, but I just can't talk to you. Out of principle and for my safety. I understand you can justify your story by saying it's your job, but all I can think is that you need another job.

"Chandler was my dear friend. She was Jana and Andy James' daughter. She was Townsend and Davis James' sister. She was a real live person with dreams and aspirations. She was precious to everyone who knew her.

"Any person or news organization that is profiting from her murder by sensationalizing events for higher ratings, honestly makes me nauseous. So, do your job. But please, I need to be left out of it. Thank you."

Kyle turned and walked in the door to Pops' waiting arms. She didn't see the man holding the camera staring after her. She didn't know that he felt the shame in his heart and she didn't see how he stuffed it down as he walked toward the courthouse. Earl Marx was being arraigned and there were pictures to take if he was going to make his deadline.

Pink bled into purple as the sun was fading, making room for the moon. Kyle never tired of the different pallets the Lord used with his masterpieces. Kyle's hand had completely disappeared in Cal's as they sat in silence on the front porch swing at the Jennings' farm. Sadness threatened every night. His mercies were new every day. Kyle was desperately grappling for normalcy.

Cal's voice broke through her thoughts, "When was the one time that you laughed the hardest?"

Kyle turned to look at him, his eyes remained on the sky. She thought for a few moments before it registered that she hadn't laughed enough in her lifetime.

"Hmm. I guess I was thirteen. It wasn't too long before my mom was diagnosed. She was a crazy garage-saler. And she was known to occasionally dumpster dive. It had to have been about five o'clock in the morning and she woke me up from a dead sleep. She told me there was a bed frame in the neighbor's trash down the street and we needed to go get it before the garbage men came to pick it up. I was furious. I had school that morning and I treasured my sleep. But, I got up because I'd do anything for her. I hated to disappoint her.

"I had my pajamas on and I was so groggy, I just put on my shoes that were next to my bed. They happened to be slip-ons with a small heel. Not exactly the best footwear to dig through a pile of junk." Kyle was smiling at the memory and Callin turned to study her.

"We got in my mom's car and it was still pitch dark. She backed out of the driveway and ran right into the stop sign by our house. She started giggling, but she knew my dad was going to be so mad. We got down the street and she parked next to the bed frame. It was so heavy. We struggled with that thing for forever, it seemed. We finally loaded it in the trunk and it was hanging out so far, one of us had to follow behind the car and hold it up.

"I was first. So, there I was in my heels and pajamas, walking down the street behind a car, holding up this bed frame. The problem was that my mom didn't know how fast or slow to drive. So, she would speed up and I had to start running, then she'd slow down and I would run into the back of the car." Kyle started laughing as she was telling the story and Callin joined her.

"That was bad enough, but then I looked over and there's this man out for an early morning walk, staring at us. He shook his head and kept walking. I got paybacks though. Halfway home, we changed places and I got to watch my mom in the rear view mirror, running behind the car, holding up the bed frame," Kyle dabbed a tear from the corner of her eye and took a deep breath. "And to think I almost missed that memory. If I would have told her 'no'."

Cal put his arm around her shoulders. She smiled up at him, "Your turn."

He leaned back and looked up at the rafters. "It was the time we all had lice."

Kyle laughed so loud she startled herself, "That doesn't sound funny."

"It wasn't at the time. I was the easiest to handle, my mom just shaved my head. But, poor Paige was a disaster. We were only in elementary school. Paige had long, thick hair and my mom wasn't about to cut it. They had worked at getting rid of the little creeps for weeks. They'd think they were gone and then one would show up. Beds were stripped, pillows went back into bags. I don't think the washing machine ever quit running. It was a nightmare. I even remember my mom at one point being so frustrated; she broke down and started sobbing.

"One night, a few weeks in, my dad got on the computer to see if there were any additional remedies they hadn't tried. He found a cure alright. This site said to shave half the head. Then set the side with the hair on fire. When the lice ran for their lives, smack them really hard.

"For whatever reason, that hit my dad's funny bone. He was doing the laugh where he was just shaking but there was no sound. I'd never seen him like that before. He was hooting so hard he was crying by the end. Then my mom started laughing so hard she started crying. Then we all joined in and it broke the bad mood of it all. The lice finally were all killed for good. We didn't even have to set anyone on fire."

Cal and Kyle were both laughing at their stories when they caught each other's eyes. There was going to be plenty of laughter in their lives together. They were both committed to make it happen.

CHAPTER 28

Summer hurried by like it knew everyone needed a new season. Football practice began as soon as school was back in and Callin felt like he hardly saw Kyle at all. He had planned to ask her to marry him over summer break, but he couldn't do it with all that had happened.

As it was, Coach Jennings stood up in front of his team of young men, flanked by his Offensive and Defensive coaches.

With all eyes on him, he spoke the words he prayed God would provide.

"We are here today, men, with a purpose. You are here today because you were chosen. Each one of you sitting before me was chosen to be here at this exact moment in time. Because you were chosen, you now have a responsibility. We have a moral obligation to be the very best on the field and off. That means that if you are caught drinking alcohol, you are off the team. If you are caught doing drugs, you are off the team. If I hear a swear word leave your mouth, you will be running stadiums until you puke. Your responsibility extends to your classmates, including the girls that you date. You are to value girls even if they don't chose to value themselves.

"We are a family, men. If you don't have a brother, look around. You now have twenty-eight brothers. You don't have a father. Look up here, boys. You now have three. We are your leaders and you can't have a good leader if you're unwilling to respect us as such. We will go through a lot together this year, and I can guarantee that your football family will impact your world until the day you die. You are faced with a unique opportunity to be a part of something bigger than yourself, that will lead to a life that is better than you can imagine for yourself. We are here to play and we are here to have fun. But more importantly, we are here to learn how to live.

"Focus, watch, listen and learn. And we will win."

The boys suited up and practiced hard. Callin's heart swelled with pride as he watched his boys gear up for a year of accomplishments. Whether they won any games at all, Cal's job was to make sure they triumphed in life.

✝

The press was finally thinning and Kyle was able to come and go without much hassle. Her classes started and she found that God had blessed her, once again, with a great group of students. It felt like life was moving on and that felt almost more painful than if it would have stood still.

The first day of school, Kyle broke down in sobs when it occurred to her that Chandler should have been in college, starting classes and beginning a brand new chapter of her life. It was taking longer than she would have liked to feel happy and secure again. But the Holy Spirit held her tight, comforting her when she needed it and renewing her when she thought she couldn't go on.

She missed Callin more than she thought possible. She realized that a football coach's social life ceased for three months of the year. She learned to appreciate the daily texts and late night phone calls. And those precious Saturday evenings where he was fully focused on her and his family.

Kyle spent every Friday night in the stands at the high school football games. She brought her portable cushion and sat with Martin, Anne, Paige and Grayson when he was off duty. She was learning a lot of what it would be like to be the wife of a coach. She heard the wannabe coaches in the seats nearby. The remarks about Callin making a bad call or being a lousy coach because he didn't put someone's son in to play, were difficult to listen to. Anne said she'd probably never get used to it, but at least she was prepared.

At the end of every game, she waited for Cal outside the locker room. The crowds dissipated and they would be two of the last to leave. They'd hold hands and talk late into the night. They were finding it more and more difficult to part.

November crawled in with unusually warm weather. While it was chilly in the evenings, a light sweater was all that was needed during the day. The unseasonable warmth soaked into Kyle's heart and she found herself smiling more, remembering less.

Greenville High's football team ended the season one win away from the play-offs. There were high hopes for an amazing next year with only a few seniors graduating. Callin couldn't say he wasn't disappointed for his players that they didn't go on and win the championship, but he was more than ready to make up for lost time with Kyle. The first free Friday he had, he invited her over for dinner at the main house.

✝

Jana James sat on her oldest daughter's bed and held her baby's teddy bear in her arms. The pain wasn't lessening. It didn't seem possible that it ever would.

The weeks that followed Chandler's murder, there wasn't a single thing that didn't remind her family of her life. Her absence. Her clothes she quickly threw on her bed the day she disappeared remained there for a month. Her cell phone, running shoes, favorite food, seat at the kitchen table. Princess roaming the house, searching for her. They all screamed for her return.

Townsend woke up nightly, frantically reaching for her sister. Jana was so exhausted from taking care of her that she was barely functioning. Davis was almost more difficult. He refused to talk about how he was feeling. He would escape to his room whenever he was home. He stayed longer at the soccer fields, longer in the weight room. He didn't want to have any spare time to be able to think.

Jana and Andy were like strangers in a mist. They spoke when they needed to, but they were both afraid to lean on one another, knowing it would be like leaning on ashes. They knew, without words, they would crumble.

The entire family had been seeing a counselor that seemed to be making a small amount of progress. He suggested that Jana and

Andy go on a date to try to rekindle the reason they fell in love in the first place. The foundation of that love was strong enough when they married twenty years earlier to make them believe they could overcome anything. They needed to realize that was true then, it was true now.

Every time Jana thought she was all cried out, the tears would prove her wrong. She cradled the bear and rocked through the sobs.

"Lord, I can't do this. No one understands…"

The bear's fur was soaked and Jana reached up to wipe her face. "I don't have anyone to talk to. No one I know has had a murdered child."

As she said the words, the vision of Jesus hanging from the cross filled her mind. Her Father knew. His Child had been murdered, too.

"Except You."

Jana jumped when she heard the doorbell sound. Kyle usually knocked. But, the bell had remained silent for weeks now. Friends and neighbors had visited daily at first, bringing gifts of food and shoulders to cry on. Lately, she felt like most everyone had forgotten but her.

She carefully replaced the teddy bear against the pillows on Chandler's bed and wiped her face again.

When she opened the front door, she was surprised to see Sutton Cassaday, holding a casserole dish.

"Hi, Sutton. Come on in." Jana opened the door wide and allowed Sutton to walk through.

"Hi, Jana. I hope I'm not bothering you. I've been feeling like I need to see you for a while now. Is this a good time?"

Jana thought of where she sat just minutes before and realized she needed Sutton at that moment more than Sutton knew.

"Perfect timing. What's this?" Jana looked at the dish Sutton held and inhaled the scents of an Italian meal.

"It's baked ziti. It's the first thing I've ever made in my whole life, so I really hope it's good." Sutton smiled and handed the meal to Jana. "I have green beans and a salad in the car, too."

"This is so sweet, Sutton. Thank you so much. Have a seat. Please."

Sutton sat on the worn couch while Jana went to the kitchen to set down dinner. When she returned she was already talking. "I had no idea what to do for supper, so I really can't thank you enough. It's been hard to get through the routines."

When Jana sat down opposite her, Sutton asked. "How's everyone doing?"

"We're surviving. Sometimes it feels like we're *barely* surviving. But we are." Jana pushed her dark hair from her eyes. "There are just so many memories everywhere. It's impossible to not miss her."

"I wish I would have known her better. I was so self-centered." Sutton looked at her hands, unsure of what else to say.

"What changed?"

"Actually, that's why I'm here." Sutton was still struggling with how to start when Kyle's words came to mind. Just tell the story. "I was in the congregation during Chandler's memorial. My world had been crashing and burning around me, my whole life long really. Everything I did to try to fill that hole in my heart cost me a piece of myself. I finally didn't have anything left. When your sister spoke of who Chandler was, her relationship with Jesus, it opened my eyes to see Him.

I was saved right then. I was saved because of Chandler."

Jana's eyes filled and she let her tears fall. In one sentence, Chandler's death proved not to be in vain.

Sutton saw Jana struggling to gain her composure and pressed on. "But, it's not just me. A few weeks after I was saved, I found out that my friend I used to go to the bars with had overdosed on cocaine. When I went to see her in the hospital, I told her Chandler's story. I explained how it was impossible to fill that void with drugs, alcohol, relationships or anything from this world. She was down enough to agree to go with me to church once she was released. I made her keep her promise.

Emily was saved on Sunday."

Jana began to weep and Sutton's tears were flowing freely. She went over to Jana and hugged her. Chandler saved her life, her eternity. As her mom, Jana would always hold a very special place in Sutton's heart.

Jana held her back and felt like a small piece of Chandler lived on in the heart of this girl before her.

A few minutes passed and Sutton returned to her seat. Jana spoke first. "Thank you so much for letting me know. I really needed to hear that today. I can't wait to tell Andy. He's so lost right now. Maybe this will help him find his way."

"I can't even imagine."

Jana leaned forward. "I think we're all a bit lost. I was just talking to God in Chan's room. He reminded me that His Child died, too. That helps in some ways. But, my biggest problem is that I don't know what to do next. I understand that she's gone. I know she's safe. But what now?"

"Well, after Jesus died, what did His Father do?"

It was an excellent question, one that Jana hadn't thought of. "He commissioned people to go out in the world and tell His Son's story, so that they might be saved."

At the same moment, Sutton and Jana were overwhelmed with the Holy Spirit. Sutton voiced it first. "We need to tell Chandler's story so that others will be saved."

Ideas started forming quickly. The women would love to take Chandler's story to the local schools, but that was impossible. They decided to approach churches with youth groups. Jana would tell of Chandler's life and death, Sutton would give her own testimony of life before and after salvation. It was exactly what they both needed.

They talked for more than an hour. Sutton told Jana what her life had been like, going to bars and clubs, living with her parents who didn't know how to love. It was obvious to Jana that Sutton didn't have much of a chance from early on.

"Are you still having a hard time dealing with the past?" Jana sensed that Sutton wasn't completely free of regret, and wanted so much to help her see how God saw her.

"It's hard to know that God has a man chosen for me to marry. I'll come to him with all this baggage. Whoever that man is, he just doesn't deserve who I was and that makes me feel like he's not going to deserve the person I am now. It's really difficult to get past."

"I have something for you." Jana stood abruptly and disappeared into a back bedroom. Sutton was curious what she was doing, but looked around as she waited. Sutton had never stayed, let alone lived, in a house as tiny as the James', but she never felt more at home than when she had walked through the door. She was so grateful for how quickly she was learning what mattered in life. If she could live in a house like this, with a family that loved like this one, her life would be a success.

Jana returned holding something small in her hand.

"I had this made for Chandler years ago. I have one for Davis and Townsend, too, but they won't need theirs for a little while." She opened her hand to reveal a white-gold bracelet. "Andy and I made this bracelet for the kids after we read a story about it in a book. Each stone on the bracelet is for a milestone in a relationship.

The small pebble represents the first time you hold his hand, the pearl represents the first time you say "I love you", the ruby represents the first kiss, the sapphire represents when you'll say 'yes' to his proposal. The diamond represents when you say "I do" and give yourself completely to that person. Every milestone you hit, you have to give that stone to the person. If you hold hands with the first person you date, you've lost the pebble. If you date someone else and kiss them, you have to give him the ruby."

Sutton studied the bracelet and watched it shine in the light. "It's beautiful."

"It's yours, Sweetie."

Sutton looked at Jana without understanding. "I can't take this. It's way too precious for me."

Jana took her hand and looked her in the eye. "Sutton, you gave me something today that my heart desperately needed. There's no way of explaining it. You gave me part of Chandler back today.

"You are an amazing and special girl, Sutton. Regardless of your past, or maybe because of it. God doesn't see your past sin. To Him, you are virginal again. I want you to have this bracelet so you'll remember that. You are starting over in every area of your life, honey. I have all the faith in the world that you will give one man this bracelet, with every stone intact."

Again, Sutton was overcome with emotion. She had only come to comfort Jana and was going to leave being comforted herself. Jana helped her with the clasp and they both stared at it. "I'll cherish it always."

Jana hugged her and said. "I believe that."

CHAPTER 29

Kyle was giddy driving over to the Jennings. It almost felt like she was seeing Callin for the first time since school began. No game tapes to watch, no strategies to talk over with Martin and Gray. It wasn't Coach Jennings tonight. It was just Cal. Her Cal.

Kyle felt like she was speeding and had to make an effort to let up on the gas pedal. She was so grateful that Callin asked her to come over early. The sun hadn't dipped too far yet and all it touched was washed in gold. She drove up the winding drive, and breathed in deeply. The scent of fresh air through her open window made her cheerful. Happy.

She parked beside Callin's truck and nearly ran to the door. She knocked twice and stuck her head in, "Hello."

Anne peeked around the corner in the kitchen and waved her on in, "Hey, Sweetie. Come on in. Callin's out in the barn, but come give me a hug before he takes you away from us."

Kyle walked through the house to where Anne was putting in a turkey to heat and potatoes to boil. "It looks like you're making a feast. I guess you're as happy to have Callin back with us as I am." Kyle smiled as she took in the aroma of butter and salt.

"It's a special night, for sure." Anne closed the oven door and turned to give Kyle a hug. "Go see that boy out there. He's been waiting for you."

Kyle went out the back door and ran to the barn. Callin had just finished saddling Duke when he saw Kyle. She ran to him and he picked her up and swung her around, kissing her on her cheek. She ran her fingers over his hair, cut short for the season.

Cal released her and smiled "I know I've seen you, but boy did I ever miss you."

"I've missed you, too. Way too much." Kyle looked at Duke

and Remington, "I didn't know we were going riding."

"I have something to show you, and we need the boys."

They walked the horses a ways down the trail and stopped at the fence enclosing the paddock. The sky was orange, threaded with ribbons of pink. They paused to take it in and took the opportunity to stand close to each other, making up for lost time.

Once in the saddles, they rode slowly down the trail. The horses didn't need leading, they had taken this path so often together. When they had almost reached the rock, Kyle and Cal jumped down and let the horses graze.

Callin took her hand until they were seated. He looked at her and touched her face. "I love you, Kyle. I love you so much."

"I love you, too, Cal."

"I've come here, to this rock, my whole life. I've prayed for every major life decision, I've cried here, I grew up here.

I fell in love here."

Kyle's eyes filled with tears. To hear how he loved her. To hear how God had so lovingly replaced what the locusts had eaten all those years before. She could barely keep from weeping.

"I've prayed my whole life for you, Ky. I prayed that God would keep you safe and that you would love Him. I prayed that you would love me and want the same things in life that I do. I prayed for my future wife."

Kyle's tears were falling freely as Callin got down on one knee and took her hand, "God has planned for us to be together since before there was time. I love you with all my heart and I promise you that I will be the best husband to you that you could ever imagine.

Cal reached in his pocket and held the ring in his hand. "Kyle Evans. You are my best friend, the most beautiful person I've ever known.

"Will you marry me?"

✝

Anne saw movement out her kitchen window and squealed with excitement, "They're back! It's time to get down to business and plan us a wedding!"

Paige laughed at her mom, "Remember, mom, she might have had everything planned out for her wedding day since she was a little girl and we'll have absolutely nothing to do."

Anne looked crestfallen for a half a second and then realized her daughter was teasing her. "Don't do that to me, you big meanie."

Martin laughed at his wife and hugged her from behind. "Just give our future daughter-in-law some space. You'll scare her off."

They watched through the window as their little boy held the hand of the little girl they had prayed over all these years.

And the little boy's mama cried.

✝

Kyle held her ring out for everyone to see. They had all seen it in the box, but it didn't look perfect until it was on her finger. Anne tried her hardest to restrain herself from overwhelming Kyle with wedding plans, but she just couldn't. Kyle laughed at her enthusiasm and was more than happy for the help.

"Ky, you just worry about finding the perfect dress and we'll take care of everything else."

Kyle was overcome with emotion to know that she wouldn't have to pay for the reception. She didn't have that kind of money saved up on her teacher's salary, and she knew she didn't have a father who would pay for the marriage of his only daughter. As far as she was concerned, Anne and Paige had full reign of the ceremony and festivities.

"What would you think of having the reception at Skip and Nancy's? We could make it elegant with table dressings, centerpieces and a gourmet dinner."

Cal and Kyle smiled at each other and Cal said, "Skip the gourmet and it sounds wonderful."

Paige and Grayson would stand up for them and Kyle had already planned to ask Pops to give her away. And the biggest decision of all was a simple one. The wedding would take place the Saturday after Christmas break began to ensure more than enough time for the long-awaited honeymoon.

Jana had prayed until dawn in the hours before she and Sutton would speak with their first youth group at a church several miles out of town. Most everyone in the area knew how Chandler had died. It was Jana's job as her mom to tell the world how her daughter had lived.

At six-thirty that morning, she couldn't take it another moment and picked up the phone to talk to Sutton.

Sutton picked up the call on the first ring "I'm so glad you called. I've been thinking about you all night. Are you okay?"

"I'm not sure. I know what I want to say, but I don't know how I'll be able to say it without breaking down."

Sutton paused "You're allowed to break down. You might break down for the first one hundred times you tell her story. But, I think it will get easier."

Jana sniffed, her eyes already red and swollen. "I know. It just still hurts so bad."

Sutton closed her eyes as the tears fell. "I'm so sorry. I can't imagine. But, it's Chandler's story that saved my soul. We are going to be talking to thirty-five kids today. Someday, I see us speaking to hundreds at a time. How many people are we going to see in heaven because you had the courage to speak up? God is going to give you the strength to get through today. And then you'll see that you can get through it the next time, too."

Jana nodded over the phone, but didn't say a word.

Sutton wiped her eyes and swiped a tissue over her cheek "And I'll be there."

Jana sniffed again and heard the Voice whisper over her heart.

So will I.

✝

Kyle, Anne and Paige had shopped for Paige's maid of honor dress and found a striking deep red floor-length gown with straight lines. It was the color of the season and it looked stunning on Paige. Anne found a classic emerald gown with matching short jacket. Things were coming together quickly.

Paige was feeling tired after the day filled with shopping and asked her Mom to drive her home. She hugged her best friend good-bye and Anne gave her a peck on the cheek. "If you find a dress, send me a picture as soon as you can."

Kyle promised and continued walking down the street. She had looked everywhere she could think of for a dress and all had been well out of her price range. She found herself standing in front of the second hand store. Everything in her wanted to keep walking. She dreamed of a brand new, bright white, off-the-shoulder masterpiece. But, she had only a used-store budget.

She opened the door and slowly walked in.

"Hello." The woman behind the counter glanced up from her magazine and said, "Let me know if I can help you with anything."

"Hi. I'm actually looking for a wedding dress."

The woman's face lit up and when she looked closely at Kyle, she jumped up from her seat and nearly ran to the back of the store.

"We just got this in. It's absolutely gorgeous and I can tell it will fit you. It's one of my crazy gifts to guess sizes." She laughed.

"My name's Dolores."

"I'm Kyle, it's nice to meet you."

"You must be so excited. When's the big day?"

"It's only a few weeks away. The dress is the hardest decision, so I've heard."

Dolores laughed again, easily, "You're right about that. Now, let's have a look." She unzipped the garment bag and opened it to reveal a bejeweled bodice of a winter-white gown with long sleeves and puffy shoulders. Kyle's fragile dreams of the perfect dress hit the floor and fractured.

Kyle closed the door of the dressing room and tried on the dress. It wasn't what she wanted, but a voice she couldn't deny kept whispering for her to buy it. And it was the only one she'd seen that she could afford. Her past haunted her as she stared at herself in her wedding dress. Maybe it was what she deserved. It was cheap, used and dirty.

And it fit perfectly.

Dolores hung the dress back in its bag and chatted on and on about how beautiful Kyle was going to be on her special day. She failed to notice the tears pooling in Kyle's eyes, or the great effort it was taking her to keep from sobbing.

Kyle paid Dolores and took the bag. It was heavy in her arms as she walked to her car.

The pain in her heart only grew as she drove the short ride to her home. Kyle hung the dress on her bedroom door and walked to the kitchen. A wedding magazine was opened on the counter, and Kyle closed it and threw it in the trash. Tears stung her eyes and she leaned against the island.

"Jesus, I know my wedding isn't about the dress. I really do know that. But, for some reason it's a really big deal for me. I guess I pray that you'll help me to be content with what I have and be grateful for Callin and the life we're about to begin."

Kyle went back to the garbage can and pulled out the magazine. She walked slowly to her room and stood in front of the opened garment bag. She opened the magazine to the bookmarked page and ran her finger over the dress of her dreams. She loved the lines and the beaded bodice. It was simple and chic. She sighed and forced herself to believe God knew what He was doing.

Look up, Child.

Kyle looked up at the dress and in the bag saw only the bodice, but not the sleeves. She gasped, "I can't believe this. It's perfect. Thank You, Lord. Thank You, thank You."

She grabbed the dress and ran from the house to her car. Her Lord cared about every detail of her dreams and provided a way to make them come true.

Kyle parked her car and rushed to the little alteration shop on the edge of town. The bell above the doorpost clanged and the door slammed behind her. A woman came in from the back room with glasses perched on her nose and a spool of thread in her hand.

"Good afternoon. It looks like you have quite a project for me." She took the garment bag from Kyle and walked to the back room. Kyle followed close behind her, "It's my wedding dress. I'm getting married the week before Christmas. I know it's short notice, but I'm hoping you can work wonders."

"I can do anything. I'm Denise, by the way."

"I'm Kyle, it's nice to meet you."

"Nice to meet you, too, Kyle. Let's see what we have to work with here. Do you need it taken in or hemmed?"

"Neither, actually. It fits perfectly. The problem is the sleeves."

Denise took the dress completely out of the bag and hung it up to inspect. "Hmm. They are quite large."

"Gaudy. You can say it."

Denise laughed, "Yes, gaudy was the word I was looking for and afraid to say. So, tell me exactly what you want."

Kyle pulled the magazine out of the purse and handed it to Denise. "This is my dream dress. "

Denise studied the picture and looked back at the dress. She checked the seams on the sleeves and smiled. "Easy peasy, Kyle. You're going to have your dream dress in about five days."

Kyle could have hugged her, "Thank you so much. Oh my, I can't thank you enough."

Kyle nearly floated out of the store and called Cal, "Hey there."

"Hi. I miss you. Are you coming over?" Callin knew the girls were looking for dresses, but the day was long without seeing Kyle.

"I am, but do you think we can meet at your mom's? I have something to show her."

Callin could hear Kyle smile through the phone, "Of course. I'm guessing you found a dress."

"I did. But, I'm pretty sure you're not allowed to see it."

"I don't need to see it. You'd look beautiful in absolutely anything." Kyle felt emotionally embraced and thought about how perfect his words were.

CHAPTER 30

Sutton had packed her last box in the truck and stepped back to look at the accumulation of her life. Clothes, purses and shoes. She felt sadness sweep over her and then resolved to move forward. What she would gain over the rest of her life would be happy memories of a life lived out for her God.

She climbed into the cab of the borrowed truck and felt her muscles tightening. She was going to be sore in the morning, but she was determined to do this without any help from her friends or family. She'd told her mother in an email that she was finally making the move to her own home. Her first step in moving on was moving out.

She had joined Kyle's Bible study and was building lasting friendships. With their encouragement, Sutton had applied for several positions as a pharmaceutical salesperson. She was so grateful for her father's insistence in her getting her degree. She never thought at the time that she would or could actually use it one day.

She put the truck in gear and slowly made her way out through the gate. She wasn't shocked by the feeling of sadness that stole her breath. When she looked back on the estate where she grew up, she began to weep. She wanted to be happy. She wanted to be excited. And maybe she was, somewhere behind the pain. But, right then, she just needed to cry.

The next five days were painfully slow for Kyle. She couldn't wait to try on her brand new dress. Anne and Paige went with her and sat outside the dressing room while Kyle changed.

Kyle emerged with tears streaming down her cheeks. Anne gasped and tears welled in her eyes as well.

"It's the most gorgeous dress I've ever seen." Paige stared at her best friend and soon-to-be sister.

Kyle turned around to look at herself in the full length mirror on the wall. It was just like Christ to take the used and abandoned and make it into a one-of-a-kind masterpiece, a new creation. Transformed into something more beautiful than anyone could have imagined. For the first time since Jesus whispered it over her heart, she believed it - she really was His princess.

✝

The Christmas season tendered the hearts of people of Greenville. The streets of the town were decorated and spoke of Christ's birth in pictures and statues. Jana and Andy James carefully opened the first box of Christmas tree ornaments and paused before removing any. They had waited for Towne and Davis to go to bed before pulling things down from the attic.

They would wait to put up the tree, but they had to prepare their hearts before they looked on anything of Chandler's in front of the others. Chandler's baby handprints. "I love Mommy and Daddy" written in a child's scrawl. Pictures of her sweet face with toothless grins and reindeer made out of clothespins. Jana remembered every one and the moment it was presented to her. Chandler's smile was unforgettable at any age.

"We have Easter, Mother's Day, Father's Day. Then we'll have gotten through all the holidays without her for the first time. This is going to be the hardest, right?" Jana's voice caught in a sob and Andy put his arms around his love.

"I think this will be the hardest." Andy held on, but he wasn't sure he believed his own words. They were all going to be the hardest.

And, eventually they would have to go through the anniversary of her death. How could they ever prepare for that? Andy felt his tears slip down his face, but he didn't let go. He'd suffered in silence over the last months. But, his silence was hurting his wife more than it was helping him. "We're going to be okay, Honey. We're going to be okay." And whether he believed it or not, he knew he needed to say it.

✝

The Friday morning before the wedding set off the typical whirlwind of events. Anne met briefly with caterers and double-checked that the cake was ordered. The photographer was arranged and the excitement was high.

Kyle's phone buzzed while she was lost in thoughts of her mom. She had tried to call her dad to let him know she was getting married, but she was forced to leave a voice mail. She didn't think he'd call her back, but when he didn't, she was angry with herself that she'd even tried. Then, just as quickly, the faces of Martin and Pops came to her mind and she understood that God gave her not one father figure, but two. It was just like Him to give her even more than the desire of her heart.

She answered her phone and didn't even say hello to Sutton on the other end, "Did you get it?"

Sutton's excitement was evident in her squeals, "I did! I start the beginning of the year. I can't believe it, Kyle. I really didn't believe in myself at all before I went to the interview."

"Well you have a huge group of friends and people that love you that believed in you. And God believed in you. You're going to be so great at talking to the doctors and schmoozing with the nurses. You know you have to bake them things so they'll let you in, right?" Kyle laughed at the thought and immediately added, "I'll help!"

Sutton was beside herself. She'd done it. But not on her own. Never on her own.

"Are you ready for tomorrow?" Sutton asked, forgetting her excitement for her friend.

"I am. More than ready. I'm very grateful for the short engagement, that's for sure."

"How are you feeling about your parents?" Sutton understood Kyle's sadness over her family as much as she did her own. Her mother wasn't dead, but some days she might as well be.

"That's funny you'd ask me that. I was just thinking about them when you called. I miss my mom. It's hard not having her here for this. This is what every little girl dreams of, right? And no one's here for me."

Sutton responded. "If I get married, I doubt I'll have anyone from my past there either. But, somehow that feels alright. Like maybe they don't really belong anymore. I might be wrong. I'm pretty new at forgiveness. But, just because you haven't known them all your life and you're not blood related doesn't mean that the people coming aren't coming for you. Of course they are. You are so loved, Kyle. By so many people. Don't let Satan work on you now when you're supposed to be the happiest. Don't let him win."

Kyle smiled at the changes in her friend over such a few short months. She needed reminding and God was using Sutton mightily.

"Thank you very much for that. I needed it. I'll see you tomorrow."

"You bet. Have fun tonight."

Sutton hung up and stared around her house, finally put together and already feeling like home. She was grateful for her friends, grateful for a place to live and grateful for a new job. Her new life was starting out better than any life she could have ever asked for.

✝

Kyle dressed for the rehearsal dinner and her spirit was light. Sutton's pep talk did wonders for her mood and she gave her anger to God. She would occasionally feel her nerves for Saturday, but then the thrill of what the next few days held overshadowed them completely. She was getting married.

Her black wrap-around dress fell just above her knees and paired with black high heels, she felt quite posh. She smiled into the mirror and whispered, "Mrs. Callin Jennings."

She heard Cal's truck pull into the drive and she opened the curtains to see him walk up the porch steps. It took her breath to watch him. He was right on time.

And she was ready.

✝

The church was illuminated and beautifully decorated for the Christmas season. Poinsettias lined both sides of the aisle and Christmas trees stood tall on either side of the stage. Large wreaths and strings of garland were hung on both sides of the church and Kyle couldn't remember ever being happier. Cal and Kyle both whispered how they wished the rehearsal was the real thing. They didn't want to wait even a few more hours.

Dinner was festive and merry. They decided on Gio's since it held such special memories. By the time Callin drove Kyle back to Pops, they were blissfully exhausted.

"I don't see how in the world I'm going to sleep tonight." Cal took her in his arms and kissed her ear.

"I know I'm not, especially if you do that again."

Cal laughed and touched his forehead to hers. "I'm going to kiss you tomorrow."

"I know. And I can't wait."

"And after that, I'm going to kiss you every single day for the rest of our lives."

They felt the heat rising all the way to their faces, scorching their cheeks as they touched.

"Wow. I love you so much, Callin." Kyle stepped back and held his hands.

"I love you, too, Ky. I'm going to show you every single moment, just how much.

He kissed her forehead, "I'm going to make you happy."

When he looked into her eyes one last time before leaving, Kyle whispered, "You already have."

✝

Her wedding morning dawned bright and sunny. The air was crisp and cool but by mid day, the temperature was supposed to warm up to be very comfortable.

Pops drove Kyle to the church where she met Anne and Paige. Paige applied Kyle's make up, making sure to keep it subtle. Anne went out to the sanctuary every few minutes to make sure the men had arrived and the photographer had started shooting. She called Martha Williams to see how the reception hall was coming along. Martha and a few other ladies from church had been at Skip and Nancy's from early that morning, making sure it was a fantasy for the couple. Martha had loved Callin since he was an infant and this wedding meant so much to her. She wanted it to be spectacular.

Paige changed into her gown and then she and Anne helped Kyle into hers.

"You look amazing," Anne touched Kyle's cheek. "I'm so grateful that you're about to become my daughter-in-law. You make my son so happy, and that makes me happy."

"Mom, don't make her cry. I just finished her make-up." Paige lightened the moment before they were all a mess of tears.

"Well, I'm grateful to be a part of such a phenomenal family. I love Callin more than I thought possible."

The girls could hear guests beginning to arrive and Paige zipped Kyle's dress the rest of the way. Anne worked the veil onto the top of Kyle's styled hair and smoothed it out down the back.

"Gorgeous."

238

Paige peeked into the sanctuary and saw the guests were seated. And just like that, it was time.

Cued by the music, Anne was escorted in by Martin. Next Paige slowly walked down the aisle, keeping her eyes locked on her husband standing next to her brother.

The wedding march sounded and the doors opened wide. Callin saw his bride, all in white, illuminated by the sun setting behind her. Tears flooded his eyes, but he didn't want to blink. He didn't want to miss a second. Kyle saw Cal at the front of the church and smiled. She held Pops' arm tighter and felt the tears wet her eyes. Pops gave her away with a hug and kiss on the cheek.

Pastor Jeremy beamed at the couple. He'd had the privilege over the past months of watching as Jesus united two of the church's family members.

Callin held Kyle's hand and squeezed it. He whispered, "You are the most beautiful girl in the whole world."

The tears Kyle had been trying to hold back, fell. The man who had promised to dry all her tears, wiped them away.

Candles flickered around them and with their loved ones watching, Callin Jennings and Kyle Evans pledged their love to each other and vowed to hold tight for forever.

Pastor Jeremy looked into the congregation and spoke with a smile, "It gives me great pleasure to now pronounce you, Man and Wife.

You may kiss your bride."

Callin put his hands on either side of her face and looked into her eyes. He leaned down and stopped a moment before he touched his lips to hers with a warmth and tenderness that stole her breath.

Their first kiss. And it was amazing.

The newlyweds were hurried away and photographed while their guests made their way to the reception. By the time Cal and Kyle arrived at Skip's, appetizers had been served and conversation was flowing.

The DJ hushed the crowd and announced, "For the first time ever in public, I'd like to introduce you to Mr. and Mrs. Callin Jennings." Shouts and applause erupted and Cal and Kyle walked in to see only smiles. They had their first dance as a married couple and Callin didn't worry about getting too close. He spun Kyle around and brought her back to him, holding her even closer.

Callin whispered in her ear, "I love you, my beautiful wife."

Kyle whispered back, "I love you, my handsome husband."

The reception followed the traditions. Dinner was served and Cal and Kyle ate at the head table with Paige and Gray. When all were finished with eating, the dancing began in full force. With everyone occupied, Cal took Kyle by the hand and led her to the back of the barn. He opened the supply room door and pulled her in. Once inside, he locked the door and grabbed his bride in an urgent embrace. They kissed with a passion that set their bodies on fire.

"We need to leave. Soon. Now." Cal said between kisses.

"Yes, I agree. Cake and the bouquet toss and we're out of here." Kyle kissed him back with the same insistence.

"Okay. I'll leave out of here first so people won't think anything." Cal moved toward the door until Kyle stopped him

"You have my lipstick on." Kyle laughed, reaching to wipe it from his mouth. He took her hand and kissed it

"Here, let me give it back. " He came back to her and kissed her gently. "Twenty minutes tops, or I'm going to lose my mind."

Cal walked out of the supply room and Kyle followed soon after. Within a half hour, Cal and Kyle were holding hands, running through a sea of bubbles. Callin helped Kyle into his truck that had been decorated for them sometime between the nuptials and the reception. The couple waved at their family and friends and Kyle mouthed, "We love you all."

Cal started up the truck and turned it toward their honeymoon.

"Are you going to tell me where we're going yet?" Kyle had no idea what her husband had planned. Paige packed her suitcase for her so she wouldn't be able to take any guesses.

"I can tell you that tonight we're staying at a suite in the finest hotel I could find within fifteen minutes from here."

Kyle laughed out loud, "You're so adorable, you know that?"

Callin attempted to keep a lawful speed, but it was proving impossible. He parked the truck in front of the hotel and gave the keys to the valet.

He stood in front of the check in desk and kissed Kyle's forehead. He'd waited his whole life for this night. It had been difficult and taxing, but at that moment, it was all worth it.

They were staring at each other when the man tried to hand them their key. He finally gave up and placed it down before them. Kyle took the key and Callin held her hand to the elevator. The bell rang at their floor and their room was, mercifully, nearby.

Kyle fumbled with the key while Cal stood behind her, kissing her shoulder, her neck, her ear. The door opened, and Callin swept her up in his arms. He walked her through the threshold, the door closed behind them.

And the wait was over.

CHAPTER 31

Their honeymoon took the newlyweds to the beaches of Florida. The condo Callin rented overlooked the ocean with spectacular views of the sunrise. They didn't miss a morning watching God wake the day. When the sun began warming the sands, they took their breakfast and a towel down to sit on the shore.

In the afternoons, the waves danced over their feet on their long walks along the water's edge. Kyle enjoyed spending every moment with her new husband. As evening would approach, they both felt the freedom in appreciating each other with lingering gazes, lying side by side in the sand.

The morning of Christmas Eve, Kyle packed their suitcases while Cal checked out. When Cal came back up for the luggage, he saw his wife standing on the balcony, looking out over the horizon.

He walked up behind her and wrapped her in his arms. A mist had settled over the waters and a rainbow was speaking for God. He kept His promises. They didn't need any more proof.

Cal turned her around and kissed her lips. He couldn't imagine it would ever get old. Maybe he was fooling himself, but he vowed to always remember how he felt right then.

"I love you. I don't think I've said it yet today."

"You did. You just didn't use words." Kyle kissed him again. "I love you, too. Can we move here?"

Cal laughed, because she was so adorable and because he was thinking the same thing. "I do wish we could stay longer. How about we come back next year for our anniversary?"

"I'll settle for that." They kissed again and Cal's arms enveloped her until they were out of time. They had somewhere else to be.

The drive to Cal's grandparents' villa took nearly four hours. Kyle had met Celia and Dallas Jennings the week before at the wedding, but couldn't wait to spend more time with the pair. Celia had a quiet wisdom that Kyle wanted to glean. Dallas rarely spoke, but when he did, he had everyone in the room in stitches. They were the kind of people that Kyle met once and they hugged her like they'd known her all her life. She felt at home being near them, and she knew Callin was who he was, not only because of his parents. The elder Jennings had a hand in it, too.

Cal pulled his truck into the drive close to three o'clock in the afternoon. The home was decorated from top to bottom with lights and Christmas décor. The entire neighborhood looked to have a contest to see who could use the most electricity during the season, and Kyle couldn't wait until it was dark to see the houses lit up.

Celia Jennings walked out door as soon as Cal cut the engine and ran up to his door. "My baby. I've missed you." She gave him a kiss on the cheek and held onto him.

"Gram, I just saw you last week. It's not like it's been a year." Cal laughed, but didn't pull away.

Gram backed up and put his face between her hands. "I'd miss you the same if it was only a day, you know that. Now, let me get to my new grand-daughter."

Kyle had walked over to where they were standing and Gram gave her a hug just as big as Callin's. "We love you, Darlin'. We're all so happy to have you as part of our family. Now, we want some great-grandchildren."

Kyle laughed. Anne had warned her that would be the first thing Gram would say. "You'll be the first one we call when we have any news on that."

"Okay. Now, I'm holding you to it." Gram led them inside to where the others waited.

Anne, Martin, Paige and Grayson all flew in the night before and were busy with dinner preparations. All work stopped when Cal and Kyle walked in.

Paige ran up to Kyle and hugged her. "Hi Friend. Hi Sister. I've been waiting a long time to say that."

Kyle was so grateful to see her best friend. And only sister. Cal set their luggage in the guest room. Paige and Gray took the pull out couch so they could have some privacy during their stay. The couch had been Cal's bed when they stayed and he thanked Kyle, since she was the reason he'd been upgraded.

After most of dinner was prepared, they dressed for service at their grandparents' church. The congregation was small and welcomed them all with open arms. Celia and Dallas had only been members for a couple years, but were deeply rooted.

Both Cal and Kyle couldn't help but feel the Holy Spirit embracing them with His presence while they worshipped and praised the King that was born to die.

Once back at the villa, the food was warmed and the turkey was taken from the oven. The smells mingled and made mouths water.

"I've been ready to eat since lunch." Martin was in charge of carving the turkey and kept taking bites between slices, until Anne slapped his arm.

"We're hungry, too. Hurry it up, mister."

Platters loaded with food were placed in the middle of the table, and everyone sat back to take it in.

Dallas blessed the food, and thanked God for the new addition to the family. Kyle blushed and they all laughed when he said 'amen' and she was still red.

"So, tell us about the honeymoon. Did you go to any amusement parks, or just hang out on the beach." Paige said, as she passed the mashed potatoes to her husband.

"We didn't go to an amusement park. It didn't seem like we had enough time, really. Next year we will. We're planning on going back for our anniversary and staying longer." Cal passed the green beans and glanced at his wife. Then he looked back at her and watched her until she looked at him. She grabbed his hand under the table and squeezed it.

"It was so beautiful. And the beach was amazing. I came to Florida with my parents when I was little. It was as neat as I remembered. I can't get over the palm trees." Kyle was so full of excitement that Anne couldn't help but smile. Her children were both happily married to strong Christian spouses. She couldn't ask for more.

It was close to two hours later by the time the dinner dishes were cleared and cleaned. It was getting late, but Paige and Kyle wrapped up in blankets and sat out on the back porch.

"How are you doing?" Kyle had wanted to talk to Paige alone. It didn't seem like they'd had a conversation since before the rush of the wedding.

"Great. We have some news." Even in just the moonlight, Kyle could see the excitement on Paige's face.

"No!" Kyle nearly jumped off her seat.

"No, I'm not pregnant." Paige's smile remained fixed, and she could tell Kyle was confused. "Gray and I decided to take foster parenting classes. We want to foster to adopt."

Kyle hugged her friend for a long time before releasing her to hear the details. She was so happy Paige and Gray had come to this conclusion. It was what Kyle and Cal had decided they would do one day. Helping a child in need, bringing them into a Christian home, growing them up to change the world.

"Oh, Paige. I'm so happy for you both. When do you start? How long are the classes? How soon will you have a baby? I have a thousand questions!"

Paige laughed. It was a sound Kyle realized she'd missed. It had been so long since Paige's happiness seemed genuine. She had remained positive through their trials and sadness, but the smile felt forced. This smile seemed very easy.

"We start at the beginning of the year, mid-January. The classes are for ten weeks, so it's not an overnight thing. It could take up to a year to have an infant placement. It might not happen ever. We're just walking with God, following Him where He leads. He could still heal me and give us a biological child. We're open to His will. There's such a freedom in that."

"Yes, there is. Have you talked to Jana? They didn't foster Townsend, but she might have some advice that would be helpful." Kyle thought out loud.

"I hadn't thought of that. I'll get in touch with her when we get home. How are they doing?"

Kyle pictured Jana and Sutton in the midst of their mission. "I think they're still struggling. The holidays are difficult, but I think Christmas will be the worst. I'm going to call her tomorrow to check in. Five teenagers were saved the first time she and Sutton spoke, and there were only thirty-five in the group. I see God working in a huge way someday with their testimonies."

Kyle thought of the upcoming trials of Earl Marx, Jimmy Aarons and Rob Tomlin. They were sure to be more painful than any of them could imagine. Kyle would have to testify, and already told Jana she would be with her every day until the three were convicted. Jana's sister and parents, along with Andy and his parents, all planned to hear every detail. It was the last hours of their beloved Chandler's life. They had no choice.

Kyle shook out of her thoughts and focused on the good stuff. It was so hard to remain happy when there was so much pain. But, Jana had said herself. They had to keep looking up. It was all they could do.

✝

Cal and Kyle woke early Christmas morning and held each other in bed until they smelled coffee. Their first Christmas together. To feel so safe. So loved. Kyle didn't want to move. Cal kissed her neck and she tingled to her toes.

"That's so not fair, Callin Jennings."

"Hmm. I've heard all's fair."

Voices drifted from the kitchen and Kyle pulled away and put on her robe. Let's get some coffee and open our presents"

"Was I supposed to get you something? I thought your present was your ring." Cal put his arms around her again and kissed her ear.

Kyle played along, "That's fine. I didn't get you anything either. But, if we don't go out now, they'll start talking."

"They're already talking. Kyle kissed him, and it took all they had to open the door and follow the noise.

✝

The ride home was long, but a vacation in itself. Neither could find anything to complain about and stopped to buy pecan rolls and oranges.

It was late when Callin turned his truck into their driveway. Kyle held Cal's hand to her chest and turned to him. How she loved the shape of his face, the lines of his jaw. The long gravel road carried them.

And led them home.

✝

He stood within the trees, watching them kiss at the door. He felt himself burn on the inside and rage spill out. He felt the weight of the knife in his hand as he clutched the handle.

She didn't belong there, kissing some stranger.

She was *his*. She'd always be his.

TORRENT'S ECHO

Book II in the *Echoes* Series

By: Courtney Baker

PROLOGUE

He stood within the trees, watching them kiss at the door. He felt himself burn on the inside and rage spill out. He felt the weight of the knife in his hand as he clutched the handle.

She didn't belong there, kissing some stranger.

She was *his*. She'd always be his.

He'd been there, waiting. Night after night since he'd found her, he'd make his way through the forest until they finally came home. He knew where they'd been. They were married now. Married. His Kyle.

The vein in his head pulsed and he grabbed at his hair. He looked at that man with his hands on Kyle once more. He was a big man. Bigger than he had guessed. Maybe this knife wasn't the right weapon.

He pulled at his hair again, trying to think clearly what to do next, when the rain began to fall. He watched the lights go on throughout the house, then watched as they went out, one by one. Now was his chance.

He faltered and looked again at his knife. No, not tonight. He'd get a gun. Then he'd come back.

CHAPTER 1

She ran to her closet and surrounded herself in darkness. The ax whapped on the door again. And again. She clutched her baby doll and rocked back and forth, willing him to go away.

She heard the ax splinter the wood and then silence. He was inside now. She could hear him breathing. Feel his presence.

The ax fell to the floor and the sound of a match sounded as it struck its flint. The wind echoed outside and pounded the windows.

Underneath the door, she saw the flames and she screamed for her mommy. Begged for her daddy.

He breathed her name.

"Sutton."

And then she woke up.

✝

Sutton picked up her phone, still groggy from her nightmare, when she heard her mom's ring sing out a melancholy tune. She rarely heard it, not even on Christmas the week before. Sutton's finger hovered over the button to ignore the call, but then answered it.

"Hi, Mom."

"Hi darling. I, I'm here by myself. What are you…? Where are you, darling?"

Sutton clutched the phone to her ear and had to calm herself to stop from throwing it. She knew by the slurred speech, exactly where her mom was, how she looked. It wasn't hard to imagine.

It wasn't even six-thirty in the morning, "I'm still in bed, but I'm planning on going over some paperwork for my job when I get up. I'm starting next week, do you remember me telling you?"

The silence on the other end made Sutton sit up and squeeze the phone in agitation. But her anger quickly turned to sadness. She wanted her mother to be healed. She wanted her to find salvation. Salvation from a life of drugs, alcohol, pain, addiction. Sutton wanted her mother to be saved the way she had been. Eternally.

 "Actually, Mom, I'm planning on seeing a counselor later this morning. Would you come with me?"

"What? Counselor? You mean a psychologist. No, I won't go with you. Never. Psychos, that's what they are. They don't help, those shrinks. They, they are worthless. We tried everything, and they are worthless. They didn't help us with that boy. They said they'd help, but they didn't help." Her mom clicked off before she finished her thought and Sutton was left to wonder what she was talking about.

That boy. What boy.

✝

Kyle nuzzled her husband's neck and made his toes curl. He wrapped his leg around hers and kissed her on lips before groaning. "You are so mean. Why are you torturing me?"

Kyle giggled and kissed him again. He tickled her until she was near tears. "That's what happens when you play with my emotions." He kissed her one last time before climbing out of bed and heading for the shower.

When Cal returned from the bathroom dressed in faded jeans and a white polo, his wife of ten days was still in her pajama bottoms and a tank top, brewing coffee.

"Tell me again why I'm going into work today instead of spending every waking minute with you?" Cal came up behind Kyle and wrapped his arms around her.

"Because, the school desperately needs you." Kyle leaned her head back on his chest until he turned her around to face him. "Plus, I'm going over to Jana's. The attorney contacted her, too. I think she needs to talk it over."

"That's true. How are you doing?" Cal stood back and leaned against the counter, studying Kyle's face.

"I'm fine right now. I'm sure I'll be more nervous when I start talking to the D.A."

"How are Jana and Andy?" Cal had forgotten he was late, but focused on his wife.

"Last I saw her, you know, she was getting stronger. They've worked so hard at moving forward. Christmas was really hard. I just hope all the talk about the trial doesn't push them back."

"They have the most important thing. Faith. We'll just stay vigilant in praying for them."

Kyle reached for him and pulled him in a lingering embrace. "I love you so much."

"I love you, too. I'll be home as soon as I can."

Kyle walked him to the door and gave him another kiss goodbye. She waved and closed the door when she heard her phone ringing on the counter.

Cal waved back and walked toward his truck parked on the gravel drive. He was almost to the driver's side door when he caught a glimpse of something shining near the tree line.

The stones crunched beneath his running shoes as he walked a hundred feet to the object. His knee cracked when he bent down to pick it up. A wrapper from a stick of gum. Callin picked it up and turned it over in his hands. He glanced a few feet into the woods and caught sight of several more.

An uneasiness rested on him and he pulled out his phone to call his brother-in-law, Chief Grayson Williams. Kyle didn't chew that type of gum and no one else lived anywhere near them other than family. He couldn't see them camping out in sight of their house, chewing stick after stick of gum. He looked around the perimeter of the property to see if anything else looked out of place.

Gray picked up on the third ring, "Hey Cal, what's up?"

Callin looked at the front door of the house to see if Kyle had bolted the door. She had. He climbed into the cab of truck and slammed the door. "I found something here at the house. I'm not sure what to make of it."

Cal pulled out and headed down the drive to the main road and explained the gum wrappers. "What do you think?"

Grayson scratched his forehead and then rubbed his nose, his tell tale sign that he was thinking. "Well, just to hear you tell it, it sounds like someone's been watching the house."

Cal ran his fingers through his hair and fell silent trying to think of what to do next when Gray interrupted his thoughts. "Cal, you have a great alarm system, right? And you have your guns. Make sure you talk to Kyle about what you found and get her out to the shooting range this weekend. Make it a date. I'll come by later today and look around."

Cal nodded to the phone. "Okay. I hate to scare her, but I guess she needs to know."

"Definitely. And, it could be something as simple as one the guys that helped on your house stood there on his breaks and chewed gum. Who knows? Marx, Jimmy and Rob are all locked up tight. Let's not freak out until we have a solid reason to. I'll check the system and see what I can find out about where her ex is right now. Are you thinking more that it's Garrison?"

"That's what first crossed my mind, but he hasn't made contact of any kind. There's been no indication that he's found her. I don't know."

"Okay, well let Kyle know what you found and I'll see you this afternoon."

Cal agreed and called Kyle as soon as he hung up with Grayson. "Hey, Sweetie. Did you set the alarm when I left?"

He could hear Kyle thinking on the other end. "Why?"

"I found some gum wrappers in the woods outside our house. I'm sure it's nothing. I've already talked to Grayson and he's coming over tonight after work to look around, but I'd feel better if you were locked up with the alarm set."

"Okay. I just set it. Now, I'm just sitting here all by myself, scared out of my mind. I guess I'll go out and visit with Pops before I meet Jana."

"That sounds like a great idea. I love you, Ky."

"I love you, too, babe. Call me when you leave the school and I'll meet you."

Kyle dressed as quickly as she could, leaving the doors open throughout the house so she could see into the adjacent rooms. She knew exactly what to do to stay safe. She'd lived like this before, not that long ago.

www.ingramcontent.com/pod-product-compliance
Lightning Source LLC
Chambersburg PA
CBHW030127180626
46812CB00002B/596